CW00428480

Clare Nonhebel, who li[v]
decided to be a writer at
the age of nine, and a w
the age of ten. In fact
public relations secretar
she wrote her first novel. *Cold Showers* was the joint
winner of the Betty Trask Award in 1984, a prize awarded
for the best first novel by an author under thirty-five.

By the same author

Cold Showers
The Partisan

CLARE NONHEBEL

Incentives

GRAFTON BOOKS

A Division of the Collins Publishing Group

LONDON GLASGOW
TORONTO SYDNEY AUCKLAND

Grafton Books
A Division of the Collins Publishing Group
8 Grafton Street, London W1X 3LA

Published by Grafton Books 1989

First published in Great Britain by
Century Hutchinson Ltd 1988

Copyright © Clare Nonhebel 1988

ISBN 0-586-20407-5

Printed and bound in Great Britain by
Collins, Glasgow

Set in Times

Contents

1

Introductions

Leon Grszinski – the halfway famous, highly promising not-so-young talent Grszinski, as he was known to the art critics; Leon with the unpronounceable surname, as he was known to his friends; that painter bloke with the reserved manner of speech and the surprisingly flamboyant way with paint and canvas – this multiple personality stood in front of his latest work of art and decided that he had missed his true vocation.

'Bus driver!' he declared. 'Road sweeper! Garbage disposal expert!'

He had had doubts like this before. His usual trick was to walk away from the painting, erase it from his mind, then suddenly wheel around and glare at it through the unrehearsed eyes of a stranger. Leon strode away from the offending canvas, stopped in mid-stride and confronted it again. Had it, in his brief absence, improved? Had he become, in those resolute steps, a painter again?

He considered it carefully. An original Grszinski would fetch a fair price nowadays; it would almost sell on the signature alone. Critics were notoriously relieved to find a familiar name. They could look up their file of previous reviews and re-word the same opinion time and again, adding only a hint of updated judgement: 'developing' or even 'blossoming' if they were in a good mood, 'losing some of his original flair and freshness' if they were feeling Monday-morningish.

On the whole, critics liked Leon. He was predictably unpredictable. They always found something different and something the same in each of his paintings. It gave them something to criticize and appraise, which was what they were paid to do, and something to recognize, so they could impress acquaintances and editors by saying knowledgeably, 'Ah, the latest Grszinski,' from twenty paces away, without having to put on their reading glasses to pick out the signature in the bottom right-hand corner.

Galleries liked Leon too. He was quiet and unassuming and unusually lenient in letting them hang his pictures much as they chose. He had let them hang two 'remarkable pieces of balanced structural form' the wrong way up once. The critics commented, and the gallery staff repeated their comments to viewers, about perpendicular and horizontal relationships of line and form for a full two weeks before Leon informed them, gravely and apologetically, that one was hung on its side and one was upside down. It was entirely his fault, he said contritely; he should of course have taken more care in advising them in the preparation stage of the exhibition. Whereupon the young deb who had recently come to work in the gallery, which was owned by a friend of Mummy's, said rather irritably (having not been educated yet that the successful artists are sensitive plants and must be treated with reverence lest they take their incomes elsewhere), 'Do you mean you want us to turn them round?' And Leon had replied courteously, 'Oh no, I wouldn't put you to the trouble. I'm sure it doesn't matter,' and then had stayed and made complimentary remarks about the other paintings, which were not only by other artists but had been hung the right way up.

This painting would undoubtedly get away with it. Certainly, it was a blob, but then most of Leon's paintings were. Inspired blobs of vibrant colour flung on to watery backgrounds, bright on dark on pale; passionate splodges with trailing drops of blood, shocking against the void, startling amid the bland; shrieks and sobs of colour tearing

8

the heart of the canvas; joyous whirls and eddies like visible pools of sound . . . they may have been formless but they abounded with life, those blobs. But this one was just a blob.

'Dustman!' proclaimed Leon bitterly. 'Sewage recycling operative!' And then, with unwonted viciousness: 'Computer software salesman!'

He rolled up the canvas and flung it away.

What could be worse, Helen wondered, than spending the evening with a group of unknown women? She wished that John hadn't told them she would go.

'I'll only just have moved in!' she'd reminded him when he phoned her in York last night. 'I won't feel like going out, and anyhow not on my own.'

He knew it was an excuse. 'I think it's important,' he said, a little reproachfully, 'for you to get to know people. They're my colleagues' wives. You want to fit in.'

'Yes.' She did of course want to fit in. 'But the first night . . .'

'I know,' he sympathized. 'But you can't start by turning down invitations. They might not ask you again. Harry only mentioned it in passing, as it is.'

Even worse. It wasn't even Marie's idea, but her husband Harry's – John's sales director. Probably Marie didn't want her at all; probably none of them did, and why should they? They were a cosy, established group, meeting each week in one or another's house for what they called (mockingly) their Gossips. Mockingly, because they were, naturally, too intelligent for such a pursuit as gossiping. Too educated, too sophisticated, too mature and too . . . 'Boring,' said Helen aloud. And then felt ashamed, for they would surely find her more boring still.

So why go? Oh . . . because John seemed to want her

to. Because he was so anxious to 'fit in' himself, in his first real job.

And because she knew that, after three months apart, he was secretly afraid she might have got used to living her life without him.

'Don't let me forget I've got to phone that girl,' Marie said, inspecting herself in the changing-room mirror. 'Do you think I look tarty in these satin things?'

'I wish I did,' said Sarah. 'Whatever I wear I look like a vicar's daughter.'

'You look very nice in them,' Marie consoled, swivelling to see her rear view.

'Wholesome,' Sarah sighed. 'Who else could look wholesome in skin-tight black satin jeans?'

'Oh nonsense,' said Marie vaguely. 'I think I might buy them. How about you?' It was a rhetorical question. Unthinkable, of course, that they should buy the same garment, to wear to the same occasions. By stating her intention to buy, Marie had staked her claim.

'No, I don't think I will.' Sarah backed down gracefully. 'You go ahead. They suit you.'

'Tell you what,' said Marie, when she had paid at the cash desk. 'We'll go and have a look at Fenwick's. They've got more your kind of thing.'

'I've got to go soon,' Sarah reminded her.

'Already? No time for a coffee?'

Sarah looked at her watch. 'A quick one. My turn to pay, remember.'

The queued in the Buttery. Marie lifted all the lids to inspect the food, although the cases were transparent. 'Aren't you eating, Sarah?'

Sarah shook her head. 'I can't face food before going to the hospital. Silly, I know.'

'What are you having done this time?'

'Oh,' said Sarah dismissively, 'Nothing much. No, let me pay, Marie.'

It was only when they had found a table and settled themselves with their handbags and carrier bags that Sarah remembered.

'What girl were you talking about, back in the shop? Someone you had to phone.'

'John Gee's wife. I have strict instructions from Harry to invite her to the Gossip tonight, to make her feel "part of the team" as he calls it. John is Harry's latest bright young thing, you know, so Harry's keen to stop his eyes wandering to other companies. So there you are; we're stuck with her, whatever she's like. I didn't even know John was married. Apparently the wife's been living on her own up north somewhere.'

'York,' supplied Sarah.

'Pardon?'

'Helen's coming down from York,' Sarah explained. 'She kept her job and stayed up there to sell their flat. You know John used to work at the York office?'

'You seem to know more than I do,' said Marie jealously.

'Only a little,' said Sarah quickly. 'I met her once when she was down here for a weekend. John brought her over for supper.'

'I was forgetting that John's a friend of Ben's,' said Marie, appeased. 'What's she like?'

'Younger than us, of course. John's only twenty-four or five, isn't he? I think Helen must be about the same age. Small. Fair-haired. Wears her hair in plaits wound round her head.'

'God!' said Marie, appalled. 'But what's she *like?*'

'Rather quiet,' said Sarah reflectively. 'But then Ben and John were talking shop all night. But she seemed nice.'

'You think everyone's nice,' said Marie. 'I can't see her fitting in. Plaits round her head? God!'

Sarah laughed. 'What's so awful? Anyway, if you don't like her you don't have to see much of her. Once you've done your public relations bit this evening.'

'Don't you believe it,' said Marie darkly. 'Harry sees me as an unpaid member of his division – Entertainments Officer or something.'

'And you love it,' Sarah teased her. 'Or you wouldn't already be shopping for clothes for the sales conference.'

Marie's eyes brightened. 'I think I might stay on here a bit longer,' she confessed. 'I saw that Marta's had some new cocktail dresses in. I didn't tell the hag-in-law I'd be back by any particular time so I'm sure she won't mind putting up with the little darlings for another hour or so.'

'You abuse that poor woman,' Sarah protested. 'She won't offer again.'

'She never does offer,' said Marie serenely. 'I tell her she's having them. If you had children you'd do the same.'

'I must go,' said Sarah, standing up. 'I'll see you tonight, Marie. Usual time?'

When Sarah had gone, Marie went back to the counter and fetched herself another coffee.

'Milk or cream, love?'

'Cream.' No point in hurrying back to the chores. She was already spoiling pleasure with business by shopping for food for the Gossip tonight. Something quick to prepare but not too exotic. Last time she slapped smoked salmon on to crackers Polly had made some remark about the standard of living of directors' wives.

Marie sipped her coffee and turned the pages of her diary, calculating the number of sunbed sessions before the date of the sales conference. With a darker tan she might get away with wearing white one evening.

* * *

Polly had ironed two dresses and now she was ironing a third.

'That was George Benson's new single,' the radio informed her. 'And now we have Evelyn Strongway on the line, from East Grinstead. Hello Evelyn!'

Polly gave the sleeves a final press and switched off the iron.

'Hello Evelyn! Evelyn? Are you there? No? Well, we seem to have lost Evelyn but we'll be having another listener on the line shortly. In the meantime, here's a beautiful ballad from everyone's favourite, Barry Manilow . . .'

Polly gave the Off knob a sharp click. She had a sudden vision of the unknown Evelyn lost not in transmission but in East Grinstead, suddenly losing her nerve on hearing herself connected to the outside world. 'Hello there, Evelyn!' But Evelyn, unused to anyone knowing she was there, was cowering in her kitchen, between the radio and the telephone, till the cheery, confident voice abandoned her – mentally cursing her, no doubt – and left her to the safety of her loneliness.

Taking the stairs two at a time was ungainly but good for the thighs, and Polly's thighs were ungainly. She undressed out of sight of the mirror then stood in front of it in one newly ironed dress after the other.

'No,' she said to the first one, and 'No' to the second. In the third, she pursed her lips. 'It'll have to do,' she told the funny-looking woman in the mirror, then caught sight of her turning her back. 'Oh no,' she said. 'Oh no. That's it. I can't go this evening. I'll have to give Marie a ring and say I've got a cold.'

Despair is a silly thing. Tea is better. Tea with no sugar and only one plain biscuit.

'Polly put the kettle on!' sang Polly, sounding happy. 'Polly put the kettle on, we'll ALL have TEA!'

She rinsed out the pot, poured milk into a dainty cup and then changed her mind and tipped it into a mug. What difference did it make, in the end? She opened the biscuit tin and selected a Cut Price rich tea. She looked at it for a long time. The kettle boiled. She opened the cupboard door, took out a packet of custard creams and threw six of them on to the tray with the teapot.

'Polly put the kettle on,' she sang, and a tear ran down her face. 'Polly put the fucking kettle on!'

Helen would have liked to go down to the park round the corner while the men were unloading the furniture, taking her sketchpad with her and sitting in the shade of one of the trees till her headache evaporated. But John had told her to be sure to supervise every stage of the removal. 'They're a load of sharks,' he said knowledgeably. 'You keep an eye on them.'

So Helen kept an eye on the unsharklike figures of Tom and George, who had bought her tea and a Mars bar at the transport café on the way down, and felt a faint pang of regret when they had stowed the last packing case in the narrow hall and bade her a friendly goodbye.

There were two ways to go about the task – or three, but John might not have approved of the third, which was to unearth a blanket and go to sleep on it for a couple of hours. The two options were to stow the essential things roughly in the right places: pans and crockery in the kitchen cupboards, clothes in the fitted wardrobe – or to spend all her energies on creating one perfect room,

Three hours later, she knew she had made the right choice, for now the sitting room gave the illusion of a complete, well-ordered home – an illusion which was only shattered when she stepped outside the door and fell over the packing cases in the hall.

The sitting room carpet had been left by the last owners

of the flat; the two-seater couch, thanks to Tom and George, was where she wanted it to stand; the curtains were up, the rugs down, the books sat neatly on their shelves and, as soon as she had knocked in the final nail, the last of the pictures (her surprise present for John) would be in place over the unused fireplace.

Of course, John might change it all when he came in. And of course she must let him, if he wanted to. She must show him she hadn't been spoilt by living with Oliver who had let her have her own way 'far too much', as John had said with mock severity.

She ran a knife round the paint-shut window, letting in dust and sunshine. The first day of April. A new month, a new home, a new city, a new . . . no, not quite a new John but a new phase of their life together. And soon a new job: she must start looking around for one. Perhaps not quite yet, but as soon as the painting was finished, the one of the old woman in the supermarket.

She had stayed up late to finish it last night, surrounded by the filled packing cases. But her thoughts had kept straying down to London, where John slept alone for the last night in his Chelsea flatlet. The old woman's face remained stubbornly devoid of character, and in the end Helen had given up and gone to bed leaving the painting incomplete.

When the clinic session was over (no medical students this time) Sarah hurried out through the fire exit and made her way to the car, stopping only to buy a magazine. A present for a good girl, she thought wryly. Some of the women who attended the clinic bought themselves clothes after every visit, or walnut whirls. Or went on the gin. You needed something. Sarah made do with a magazine.

In the car, she thumbed briefly through it. 'How Motherhood Changed My Life' cried the centre-page headline, above a full-colour photo of a famous actress, holding a baby that looked like everyone else's.

'I went back to work when Gemma was three months old,' Sarah read, 'and it broke my heart. I'm an actress. I have to work; it's in my blood. But motherhood means everything to me.

'While I was rehearsing my new TV series (*A Plaintive Sound*, BBC 1, Wednesdays from 21 September) Gemma went down with gastroenteritis, and do you know I was on the phone to that nanny at least twice every day?'

Sarah started the engine and looked in the driving mirror before she began to reverse.

'Jake,' said Eleanor into the phone, 'just a quickie. Did you get Gaby's medicine or do you want me to pick it up on my way home? Sure? Okay. I'm just off to this meeting now. Great Newport Street. Home about seven-thirty, okay? What? Oh God, I'd forgotten. Marie's isn't it? All right – no, don't do supper for me; I won't have time. See you later, love. Kiss to Gaby. Bye. Jeannie!' she called, putting down the receiver. 'I'm off. Where's the agenda for the meeting?' She collided with Jeannie in the doorway between their offices.

'I put it in your briefcase.'

'Good. Let me just check – yes, fine. I'll see you tomorrow, Jeannie. Did you get through to Bowers?'

'Mr Cowdry's still at lunch.'

'At quarter to four?' Eleanor arched her eyebrows. 'Keep trying his number, will you? Good.'

The phone began to ring. Jeannie picked it up. 'Hello, Mr Savage.' She looked at Eleanor inquiringly. Eleanor shook her head.

Mr Savage's voice resounded down the phone. 'Can I have a word with your lovely lady boss?'

Eleanor tucked her briefcase under one arm and waved with the hand that was holding her car keys.

'I'm sorry, Mr Savage,' Jeannie said. 'I'm afraid she's just left the office.'

From the doorway into the bedroom, the portrait over the fireplace looked even better. She had caught the hunch of John's shoulders as he sat at the computer, a wad of printout in his left hand while his right hand hovered over the keyboard and a shaft of light glinted on his gold-rimmed spectacles. He looked young and keen and vulnerable like that. It was the way she had liked to remember him while they were apart.

The sun spilled wastefully on to the bedroom floor. Helen lay down on her back and caught the rays in her upturned face. It's not such a bad place, she thought. I probably won't miss York all that much.

She would tell John, when he arrived after work, that she felt a bit tired. Not too tired, but just not like going out. They would get fish and chips and sit in their little sitting room and discuss his plans for the rest of the flat. They would have a quiet evening together and then they would go to bed.

She had fallen into a doze when the phone began to ring. After a few bemused minutes she located it behind a portfolio. 'Yes? Hello?'

'Helen,' said an unfamiliar voice. 'Marie Kusek. I have strict instructions from your husband and mine to confirm that you really are coming tonight. Half-past eight. Don't bring anything. Okay? See you later then; I must fly.'

2

Setting Out

'Ben!' called Harry, catching sight of him in the car park.
'I won't keep you,' he added, as Ben obediently came
over. 'John Gee. Do I approach him or do you want to
handle it yourself?'

Ben had no intention of letting anyone but himself offer
membership of his team, but he made a play of considering the question.

'I'm seeing him tonight,' he said, as though this fact
had just occurred to him. 'How about if I sound him out,
just off the record? Of course the job offer has to come
from you, but it might be as well to give him a chance to
sleep on it before he has to give an official answer.'

'Good thinking, Ben.' Harry slapped him on the shoulder, in the paternal style he liked to affect with his
younger managers when they were in favour. 'You do
that,' he approved, getting into his Mercedes. 'By the
way,' he said as an afterthought, depressing the electronic
window switch, 'where are you going this evening – you
and John?' He had just remembered that Marie wanted
him out of the house. Gossip nights excluded husbands,
even if they wanted to stay.

'I'm helping him move flats,' Ben said.

'Ah. Well, good moving,' said Harry, moving off
himself.

'You can stay up and see Mummy,' said Jake, 'as long as
you're ready for bed. Teeth brushed, nightie on, okay?'

'And stay while she's having her supper?' Gaby
bargained.

'She's not having supper tonight; she's going out.'

Gaby stamped her foot. 'I don't *want* her to!' she shouted. 'I want her to stay for supper!'

'Tomorrow,' said Jake. 'Promise. Come on; we'll run your bath.'

Gaby looked at him out of the corner of one calculating eye. 'Tomorrow and tomorrow, and the day after too,' she said.

'You take after Eleanor,' said Jake. 'A businesswoman at seven. All right, you win. Now come and have your bath.'

Oriel had promised Polly she wouldn't linger on the way home from school. She sauntered slowly (which was not the same thing as lingering), swinging her bag. She had removed the belt of her school dress and tied it round her head, sweeping back her long fair hair and its dyed blonde fringe.

On the corner, Elvis Simpson waited with his mates – for Oriel, or for any other girl. In unison, they began to whistle.

'Oriel!' chanted Elvis. 'Or-i-el!'

Head in air, bag swinging nonchalantly, she passed them.

'Care for a bit of oriel sex?' said Elvis, and they all cheered – or jeered. Sometimes the dividing line between the two was thin. A girl had to be careful. Too eager to please and she was a slag; too haughty, and she was a pain in the four-letter word. Today, Oriel had to be indifferent, because yesterday she had looked at him.

'Oriel!' sang Elvis, as she crossed the road. Then, in a lower voice, 'Oriel, Bore-iel!'

That did it. You couldn't afford to let them coin such a phrase or it would be all over everywhere before you knew it. Halfway across the road on the traffic island she

paused and, calculating the exact location of Elvis behind
her back, turned swiftly and, looking straight into his
eyes, she smiled.

'Way-hey!' cheered the gang. 'You're in there, Elvis!'

Oriel turned the next corner and walked quickly down
the street. Her heart was pounding and her hands were
covered in sweat. What would she do tomorrow, having
gone so far today? What would he do? She would do
anything for her class to see her out with Elvis Simpson.
Anything.

'Oriel, is that you?' Polly called, coming into the hall.
'Have a nice day?' She leaned to kiss her, but Oriel
ducked her head.

'All right,' she said, without enthusiasm.

'What did you do?' Polly inquired.

Oriel shrugged her shoulders, turning away. 'Nothing,'
she said.

'Want a cup of tea?' Polly said. 'I've put the kettle on.'

'No, thanks,' said Oriel. 'I've got my homework to do.'

Ben, watching Harry drive off, felt sore without knowing
why. John Gee, he thought, getting into his car. Logodata
Inc's new programming genius, soon to be – if everything
went as planned – the new software genius, in Ben's own
team.

There was the sore point. Ben was not at all sure he
wanted a genius in his team. Better in his team, earning
him commission and praise, of course, than in someone
else's, but still . . . It was only two years ago that the
name on everyone's lips, the hot tip for fast promotion,
was Ben Jepson. Not that Ben had not fulfilled his early
promise. Regional sales manager for a firm the size of
Logodata by the age of twenty-eight was not bad by
anyone's standards. He had nothing to fear from any up-
and-coming young men. Especially not from John.

It was Ben who had persuaded John – an ex-rugby-playing friend from his school Old Boys' team in Darlington – to join the firm. Ben had claimed the £50 bonus offered to staff who introduced a suitable friend to the company, and John was suitable. So suitable, in fact, that after only six months in the northern branch, John had been invited to join the central programming staff at the London HQ. And when Harry, as sales and marketing director, had talked to Ben about Logodata's plans to expand its software sales, Ben had thought immediately of John. There was no doubt that John would be an asset to the team and an asset to Ben as its leader. So why did the prospect make Ben feel insecure? 'Soon be time I was moving on,' Ben said aloud.

He felt reluctant to face John before he had had a chance to work out the proposal; he needed more thinking time. He considered calling in at a pub on the way to John's digs, but pubs were no place to think.

Ben found that the car, as if with a mind of its own, had taken the usual turning for home. Well, why not? he thought. He could use a cup of tea before he started shifting furniture, and what was a wife for if not to act as a sounding board for ideas?

If Ben didn't turn up soon, John thought, then by the time they had loaded the van and driven from Chelsea, Helen would have gone out to this women's thing.

He looked at his watch again and, for the third time, checked that the stereo deck was well protected with the polystyrene sheeting he had taken from work. His thoughts were with the new flat, with Helen waiting for him. Would she be pleased with his choice? Today would be her first chance to see the flat. Would she think he had got a good deal? Would Helen have made the flat look like home? Would the furniture from York look out of place – or worse still, out of date – in a London flat? Would Helen feel as nervous as he unaccountably did, at moving in together again? Would she have put up the bed . . .?

John stood by the window and looked for the last time, out at the rooftop view of his 'bachelor pad'. A bachelor, he had been in effect, for the last three months. 'Best of both worlds, lucky bastard!' the lads at work had said. Not that it hadn't been fun at times, doing the clubs some nights with Ashok and Steve – and Ben had been only too keen to join him at playing bachelors, when he could get free.

But it had been lonely too, especially when Helen had had to work overtime and couldn't come down for weekends. He had gone up there one Sunday, although she had said she would hardly be home at all, and had waited in for her with increasing agitation – not helped by that poofy idiot Oliver yattering on – until he had heard her key in the door at twenty past nine. He had been so relieved to see her (would anyone really work till twenty past nine, even the day before an important audio-visual show?) and also so afraid that she would find it strange that he had driven all that way just to see her for a couple of hours, that instead of greeting her lovingly he had snapped, 'What kind of time is this to get home?'

But Helen had been unmistakably happy to find him there. She had cooked him spaghetti and made a fuss of him, and they were in bed by half-past ten, and even Oliver playing heavy music in his room had not disturbed the harmony between them. He had had to get up at five o'clock to drive down to London in time for work the next morning, but it had been worth it. A good seven hours. John smiled to himself at the memory.

But where the hell was Ben?

* * *

22

'Darling,' said Sarah, kissing him. 'But aren't you meant to be helping John?'

'John can wait,' said Ben. 'I've had a lousy day. Make us a cup of tea, love.'

He kicked off his shoes, shrugged out of his jacket and tugged his tie to half-mast.

'What kind of day did you have?' he inquired, following Sarah into the kitchen.

She took a deep breath. 'Well . . .' she said.

'Where are the matches?' Ben asked.

'Here.'

'Fucking lighter ran out of fuel. Fucking car's not ready either; I'm still in that bloody hired one. It's a joke.'

'When will they have yours done?' Sarah asked.

'They *say* tomorrow. And then it'll take me a couple of days to get used to it, after the stupid buggers have tightened the brakes almost rigid, like they did last time.'

'Never mind, love,' Sarah said absently.

The phone rang.

'I'll get it,' said Ben. 'You make the tea.'

Waiting for the kettle to boil, Sarah ran her eyes over the calendar. It had become a habit, charting the days neatly, writing her own personal dates in above the universal ones: 4 April – day 12 of her cycle; 5, 6, 7, 8, 9 April – the all-important days, according to the clinic.

Ben had bought her this large-scale calendar, had entered into the spirit of the exercise, until the day the doctor had chided Sarah for not having intercourse on the 'right days' and she had returned home in tears.

'Bloody nerve!' Ben had exclaimed. He had been the one, that time, who had said he was too tired for sex five nights in a row, and he feared that Sarah had made this known to the doctor, and publicly slighted his manhood.

So after that, Sarah had not told him, directly, on which days he was expected to satisfy the clinic's requirements

23

for attempted fatherhood. She merely continued to write the figures in, above the dates on the calendar – day 13, 14, 15, 16, 17 – and Ben too had acquired the habit of glancing at it when he came in. He was stern with her, and with himself, over 'missing the right days', sterner really than the half-disinterestd doctors, though Ben blamed his own strictness on to them.

'We'd better leave the party early tonight,' he'd say mockingly, 'or you'll have old Hitler on to you again.'

He had even started referring to sex as 'collecting ticks on your chart to please the clinic'. Sarah wished he wouldn't.

Ben returned. 'Your mother,' he said shortly. 'I said you'd call her back.'

Sarah looked questioning. 'I could have spoken to her now.'

'No you couldn't; I want to talk to you. Call her when I'm at John's.'

'I'm going to Marie's,' Sarah reminded him.

'You'll have time before you go! Bloody hell!'

Sarah carried the tray into the sitting room and pulled a small table close to Ben's chair.

'Here. Relax, and tell me what the trouble is.'

He sat for a couple of minutes in restless silence, tapping ash from his cigarette before it had accumulated any.

'By the way,' he said, 'how was the hospital?'

'Well . . .' Sarah hesitated again. 'Look, why don't we talk about that later? That isn't what you wanted to say.'

'It was a perfectly simple question,' Ben said, 'which needs a simple answer. In fact, you could have bloody well told me when I came in the door, instead of waiting till your bloody mother phoned to ask how you got on and made me sound a bloody idiot for forgetting your appointment was today.'

Sarah stirred his tea for him and placed the cup beside him, handle towards his hand.

'It doesn't matter,' she said. 'We'll talk about it later. It was okay.'

'Either it was okay, in which case there's no more to be said, or something's wrong that we need to talk about later; you can't have it both ways,' Ben insisted.

Sarah suppressed a sigh.

'They've completed the tests,' she said, 'and found nothing wrong with me. They suggest re-running all the ones they did at the beginning, two years ago, in case there's anything they missed.'

'So?'

'We'll think about it, shall we?' Sarah suggested. 'What did you want to . . .?'

'What's there to think about?' Ben interrupted. 'You've done every bloody thing they've ever said.'

'Ben, let's not go into this now.'

'Go into what? Where's the problem? Our lives are run by that clinic; what's another two years of it?'

'Well, that's what I was thinking,' said Sarah, with relief. 'We've done all we can to try and have a child, and maybe we're just not meant to, and it's time we . . .'

'Oh, I knew it!' Ben exclaimed, 'I knew you'd bring bloody religion into it somehow. Two years of subjecting yourself to the wonders of medical science, and at the end of it all, you say, "It's just not meant."'

'If they say they've missed something, then they obviously have, haven't they? Women are meant to reproduce. If they don't then there's something wrong somewhere. It's obvious, and the doctors haven't found it yet. So we'll have to allow for their incompetence and live our lives by the bloody calendar, if not the stopwatch, for as long as the clinic requires. Because it's the clinic you're relying on to cure you; it's not some imaginary God.'

Sarah sipped her tea, sitting on the edge of her chair with her skirt drawn over her knees.

'Well?' he said.

'I think,' she said carefully, 'that it needs more thinking about. Let's leave it.'

'No, let's not leave it. Let's sort it out. What exactly are they wanting now?'

'It's what we want that counts,' Sarah said. 'They will keep on trying to help, at the clinic, if we want to go on. But I can't see much point in going on indefinitely. It's a strain on both of us, and the tests aren't exactly pleasant . . .'

'So?'

'So maybe it's time to accept it, that we may not have children of our own.'

'Have they said you can't have children?'

'No. They can't find any reason against it. That's why they want to re-test us both.'

'Both?' Ben's face darkened. 'There's nothing wrong with my sperm count. They tested that first, and it was bloody embarrassing, but they said it was perfectly normal.'

'But my results are, too,' Sarah pointed out.

'What is this? Some kind of trial?' Ben demanded. 'Who's to blame? Which one is deficient? Do we get a jury?' He was leaning forward in his chair.

'Ben,' Sarah said. 'It isn't like that. Don't you think it's better to leave it? Have your tea.'

'I'm going out,' Ben said, 'I'm late as it is.'

'But didn't you want to talk to me about something?' Sarah pleaded.

'Forget it,' said Ben. 'I'll work it out for myself.'

'I got ready-made quiche and frozen cheesecake,' Marie said. 'I'm too tired to think of making things. And Polly turned her nose up, the last time I did smoked salmon.'

'She's only jealous,' Harry said, putting his arm round her shoulders and squeezing her.

'And there'll be one extra, thanks to you,' Marie complained. 'I hate having strangers at the Gossips; it spoils the atmosphere.'

'Good thing,' said Harry heartily. 'Stops you all getting smutty and swapping anecdotes about your husbands.'

'We've got better things to talk about. And if Polly brings that snotty-nosed daughter of hers I shall tell her where to go.'

'No, you won't,' Harry said confidently. 'You'll say, "Oriel, what a nice surprise; do come in!"'

Marie laughed. 'Well I'm not feeding her,' she warned. 'She wasn't invited and I haven't catered for six.'

'How about feeding me?' Harry wheedled. 'Just a little taste, to make sure it's all right?'

'After that big business lunch?' she scolded. 'You'll get heart trouble. It's bad for middle-aged men to eat too much.'

'Less of the middle-aged!' he said, smacking her on the bottom. 'Just because I snatched my wife from the cradle!'

'You can have some of yesterday's pâté,' she said relenting. 'It's in the fridge. Where are you going this evening?'

'I'll just stay up in my den,' Harry said, with his back turned.

'Oh no, Harry, come on! All the other husbands go out when it's their wife's turn.'

'That's different,' Harry claimed. 'They're young men. You've just accused me of being old; now you want to turn me out of my own house after a hard day's work.'

'Okay,' she bargained. 'On one condition: you don't mention the price when I show you what I bought today.'

'You'll ruin me,' he groaned, but he was smiling. 'Go and put it on and show me. I hope it's sexy.'

'And glamorous,' Marie promised him. 'I got it for the sales conference.'

'That's months away yet! Don't remind me.'

She kissed him on the lips. 'As my husband's ex-secretary, I believe in forward planning. My boss taught me everything I know.'

'In the days when I still was the boss,' he grumbled, 'and not just the bankrupt husband.'

'I'll show you the dress,' Marie said. 'You'll say it was worth double – whatever it cost. It's got no back to it, and not a lot of front.'

He wound his arm around her waist. 'Have pity on an old man's hormones,' he begged. 'Can't you get rid of these gossiping women tonight?'

'Later,' she said, waltzing out of his grasp and giving a little wave as she left the room.

It amused them to play the old game still – the older man lusting after irresistible young girl – just as though they were not three years married now with two little girls; just as though Harry were not under some strain at times, by eleven o'clock, not to be 'too tired'; as though Marie had not discovered her first grey hair the other day; and as though Harry had never quite managed to lose (although he did disguise) his shameful taste for Horlicks at night.

Marie waited until she was sheathed in the silky off-white backless, thin-strapped dress before peeking in the children's bedroom to check that three-year old Sorrel and baby Sacha were safely asleep. It was one of her concessions to motherhood.

'I'm too old to be going out with Mother,' Oriel said. She was curled up on her bed, her long fair hair falling over the page of the teen magazine she was engrossed in.

28

'Well, you don't have to come,' Polly said. 'I expect you have homework to do, anyway.'

There was an unspoken promise in this one: come with me and I'll turn a blind eye if your homework doesn't get finished, just for once.

Oriel knew she would go, but she wasn't going to let Polly win that easily.

'They'll all be so boring, your friends,' she said. And didn't add, 'Like you,' but simply, 'They're so middle-aged.'

'Oh no,' Polly protested. 'They're quite a bit younger than me, most of them.'

Younger, prettier, smarter, more successful, more self-assured.

Oriel kicked the wall idly. 'I know they're younger than you, but they're still middle-aged.'

'Not Marie,' Polly said. She sat on the end of the bed, tentatively, glad that the conversation was being continued. 'I don't think Marie is even twenty-nine yet. You can't call that middle-aged.'

'She probably lies about her age,' said Oriel. 'That type would. And Sarah must be at least forty.'

'Thirty-three,' Polly corrected. 'Five years younger than me. And Eleanor's thirty-four, and . . . well that's it; that's everybody, isn't it?'

'Boring,' Oriel said. 'Same old faces every time. Same old boring talk. And Marie's week is the worst. She wouldn't even let me watch the rock concert last time.'

'The television was in the same room as us,' Polly excused her. 'It is hard to talk while it's on.'

'It would have done them good to shut up for a while and listen to something good,' Oriel pronounced. She lay back on the bed and yawned dismissively. 'Think I'll wash my hair,' she said.

Polly became nervous, as Oriel had intended. 'Oh, but would it be dry in time, that is if . . .?'

'I don't think I'll come with you this time,' Oriel said. 'You go on your own.'

'I was thinking of not going anyway,' Polly said. 'I've nothing to wear to it really. Which do you think looks least awful on me, the green or the blue? Not that anyone's going to look at me,' she said, laughing self-deprecatingly.

'Exactly,' said Oriel. She went back to reading the comic. From the posters above her bed, satin- and leather-clad men snarled and pouted into microphones. Polly felt rejected.

'If I'm going,' she said, standing by the door, 'I'll be leaving at twenty past eight. If you change your mind and decide to come too.'

Oriel didn't raise her eyes from the page. 'I'll think about it,' she said.

The April evenings were lengthening, holding on the fading light till later every day.

Helen, leaning out of the window, watched the chilly sun sinking in deceptively warm pink streaks above flat and sloping roofs, the chimneys, television aerials and trees. Tomorrow she would go and look at the park. The eyes grow tired without their soothing dose of green, and Helen's felt sore and prickly from gazing on too much concrete and wood: too many browns and greys. The pink and gold of the sky revived them now, but they ached from desire to sleep. Another four hours, she calculated, before she could. What excuse could she find for not going this evening? Or would John's disappointment in her trouble her more than a couple of hours of forced conversation with strangers? She didn't know.

She resolved to go tonight, to behave impeccably, and

to make it clear, politely, that she was not suitable for them and they need not feel obliged to invite her every week. John could hardly expect her to go if she wasn't invited.

It wasn't, she told herself, that she was not prepared to like them – just that she wasn't eager to get into a routine as soon as she arrived. So, after tonight, no Gossips, no all-girls-together evenings, no – Helen shuddered at the thought – coffee mornings.

Snob! A voice within her accused. But, 'What if I am?' she said aloud. 'It's my life.'

As if looking for confirmation, she went over and stood in front of her painting of John. The fact of its accomplishment reassured her. She was an artist. She had just resigned from a good job in York, in graphic design. She was a person in her own right; she would never be a company wife.

At twenty past eight Polly gave a final despairing look into her mirror and wished, with utter hopelessness, that she was Sarah.

What she saw was not a reflection of her success in being Polly: generously built, with naturally wavy hair, a warm if rather tense mouth, and a nice face. She saw only confirmation of her failure to be Sarah.

The object of her envy, Sarah herself, was still sitting as Ben had left her. Suddenly recollecting herself, glancing at the carriage clock on the modern teak mantelshelf above the realistic fake log fire, she went out into the hall and, standing in front of the mirror, ran a comb through her hair, which was fine, dry and fair.

For a moment she wished she could have hair like Marie's buoyant dark curls that sprang back into shape even when she got caught in a shower of rain.

In fact she wished, just fleetingly, that she could have

the personality that went with those curls. It was hard to imagine Marie being flattened by life, failing to spring back after any setback. Marie had proved her buoyancy well enough during the long-drawn-out episode of Harry's divorce, which coincided with Marie's pregnancy and included a series of at first tearful and then abusive phone calls from Harry's wife.

Through it all, Marie's curls had lost none of their bounce, her conscience and even her figure showed no sign of stress, but simply swelled out a little, comfortably, to accommodate the added burden.

Sarah stared at her own worried face, and wished with all her heart she was Marie.

Marie, at twenty past eight, gave one last look in the full-length bedroom mirror and wished that she was Bo Derek, or at least that Polly's daughter Oriel didn't make her feel so middle-aged.

And Oriel, following Polly out of the house with a show of reluctance and a sullen goodbye to her dad, wished she was Susie Howard, who had a thirty-six inch bust and a different boy every week and never had to go anywhere with her mum just for the sake of going out.

Eleanor wished, briefly kissing Gaby and Jake, that she could be more like her husband and child, with their ease in each other's company, their simple enjoyment of life, and their freedom to waste time.

Only Helen, setting out from the new flat on her way to her first-ever Gossip, was wishing that she could be herself – the one she seemed to have left behind in York.

3

The Gossip

Eleanor didn't arrive at the Gossip. Helen could sense that this was a major disaster.

'Why don't you phone her?' Polly suggested. 'See if she's left?'

'I'll give it another ten minutes,' Marie said. 'I'll just take the quiche out of the oven. I can always reheat it in the microwave when she comes.'

'If she comes,' said Polly.

'She would have phoned,' Marie said, a shade snappishly. 'She always does.'

Helen wondered what was so important about Eleanor that they could not eat a slice of quiche without her. Helen was hungry.

'What's she like?' she asked.

Marie, Polly and Sarah gazed at her. Only Oriel continued to tug at tufts of the pale pink carpet where she lay sprawled, ignoring them all.

'Eleanor?' said Sarah. 'What is she like?'

'Yes,' Helen assented. It seemed a simple enough question to ask.

'Oh,' said Sarah, 'she's very nice. I'm sure you'll like her.'

Oriel clicked her tongue and raised her eyes skywards.

'Well it's difficult to describe someone you know well,' said Sarah defensively. 'Where do you start?'

'She's elegant,' said Polly. 'And successful. She has an important job with a company car.'

This was said with rancour. Helen wanted to ask

whether Polly's husband didn't qualify for a company car, but she didn't like to.

'She's had a lot of luck, though, with her job,' Marie added. 'She was around at the right time, when there was all this fuss about women being promoted, and equal opportunities, otherwise she'd probably still be a sales rep.'

'What does she do?' Helen asked.

'Public relations manager,' Marie said. 'I'm going to serve the quiche.'

Helen felt slightly bewildered. For someone so anxiously awaited, Eleanor had not been spoken of with any marked affection by anyone.

'She's a very sweet person,' Sarah said.

'Sarah thinks everyone's sweet,' said Polly with a little laugh, 'because she's so sweet-natured herself.'

'She's a bitch,' Oriel contributed.

'Oriel!' said Polly.

'I don't mean Sarah,' said Oriel impatiently. 'I meant Eleanor.'

'That doesn't make it any better,' said Sarah in reproof.

From the hall, they heard the sound of the telephone receiver being lifted.

'Lovely flowers,' Sarah said, to make conversation so that it didn't seem they were listening in on Marie. 'Marie always has fresh flowers in the house,' she added, addressing Helen. Helen nodded but couldn't think of a reply.

'Jake?' said Marie, on the phone. 'Hi, darling, how are you? Oh fine, thanks. Listen sweetie, we're having our little girls' gossip session tonight and we're missing your wife. Not ill or anything, is she? Sorry? Really? Oh, I see.'

'Mum,' said Oriel. 'Can't we go home now?'

'Ssh!' said Polly, but it was too late. They heard Marie replacing the receiver, then going into the kitchen.

They smiled at each other sociably.

'How's the flat coming on?' Polly asked Helen.

'You asked her that already,' Oriel said. 'I doubt if a flat can change much in ten minutes.'

Helen, who had been thinking that herself, wondered how Oriel had lived so long, and said to Polly, 'You'll have to come and see it.'

Polly lit up. 'I'd love to. When shall I come?'

'Oh, whenever you like.' Damn, Helen thought. And I said I wouldn't start getting involved with them.

'Tomorrow morning, elevenish?' Polly asked.

Helen was about to think of some excuse when she saw Polly's face, bright and anxious, like a spaniel that had been kicked and yet kept making friendly overtures. A glance at Oriel showed who had done most of the kicking.

'Fine,' Helen said. 'As long as you don't mind the mess.'

'Oh, I don't mind.'

Sarah was studying the wall.

'Sarah,' Helen said, 'would you like to come as well?'

Sarah's face brightened; Polly's fell. Oriel sneered. Helen longed for her little flat back in York, where people dropped in when they liked and life was simple.

'Yes,' said Sarah. 'Thank you. Shall I bring anything?'

'I'll bring something,' Polly said quickly. 'Do you like scones?'

'It's not a fucking dinner party!' Oriel said, and once again Helen was ashamed of both disliking the girl and hearing her voice her own thoughts.

Marie returned bearing a tray of quiche and four little china plates, so fragile they were almost transluscent.

'What have you all been discussing while I've been in the kitchen?' she said brightly.

35

'What did Jake say?' Oriel inquired. 'Has the Lady Eleanor sneaked off to her lover?' She and Polly turned expectant faces towards their hostess, and for a fleeting moment Helen had the absurd impression that Oriel was a ventriloquist's dummy, brought along by her mother to make all the rude remarks Polly would like to make but didn't dare.

Marie handed a plate each to Polly, Helen and Sarah, and kept the fourth for herself. She did not look at Oriel. She handed round the quiche and four little bone-handled cake forks.

'You've forgotten Oriel,' Polly said.

'So I have,' said Marie.

'I don't want any,' Oriel said. 'I feel sick. Where is Eleanor, Marie?'

The door opened a crack.

'Sorrel!' said Marie. 'What are you doing out of bed?'

'I want to see Oriel,' the little girl said.

'Go back to bed,' Marie told her. 'I'll come up in a minute and give you some sleepy medicine.'

But Sorrel had already run to Oriel and climbed on her legs, smiling happily. Oriel returned the smile. Helen had doubted whether she had one. Perhaps Oriel had just been bored, she thought, with a pang of fellow feeling.

'Babies love Oriel,' Polly commented.

'They don't,' Oriel said. 'Not all of them. Come on, Sorrel, come and play with Oriel. I'll take you upstairs.'

'Don't disturb Harry, in his study,' Marie cautioned.

'I wouldn't go near him,' Oriel assured them all. She went out with the little girl clinging to her hand.

Helen thought she saw steam coming out of Marie's ears, but it could have been rising from the quiche.

'Marie,' said Sarah. 'Is Eleanor all right?'

Three things happened at once then. The phone rang, the doorbell rang, and Harry came downstairs.

'I couldn't resist all you lovely ladies,' he said, but his eyes were on the quiche.

'Answer the phone, will you, Harry,' Marie said, 'while I get the door.'

Helen missed her first glimpse of Eleanor because the phone call was for her.

'It's John,' said John.

'Anything wrong?'

'No, just that you'd left by the time I got in with Ben. How's it going?'

'Oh,' said Helen. 'Fine. I expect I'll be leaving soon. Why don't you walk down and meet me? Give me a reason to leave.'

'Ben's still here,' John said. He had lowered his voice.

'So? Can't he wait for us, or walk down with you or something?'

John laughed. 'You've got a lot to learn. Ben wouldn't dream of crashing a Girls' Gossip.'

'We're hardly girls,' said Helen irritably, 'and there's not a lot of gossip, so don't hold back. Just come and ring the doorbell and I'll walk home with you.'

'Oh, I'd better stay with Ben,' John said. 'We'll see you when you get back.'

'Fine,' Helen said. 'What was it you rang for, John?'

'Just to say hello and see if you were okay.'

'Oh, well, see you later then.'

When Helen came back into the room, Eleanor was perched on the edge of the coffee table, talking to Harry.

'Helen!' Marie cried. 'Come and distract Eleanor from all this shop talk, then we can banish my husband and have some peace. Eleanor, meet Helen.'

Eleanor, tall and immaculately dressed in a dark linen suit and flowered blouse, turned her attention from her company director to the newcomer. She did not, as Polly and Marie had done, look Helen up and down, from the tousled plaits coiled on top of her small blonde head to the strips of red sock between jeans and striped canvas boots. Instead, she looked Helen straight in the eye and said, 'Hello Helen. I work with John. Nice to meet you. When did you move down here, finally? Today? Good God, what are you doing here? You must be shattered!'

This could have been Helen's cue for saying. 'Yes, I am tired,' and leaving, but somehow she sat down again. It wasn't that it seemed rude to walk away from Eleanor, rather that it seemed unnatural.

Eleanor had abandoned Harry now, who was helping himself to quiche, and began to question Helen as thoroughly as if she was interviewing her. How had the move gone, she wanted to know? How long had Helen stayed in the flat in York, after John had left? Three months? Would she find it difficult to adjust to living here?

Helen answered, and the others listened, with the exception of Harry who, having sneaked into the kitchen and helped himself to a portion of pudding as well, was content to leave the company of the 'lovely ladies' he'd claimed to find irresistible and return to his den upstairs.

Helen was slightly embarrassed to find herself the centre of attention, but Eleanor's questions were friendly and her interest genuine. Sarah, listening, envied her. Why couldn't I think of asking Helen those things, she wondered? Eleanor covered all the details of the move, asking everything, Helen noticed with gratitude, except, 'How's the flat?' Now she moved on to Helen's job in York.

'She worked for a design firm,' Marie put in quickly, to show that Eleanor was covering old ground here.

'Oh? What did you do?' Eleanor asked.

'Secretary,' Polly said.

'Graphic designer,' said Helen.

38

Polly looked affronted. 'I thought you were a secretary,' she said.

'No,' Helen said.

'I'm sure you said you were a secretary!' Polly insisted. 'When I asked what you did.'

'She didn't,' Marie said. 'She said she worked for a company. You didn't ask what she did.'

'What sort of jobs do you handle?' Eleanor asked.

'I was the junior, so I mostly got the less creative jobs,' Helen said, 'like diagrams for instruction manuals and layout of copy for brochures, but I did do one or two letterheads and company logos.'

'And you're looking for the same kind of job here – or have you got one already?'

'No,' Helen said, 'I'll be looking.' But not just yet, she added mentally.

Marie brought in the dessert, a raspberry cheesecake.

'Marie, that looks lovely,' Sarah said.

'It would do,' Marie said tightly, 'if Harry hadn't dug into it first.'

'I shouldn't have any,' said Polly wistfully, but Marie said, 'Oh Polly, you must!' and cut her a large slice.

'I won't have any,' Eleanor said. 'I haven't started my quiche yet. Delicious, Marie.'

'It's not home-made,' Marie said. 'I'm not one of these dedicated housewives, like Polly and Sarah, I'm afraid!'

'I'm a terrible cook,' said Eleanor. 'Jake's much better than I am. I buy everything ready made.'

'It's all right if you can afford it,' Polly said.

Eleanor wrinkled her nose. 'It'd be nice to have the choice. You couldn't buy scones like your home-made ones, Polly. Get Polly to make you some scones, Helen,' Eleanor advised her. 'As a moving-in gift. They're so light they float off the plate.'

39

'I'm going to make her some.' Polly said, 'Tomorrow morning. I'm going round for coffee, to see Helen's flat.'

Marie looked at Polly, then at Helen, but it was Helen's turn to study the pictures on the wall. I'm not inviting everyone, she thought; I don't see why I should ask Marie as well. She leant back in the chair, suddenly overwhelmed by tiredness. She felt too tired to make her goodbyes and walk home, so she just sat and let the conversation flow over her.

It was not that Eleanor talked a lot, she reflected, but she seemed to say things that got everyone else to talk. It was twenty minutes before even Polly remembered to ask, 'What kept you tonight, Eleanor? We were all getting worried.'

'Oh sorry – were you? I was at Leon's.'

'Leon?' said Marie, on a rising note. 'Eleanor, you naughty girl, now who's Leon?'

'I'm sure I mentioned him before,' said Eleanor, and Helen detected an undercurrent of impatience in her voice. 'The painter who's doing me a picture for Jake's birthday. I called in on the way here to see how it was going.'

'And two hours later she left,' Marie told Sarah.

Eleanor's wine glass shook very slightly in her hand. 'Well, I hadn't meant to stay at all,' she said. 'But the man is having some kind of mental block and he said he'd been starting paintings all day and throwing them away. He seemed quite depresssed, so I stayed for a drink with him and a chat. Partly out of self-interest, I must admit, because Jake's birthday's on the twenty-third, so I really hope Leon gets started again soon.

'By the way,' she added, 'don't mention to Jake that I was late getting here, will you, or he'll ask where I was and that'll spoil the surprise.'

There was an uncomfortable silence. They all looked at Marie. Marie looked back defiantly.

Eleanor summed the situation up. 'You phoned him, did you?'

'Well, I thought there must be something wrong,' Marie said angrily. 'I thought you would have phoned or something otherwise.'

'Of course,' Eleanor said, 'it was thoughtless of me. Never mind.' She looked at her watch. 'Is that really the time? Helen, can I give you a lift home? You look exhausted.'

In no time, it seemed, they were all putting coats on in the hall, and Polly had gone upstairs in search of Oriel, and Marie, with a grimly smiling face, was kissing them all goodbye.

Helen found herself in the passenger seat of Eleanor's car without knowing how she had got there.

'Which end of Sanderstead Road? Eleanor asked. 'The top? No, no trouble at all. We don't live far from you.'

She drove swiftly, not talking, but as she pulled in by the door of Helen's block of flats, she said, 'Graphic design. I'll ask whether they need anyone in graphics department at work. Worth a try, isn't it?'

Helen was half asleep. 'Thanks. Thanks for the lift then. Bye.'

'I'll see you again soon, Helen. I must come and see the flat sometime.'

'Yes, you're welcome.' They were obsessed with where you lived, Helen thought. A flat was a flat, wasn't it? Walls, ceiling and floors. And pile of packing cases to return to now. 'Goodnight.' She waved at the departing car, but Eleanor didn't look back. The street seemed suddenly deserted.

Halfway up the stairs, Helen was seized by a sudden premonition that something was wrong – that everything

41

was wrong about this place, and life would never be the same again.

She forced herself to climb the rest of the stairs. I'm tired, she told herself. I'm imagining things.

She took out her key, the key that the previous owners had left for her under the mat this morning. John already had his key, for he had called to see them the night before. He had met the young couple, knew their names, had heard from them how happy they had been in this little flat.

Perhaps if Helen had met them, she would feel differently. Perhaps if she had seen this flat, chosen by John for them both, before she had to accept it as their home . . . But she had been the one who said she didn't care where they lived, 'As long as we don't have to go on living apart.'

And now, after the three-month separation, here they were. Back together again, as though they had never been apart. Their own little home, a brand new start in the big ambitious city, with John doing so well in his job.

She had felt lonely so often, up in York, and had missed him on so many nights and early mornings, that she couldn't understand, now, this strange chill in her heart, a mixture of dread and homesickness.

Tired, she told herself firmly. That's all. Just tired.

She turned the key in the lock and went in to find John in their new home.

'Total disaster, if you ask me,' said Marie disgustedly. 'I don't know why I bother, I really don't. Harry, if you don't tell that child to stop her screaming and get into bed, she'll get the back of my hand . . .'

'I'll go,' he said.

* * *

Sarah gave Polly and Oriel a lift home, as she did every week, and Polly said, as she said every week, 'Come in for a coffee before you go home?'

She was half out of the car as she spoke, for the invitation had become a formality. Sarah always declined it: she must get back, she would say; Ben would be expecting her.

This time, to her own surprise and Polly's, she suddenly said, 'I'd love to. Do you mind?'

'Of course we don't mind!' Polly was delighted.

She led the way in. 'Go through and sit with Richard, while I put the kettle on. I won't be a moment.'

'Polly,' Sarah stalled her. 'I won't disturb Richard at this hour. I'll just have a quick cup in the kitchen with you, and then I'll go home.'

'You won't be disturbing him. Don't be silly! He's always delighted . . .'

'Polly,' Sarah said, 'please.' She could feel herself starting to cry.

Polly looked at her, startled. 'What's wrong?'

Sarah shook her head and couldn't answer. Polly took her arm and led her into the kitchen.

'Sit down here,' she said, 'and I'll make you a coffee.' Polly put the kettle on, this time for someone else, she thought. Somewhere inside her, a voice began to sing. Sarah's in trouble, and she's chosen to confide in me. Polly felt ashamed of her joy.

'Mum,' said Oriel coming in. 'Dad's watching some documentary and you said I could see *Late Latest* when we got in. Tell him . . .'

'Oriel,' said Polly, 'don't disturb us. I'll bring you in a coffee in a minute.'

'You're not listening to me!' said Oriel furiously. 'I want you to tell Dad . . .'

'Ask him yourself,' Polly said, 'nicely. But just leave us in peace for the moment, darling, will you?'

Oriel looked at Sarah. 'What's the matter?' she said.

'Oh, nothing,' Sarah said, 'really.'

Oriel went out. They heard her shouting at her father, then slamming the sitting room door. 'If you'd let me have a TV in my room, this wouldn't happen!' she shouted. 'I've told you before!'

'I shouldn't have come in,' said Sarah. 'It was thoughtless of me, Polly. I'll just go home and let you get to bed.

'You sit down,' said Polly firmly. 'Oriel and her father argue all the time. Just take no notice.' She set the coffee down on the table, with a plate of custard creams. 'Now,' she said. 'Tell me what's upset you.'

'Oh, I don't really know,' said Sarah helplessly. 'I didn't even think I was upset. I expect it's just things getting me down.'

Polly wasn't letting her get away with that.

'Is it something to do with Ben?' she asked. She had never trusted Ben to look after Sarah.

'No, no,' said Sarah quickly. 'Ben's fine.' She couldn't talk to Polly about Ben, because she couldn't trust Polly to like him as he was. 'No,' she continued, 'it's just me. The hospital tests have been going on a long time, you know, and I suppose I just feel I've had enough.' She started to cry again.

'But Sarah,' Polly said, touching her arm tentatively, 'it'll all be worth it if it works, won't it? If you and Ben have a baby. Doctors are so clever, aren't they? They can do such wonderful things these days.'

'I don't know,' Sarah sniffed. 'I'm beginning to wonder whether there aren't reasons why women don't have babies, and doctors have no business to poke you around and call you infertile. Maybe I'm very fertile, and my babies just don't get born.'

44

Polly was nonplussed. 'What do you mean?' She began to wonder if Sarah, so cool and calm normally, was having some kind of breakdown. Sarah was Polly's ideal, her idea of normal. If Sarah wasn't normal, then who on earth was? Certainly not Polly.

She spooned sugar into Sarah's cup, and stirred it for her. 'Drink your coffee,' she said encouragingly, and Sarah, out of habit, did as she was told.

Polly nibbled a biscuit and watched her. Sarah didn't usually talk rubbish. 'What sort of reasons,' Polly said cautiously, 'would there be for children not getting born?'

'Oh, ignore me, Polly,' Sarah said. 'I'm just confused. I don't know what I'm saying.'

'No – go on,' Polly was intrigued. 'I couldn't have any more after Oriel, and we never knew why.'

'Well,' Sarah said slowly, 'there are all kinds of medical explanations, and all kinds of things that can go wrong – low sperm count in the husband, poor ovulation in the woman – quite apart from obvious problems like blocked tubes. But nobody tells you why these things occur.'

Polly was letting her coffee go cold. 'Why do you think it is?'

'I think,' Sarah said, 'you can't just put it down to mechanical faults, or failures in the way you're made.'

'No,' Polly agreed. 'Some people have babies when they're considered infertile, and some people with nothing wrong with them just don't. They say it can happen when you stop worrying about it,' she added. 'Some couples adopt, and then . . .'

'I know,' said Sarah hastily. She was sick of miracle stories about couples who adopted a baby and then had their own. 'But I just don't think it's that simple. It doesn't take people's souls into account.'

Polly blinked. 'Souls?' she said faintly. She started to wish that Oriel would come in.

'Well, what about if you remember coming into the world yourself, and never really wanted to?' Sarah demanded. 'How could you forgive yourself for doing that to another child?'

'But Sarah . . .!'

'What if the father, when he was a little boy, was gentle and sensitive and spent his whole time, when he grew up, pretending to be tough? How could he teach his own son to do the same? And what if the son wouldn't play the game and showed him up?'

'But Sarah, a child is a gift . . .!'

'And what if,' Sarah continued, warming to her theme, 'the mother didn't really like herself very much, and had a daughter and couldn't like her either? How could she teach the daughter to like herself and to want to have children like her?'

Polly started to laugh, despite herself. 'Oh Sarah, if everyone went into all this, no one would ever have children at all! I mean, nobody's perfect, are they? You can't say you wouldn't make a good mother, because I'm sure you would. And Ben . . .'

'And Ben would have to stop being the child,' Sarah said. The words slipped out before she could stop herself. 'I must go home,' she said quickly. What had she said? Ben was always insistent that she must be loyal to him. But if Ben wouldn't listen, she had to talk to someone, surely? 'Polly, do me a favour,' she begged.

Polly was serious at once. 'Of course I will; what is it?' I'd die for you Sarah, she wanted to say, but it sounded embarrassing and melodramatic.

'Forget what I've just said. I was just upset after the hospital today, that's all.'

'Yes. Of course.'

Polly followed her to the door.

'Do you think I'm getting unbalanced about this?' Sarah

said, on the doorstep. 'You think I should see someone, or something?'

'There's nothing wrong with you,' Polly said staunchly.

'You're not just being nice?'

Polly hesitated.

'Go on,' Sarah prompted. 'Be honest with me, Polly.'

'There's nothing wrong with you,' Polly repeated. 'What you said sounds a bit funny, but I'm sure you could be right. But what can you do about it?'

Sarah sighed. 'That's just it,' she said. 'I mean, we've pinned all our hopes on having children, and blamed everything on the fact that we can't. But if we did, I've a feeling that things could be worse. But Ben just won't give up.'

She opened the gate and stood by the car.

'Sarah . . .' Polly called, but Sarah didn't look up from opening the car door. She waved before she drove off.

It was just as well, Polly thought. She had no idea of what she would have said. If I was Eleanor, she thought wistfully, I could have found the right words. Sarah would have done better to go home with her.

When Eleanor got home, Jake was already in bed. She went in and kissed him on the forehead. 'Want a coffee or anything, love?'

'No thanks.'

'Okay. I'll just have a shower and then I'll be in. I feel dead.'

On her way to the bathroom she looked in on Gaby. I hardly ever see her awake, she thought. The child, so active during the day, slept motionless, one hand raised on the pillow, with Eleanor's old teddy resting against her cheek.

When Gaby was a baby – Gabriella Sophie Louise, their first and only child, born when they were both

47

established in their careers – Eleanor used to stand by the cot, anxiously waiting to hear the child breathe.

I'm not a natural mother, she thought. I always worried too much. Eleanor's mother told her she was cold. 'Why don't you pick the child up? Show her some affection?' But Eleanor, so competent at work, had been afraid of the child's dependence, the need to keep her alive.

It was Jake who, with complete assurance, cuddled her and tickled her, taught her to make noises, threw her in the air, reducing them both to helpless giggles. Eleanor washed nappies, filled bottles, bought clothes and toys. Jake was always ready to help with the chores. 'I'll do that,' he would offer. 'You go and play with her.'

But Eleanor would sit on the floor with Gaby, uncomfortable and unsure of what to do, till Gaby yelled for her daddy or, later on, crawled off in search of him. Eleanor, who had kept an open mind about whether or not to go back to work after the baby was born, decided she would. In her job, she knew what to do and was only expected to do it, not to produce an alien range of emotions and become a model of motherhood. She had taken Gaby, in the early days, to a mother and baby group, in an attempt to integrate both of them with their peers, but the talk of teething troubles and feeding habits and colic had left her bored, and the noise had made her long for the peace of a busy office. At work, few of her colleagues even knew she had a child.

Jake had been sympathetic about her aversion to motherhood, but opposed the idea of employing a nanny. He took a sabbatical year away from the college where he taught, ostensibly to do research, and worked in the evenings, spending the day looking after Gaby and keeping house.

When the year was up, they made a major decision: Jake would give up his job till Gaby was settled at school, and spend his free time writing textbooks, which would supply him with useful credentials to help him apply for teaching jobs at that time.

It had sort of worked, except that Eleanor's job had increased in importance, with unexpected promotions to junior and then senior management, and growing encroachments on weekends and evenings. But Gaby had taken easily to playgroup and then, at five, to school. Eleanor organized the shopping, stocking the freezer methodically, so Jake was still able to do his writing.

That was how it worked, in theory. In practice, Jake found that he kept on falling asleep; that the trips to deliver Gaby to school in the morning and collect her mid-afternoon divided up his working day, and that often it proved impossible to make the mental gearshift from Care Bears at eight A.M. to economic theory at nine-thirty. And even if there were no additional chores (dry cleaning to be taken in, library books to return, a visit from the washing machine repair man) there was his share of the house to clean, and Jake had found himself becoming houseproud. 'I'm becoming a neurotic house-wife,' he joked one day, when Eleanor came home unexpectedly and caught him ironing tea towels, but she thought that it was only half a joke.

She liked him being at home and so did Gaby and so, he said, did he. 'Don't worry about it,' he reassured Eleanor. 'If I really burned to write textbooks, I'd find time somehow.' But she knew how hard it must be to summon up the enthusiasm and will to get down to work, when there were no bosses, no deadlines, and Gaby had begged him to make her a dolls' house instead.

The dolls' house stood in the corner of Gaby's room now, a work of love rather than art, and the economics textbook was still unfinished. Gaby had been happily settled in school for a year and a half now, and nothing had been said about Jake finding another job.

Eleanor left the door of the child's room ajar and went to have her shower.

Ben was half-lying across the two-seater sofa in Helen's sitting room, wide awake and belligerent. John had consumed the same amount of drink, but it had just made him sleepy.

The flat was in the same state as Helen had left it, except that the sitting room – her one perfect room – was all changed round. The picture above the fireplace had been taken down and stood on the floor, face to the wall.

'Well, hello!' Ben declared. 'The lady of the house! Welcome to the new abode.' His tone suggested he didn't think much of it.

Helen leaned against the door. Ben made no move to make room for her on the sofa, and John occupied the only armchair.,

'Hope you don't mind,' Ben continued, 'but we made a few improvements. The rest will have to wait till you build the extension. Just don't buy a cat that likes swinging, because there isn't much room to swing it.' He threw back his head and laughed, unpleasantly, Helen thought.

John joined in. 'Oh, we won't be staying here long,' he said, 'but this will do us till we find something bigger.'

'It seems all right to me. There are only two of us,' Helen pointed out. 'What happened to the picture?'

John looked embarrassed. 'I thought it might look better in the bedroom.'

'No, you didn't!' Ben contradicted loudly. 'You liar! I took it down, Helen my flower, because it was driving me mad trying to work out what it was meant to be.'

Helen went over and held it up. 'It's a picture of John,'

she said, 'at the computer. I was quite pleased with it, myself.'

'Oh-oh!' Ben chortled. 'Ben's made a boo-boo. I thought it was a kiddie with a handful of outsize bog-paper.'

'Don't be an idiot, Ben,' John laughed. 'If you can't recognize a computer print-out by now . . .'

'Well, with the programmes you wallies design, it's only fit to wipe your arse with, anyway,' Ben asserted.

John threw back his head and laughed, in exactly the same way Ben had. Helen's nerves were on edge. It was bad enough having to be in a room with one Ben, let alone two.

'Did you get the bed put up?' she asked shortly.

'Now there's a question!' said Ben. 'Passion time! Can you get John up, that's the real million-dollar one, eh John?'

Helen addressed herself solely to John.

'There's no bed then?' she said bluntly.

'I'll see to it,' he said. 'Sit down and have a drink.'

'No thanks,' she said.

She went into the bedroom. The divan was in the corner, where the removal men had put it, but John had put most of his belongings on top of it, and on top of the packing cases containing the bedding.

'John,' Helen said, returning to the sitting room, 'I'm going to need a hand to move the stuff off the bed.'

'Bed crazy, this one,' Ben remarked. 'You know how to pick 'em, friend.'

He and John laughed.

'Listen,' Helen said. 'Pardon me if I'm missing the funny side, but I've been up since five this morning and I want to get to bed, so could you please just give me a hand . . .'

'I could make an answer to that,' Ben said, 'but

somehow I think it wouldn't be appreciated. So I'll leave you lovebirds to it and be off to my own little home, God bless it, and my own little wife, God help me.' He swung his legs off the sofa and slid his feet into his shoes.

'Oh, you don't have to go,' John protested. 'Have a coffee?'

'I'm pining for one,' Ben said. 'But I'll go home. I can tell that your wife doesn't like me.'

John saw Ben to the door, and Helen could hear him denying this all the way.

She shifted one of his suitcases off the packing case which contained the pillows and double duvet, pulled them out, dragged them into the sitting room and threw them on the floor. She emptied the ashtrays out of the window.

'Don't do that!' John exclaimed, coming in as she was doing it. 'We've got to meet the neighbours here yet.'

'But not tonight,' Helen said. She lay on the floor and rolled herself in the duvet, fully clothed.

'Helen!' John said. 'Don't be like that. I meant to get the bedroom sorted out. I was just going to do it.'

'Leave it,' Helen said. 'We'll sleep in here.'

'I'm not sleeping on the floor,' he said mutinously.

When he got no answer from Helen, he poked her with his toe.

'Helen. It'll only take a minute to . . .'

She mumbled something that sounded like 'Gerroff.'

'Oh, fantastic,' he said, in Ben's tone of voice. 'Some reunion night this is going to be.'

But Helen was either asleep or pretending to be.

4

The Company

Ben arrived at the office next morning at a quarter to eight. He would make a story of it later. 'The best cure for a hangover is work,' he would tell his young sales staff. Ben Jepson, workaholic, legend of dedication to high standards and high income, company record-breaker in the fast promotion stakes.

His true reasons for arriving at work at such an unearthly hour were more complex than a hangover cure or the enhancement of his reputation.

Ben, who never flinched from confronting the most hostile and unco-operative customers – regarding them, in fact, as a welcome challenge – had lacked the courage to return home sober after the row with Sarah, and quailed at the prospect of waking to her mute forgiveness this morning.

His office was a refuge. Here his authority was not questioned – not openly, at least – by his staff. If there were arguments with colleagues and superiors, everyone recognized that the aim was to win. With Sarah, it was not enough to win the argument, to have the last word. Usually, with her, he could get his own way so easily that there was no triumph in winning, and as if that were not bad enough, she invariably made him feel that he was in the wrong.

She was so guiltless of ordinary human faults, like irritation and resentment, that he sometimes felt guilty just for being with her, for sullying her self-controlled calm with his selfishness and bad temper.

Then it was a relief to seek the security of his office,

with his double-drawered kneehole desk (instead of the single-sided ones accorded to junior staff) and the plaques on the wall recording his over-achievement of sales targets. Ben needed these plaques to cover the space on the walls which other managers in other offices filled with pictures of their children. The huge sales-projection chart, a year-planner calendar, and a map of his sales reps' districts within Ben's region, filled still more space and bore witness to more prestige.

Here he was safe, successful. It was even a virtue, in business, to be demanding and selfish. Ben's team did not achieve the success it did by having a regional sales manager who made allowances for weakness. He recruited staff who were dynamic, discontented, assertive and selfish. John Gee, he thought, might prove a little too soft to start with.

Two more reasons for his being seated behind his desk at this hour of the morning, playing with the executive toy Sarah had given him (his choice) on his twenty-eighth birthday: one, that title, 'regional sales manager', and two, John Gee.

If John was to join the team, Ben wanted some compensation, in advance, for possible damage to his ego. Recruiting a whizz-kid was a point in Ben's favour, but working so close to one was a disadvantage. It invited comparisons, and John had novelty value and three years more youth on his side.

Properly motivated, John could become a credit to Ben's team, but also a threat to Ben's personal record. To maintain his own status, Ben felt he needed some sign of promotion, ideally a rise in salary, but in any case a change in job title. That would merit at least a line and perhaps a photograph in the Promotions section of the in-house magazine, and a congratulatory paragraph or three in the bulletin sent to customers. It would be a sign that

Ben Jepson, however strongly rivalled, could not be overtaken.

Ben mused. He had not, after all, said anything to John last night about the prospect of the new job. Damn it, the guy was so pleased with himself already, with his new flat and his Helen, and that bloody stupid portrait she'd painted of him that made him look like a computer genius or something. Why should Ben add to his glory?

But now he had to speak to John before Harry beat him to it. It was unthinkable to admit to Harry that he had not done as he himself had offered, and intolerable that news of the job should come to John from the top instead of through Ben.

For a full five minutes Ben pondered the question of whether to leave a memo on John's computer terminal, requesting – no, instructing – him to come straight to his office on his arrival.

Eventually, he decided against it. It would look more official to get his own secretary to phone John's supervisor and have the supervisor call John out of the open-plan office, in front of the other staff. A summons from one of the Powers-That-Be.

Pleased with the fruits of his thinking, Ben treated himself to a coffee – black, no sugar – to celebrate the success of his careful planning. Another maxim he fed to his sales staff was 'Never neglect the detail. Detail pays dividends.'

Harry Kusek's reputation could just as easily be enhanced by arriving late at the office as by arriving early. As sales and marketing director, he could turn up when he liked, and no one would question it.

Today he arrived just before the official start of the working day, which was nine o'clock. He walked directly from the lift to his office, looking straight ahead. The sales staff and secretaries had learned that they were expected to wish him good morning but should not expect a reply.

It was common for Harry to walk past a salesman's desk, or even a manager's office, completely ignoring him, only to send for him a few minutes later and welcome him affably from behind his leather-topped desk.

Harry installed his briefcase in its accustomed place. There was even a briefcase-shaped dent in the carpet at just that spot. Harry was nothing if not methodical.

He pulled back his chair, sat down, and drew the chair up to the desk in a businesslike manner. The desk was perfectly empty. He always left it cleared the night before.

He fixed his gaze on the silver-framed photograph of Marie, and thought about work. He never thought about his wife when he was in the office. He told his staff so.

'You can bring work home,' he said, 'but never bring home to work.' Harry Kusek had been creating maxims before Ben Jepson was born, and he was proud of this one, which had taken him a while to perfect.

It had originally been, 'Leave the wife at home, son, and don't remember her till it's time to go home.' This had become outdated when he realized that most of the salesmen's wives would not stay left at home but were out at work themselves. 'Leave the wife at work' did not have the same ring about it. The phrase had then become totally redundant when he found himself on the point of quoting it to a newly recruited sales rep – then noticed that she was female, and therefore unlikely to 'leave the wife' anywhere.

The trouble was that, like most maxims, it was easier to quote than to live by. Harry's first wife, Biddy, had been happy to be left at home, and left behind in his thoughts, while her husband went out to earn their living and pursue his career. At least, she had seemed happy enough, until that astonishing outburst . . . still, that had nothing to do with work.

But Marie, now, was a different proposition – though 'proposition' was an unfortunate choice of word, since it was a proposition to his pretty young secretary, Marie Smith, that had led to his breaking his own rule and entangling business with pleasure, home and work, irrevocably. It had occurred to him since then that the one thing he had failed to appreciate in Biddy (though she would not agree that this was the only thing) was her total ignorance of what her husband did at work.

Marie, having been his secretary, or personal assistant as she preferred to be called, seemed to have Harry's timetable still engraved on her brain. If he said he could not be home early to help prepare for a dinner party, she would cross-examine him about what exactly he had to do and even suggest names of staff to whom Harry could delegate some of the tasks. Taking orders from his secretary was something he would never tolerate, but taking orders from his wife was far worse. Biddy, for all her faults, had never expected that. Nor had she, for that matter, ever expected him to contribute more to a dinner party than hearty conversation and an unhealthy appetite.

Not that Harry had ever regretted his divorce and remarriage. No sir! In fact, after years of lecturing his young salesmen on the necessity of moral integrity and discretion, if not fidelity, in the marital sphere, Harry had been pleasantly surprised by his lack of regret and guilt. The salesmen, too, had not treated him with the scorn and disrespect he felt he deserved, but rather with amusement and a certain fellow feeling – almost as if, he thought, they had never really believed in his moral pronouncements and were not surprised in the least to see another one fall off the perch.

Yes, definitely one of the perks of the whole affair,

which otherwise might have risked being seen as sordid, was that Harry once more became 'one of the lads'. It was this that had, unexpectedly and undeservedly, in spite of divorce and despair, grief-stricken phone calls from Biddy's elderly parents and that one hysterical outburst from Biddy herself, rendered Harry absurdly happy for a few months.

Eleanor didn't go in for maxims and kept her working methods, such as they were, to herself, not expecting her views to be of very much interest to anyone else.

One maxim she had learnt to ignore was 'first things first', finding it more convenient, very often, to carry out the least important tasks first to clear the way for the major ones later on.

So on entering the twelve-storey Logodata Inc. office block this morning, she called in first to the graphics department on the third floor in search of Bob Fraser, to make a casual inquiry about a job for Helen.

Despite the fact that it was nine A.M., the graphics workroom was deserted. Eleanor was about to go out again, when she saw that the red light above the door of the darkroom was on. Logodata did much of its own photography, for press and publicity purposes, and it was not unknown for the graphics department staff to make use of the darkroom to develop their own snaps as well. Eleanor suspected that this was the case now. It was unusual for Bob Fraser and his assistants to be at work on time.

'Anyone in?' she called through the door.

'Hold on!' came the prompt answer. 'Just finishing.'

A few seconds later, the burly form of Bob Fraser eased itself through the door.

'Well now!' he said. 'If I'd known it was you I'd have been through my work even faster.'

'Are you sure it's work, Bob?' Eleanor teased. 'At nine o'clock in the morning?'

'It is, believe it or not! Take a look.' He reached in to the little room and drew out a still damp black-and-white print, holding it by the corners. 'Isn't that artistic, now? I'm trying a little experiment, to liven up these dreary old photographs we keep boring the technical press with.'

'I'm all for that,' Eleanor approved, 'But what is it? Are you holding it upside down, Bob?'

'Am I heck!' When aggrieved, Bob's Aberdeen accent grew broader. 'It's the printed circuit board of the Maxitronic 5000L, seen through a fish-eye lens. Tell me you love it, girl.'

'I love it,' Eleanor said. 'I've an even more lovely idea of what to do with it.'

Bob looked pained. 'I hope you're not going to get coarse,' he said in mock-refined tones.

'I was only about to suggest,' Eleanor reassured him, 'that we sent it to a trade magazine as one of those "Guess what it is" competitions.'

'It's not that bad!' Bob said. He turned the print upside down and looked at it critically. 'Though from this point of view, I admit . . .'

'I was only joking,' Eleanor said.

'No, no!' Bob said, enthused. 'That could be really good. I could put in a little clue. You see down here in this corner, a tiny M5L sign? It would get people thinking about our machines.'

'Yes, it could be worth thinking about,' said Eleanor hurriedly, wondering how she had managed to get into this. She made a mental note to avoid making jokes with Bob Fraser again. 'What I really called by for, Bob,' she went on, 'was to ask how far you'd got with the idea of taking on an extra graphics assistant.'

Bob threw his hands dramatically into the air, then

paused to lay down the photo carefully on a bench. 'Catastrophe!' he declared. 'We waited weeks for an answer from Harry Kusek – though, by-the-by, you tell me why it has to go through him at all?'

'He's sales and marketing director,' Eleanor said patiently. 'Graphics design is a part of sales promotion so it comes under marketing.' The graphics department had voiced this grudge many times. One of Bob's assistants had even stuck a cartoon on the workroom door, bearing the message 'Home Rule for Graffiti Depot'. This witticism had unfortunately come to the notice of the managing director, Peter Halliday, who instructed Harry Kusek to lecture the whole department on its deplorable spirit of anarchy. Bob Fraser, not in the least abashed, had countered it with a good-humoured defence of 'this poor little bastion of artistic spirit, struggling for survival in the heartless commercial jungle of Logodata Inc.' And his memos to Eleanor, with whom he felt more at liberty to joke, were invariably signed 'Head Boy of Graffiti'.

Eleanor was not prepared to tolerate another time-wasting skirmish in the field of graphics department versus the rest of the company, so she recalled Bob to the subject. 'What was Harry Kusek's reply to your request for more staff?'

'Half a person more,' said Bob disgustedly. 'One part-timer. I ask you! We're worked off our feet.'

Eleanor looked pointedly round the still-empty office, and then at her watch.

'Oh, I grant you, not right now!' Bob agreed. 'But the work is almost seasonal here. Come the sales conference, we'll be a good six weeks preparing for that, working ten or so hours a day, then all the last-minute rush . . . And all Harry Kusek will say is, "Recruit a few temps for a couple of weeks". Temps! This is a highly skilled job, and it's not just anyone who . . .'

'I know, I know,' Eleanor interrupted. 'I do sympathize with you. But if Harry gave the go-ahead for as many permanent staff as you need for those two months, you know they'd be twiddling their thumbs for most of the rest of the year.'

'What you management people don't understand . . .' Bob began.

Eleanor felt herself beginning to get annoyed. She was wasting valuable time here on a minor inessential errand, while a pile of important work awaited her upstairs. She decided to bring the discussion to an end.

'The alternative,' she said bluntly, 'is to scrap the graphics department altogether and employ an outside agency for all the photography and design, so I honestly wouldn't make too many demands of Harry Kusek if I were you, Bob.'

Bob Fraser stopped, looking shocked. 'Is that what he's said?'

'Not in so many words,' Eleanor allowed, 'but it is what a number of companies have changed to recently.'

'Not the bigger ones, surely?' Bob protested. 'The computer giants? Using agencies?'

'It's possible,' Eleanor said. 'Well, what about this part-timer, anyway, Bob? Have you found someone yet?'

'It's not even advertised. We only heard yesterday that this was to be our generous staff allowance. Why? Do you know of anybody?'

'I thought I did,' Eleanor said, 'but she's young and newly married, I think. She'd probably want a full-time job.'

'Well, if you could swing it with Harry so's we get a full-timer, then?' Bob wheedled.

'I could not,' said Eleanor firmly. 'Harry Kusek's my boss, not the other way round.'

'Okay, I give in! What's this young friend of yours like?

I mean, apart from being young and regrettably no longer single, is she qualified to work with the likes of me?'

'I couldn't really tell you,' Eleanor said. 'All I know is that she worked for a graphics agency in York, and she's the wife of one of our best young software staff.'

'Software!' Bob groaned. 'Soft in the head, they get in that department, writing programs all day for these bloody machines. They can only talk to you in computer jargon. I think they turn into robots themselves.'

'Yes, well, that's only her husband, so I doubt it affects Helen's work.' Eleanor glanced at her watch again. 'I tell you what, Bob, I'll give her a call anyway and tell her you've got a part-time vacancy, and she can contact you direct if she wants. The name's Helen Gee, if she does phone you, but as I say, I doubt she'll be interested.'

'Okey-dokey,' Bob said.

'I'll be seeing you, Bob. Have a good day.'

'See you soon,' Bob returned.

Just as she thought she was safe from further delay, having reached the end of the corridor, she heard Bob call after her, 'Hey, what about this competition, for my photo?'

Eleanor waved a hand at him, part friendly and part dismissive. 'I'll talk to you later about it,' she promised, with total absence of sincerity.

John Gee, arriving for work that morning, was surprised by his lack of all emotion as he removed the cover from his mini-computer. Gone was the usual surge of pleasure and excitement, and the little inner voice that congratulated him on having found a job which paid him handsomely for pursuing his favourite hobby of creating computer programs.

Could it be the depressive effect of last night's drinking? No: his excitement in his achievements at work had

62

survived many other late nights, and greater excesses than yesterday evening's.

He knew what it was. It was something to do with Ben Jepson, and the way he had talked about the prestige of sales reps, the fabulous rates of commission and exciting incentives – company cars, free holidays for those who exceeded their sales targets. He had used words like kudos, perks, fringe benefits. He had also, John registered uncomfortably, made fun of programmers and even what good programmers grew into – systems analysts – and called them, if he recalled the phrase, 'street-dumb square-eyed boffins'. Not that phrases like that actually meant anything, but still, it was said with a certain scorn . . .

The scornful tone of his voice had been matched by the expression in Ben's eyes as he had looked round John and Helen's new little flat last night. There had even been (or perhaps John was imagining this) a touch of that expression on Ben's face when he had looked at Helen herself.

Of course, Helen was not used to London ways, and Ben was surrounded by smart and sophisticated office girls. But Helen would learn to adapt. John had no doubts about Helen.

'John,' said Eleanor, suddenly beside him, 'are you on the phone yet?'

She made him jump, appearing from nowhere like that. Stupidly, he looked at the phone on the desk.

'In the flat,' she elucidated. 'Is it connected yet?'

'Yes,' he said. 'It is. We had it . . .'

'Can you give me the number?'

He had to look it up. Eleanor waited while he leafed through scraps of paper in his wallet.

'Here it is,' he said finally. He couldn't find the courage to ask why she wanted it.

'Fine,' she said. 'I'll give Helen a ring. Settling in?'

'Sorry? Oh, yes the flat. Yes, yes. Boxes and things, you know. Bit of a mess . . .'

'Fine,' Eleanor said. 'Have a good day, John.'

John sat down and punched up the last few lines of yesterday's half-finished program on the computer's visual display screen. He scanned the text, full of familiar key words and abbreviations, but it looked strange to him and seemed suddenly meaningless. He felt like a man he had once seen on television, who had been brainwashed and could no longer make sense of things which had formerly seemed quite ordinary and simple.

By the time the supervisor came to tell him that Ben Jepson of the sales department wanted to see him, John was feeling completely demoralized. At that moment, he would probably have agreed to anything.

Richard Shaw phoned his wife Polly every lunchtime, but this morning he was tempted to phone her at five past nine, because the pain in his diaphragm frightened him so much.

He knew what it was. The doctor said it was an ulcer brought on by stress, and that Richard should eat light and regular snacks and learn to relax.

This advice left Richard powerless. He had no idea how anyone, working in sales administration for a company as important as Logodata, could possibly relax for a minute. People who relaxed got made redundant. To be seen as indispensable you had to seem permanently, and frantically busy.

As for the second point, wouldn't it look inefficient to be consuming snacks in working hours, to say nothing of sloppy? Packets of crisps at the desk? Richard shuddered.

Also, if he should be seen changing his fifteen-year working habits so drastically, questions might be asked, and Richard feared letting anyone know about the ulcer much more than he feared the pain. Not only did the fact of it make his body seem unreliable, in displaying such evidence of human vulnerability, but – worse still – it could be construed as arrogance, to have such an ailment.

Ulcers, as anyone knew, were for executives. Richard, as a plodding administrator, occupied too lowly a place in Logodata's hierarchy to be eligible for contracting Executive Stress.

Richard's younger colleague came into the little glass-partitioned office. Richard abandoned the idea of phoning Polly, and left the magnesia tablets in his briefcase.

'Morning, Richard,' said Stevie breezily. 'How are we this bright fair morning then, may I ask?'

'Oh, fine,' said Richard. 'Never better. Fine.'

Harry Kusek made phone calls, dictated letters, made appointments, had a brief word with the managing director, Peter Halliday, about the probable programme and arrangements for the sales conference, gave a few moments of his time to one of his regional sales managers, Ben Jepson, and paid a visit to the office of the public relations manager, Eleanor Farringdon.

There was no real need for this chore, except that he felt he'd earned a coffee break and Eleanor's office was a pleasant place to take it. Also, some devilment in Harry had been aroused by that cocky young Ben Jepson's request, and Harry would enjoy rubbing salt in the wound he had caused Ben, by offering Eleanor a post he had had in mind for her for some time. This would be a perfect moment, straight after turning down Ben's nonchalant request for special status – as though it were not enough in itself that Harry had given him the chance of having this bright young software spark, Gee, on his team. Status! The boy ought to be glad he had a job.

He told Eleanor about it. Eleanor was not delighted to

see him. She was having a meeting with the account executive of the advertising agency which Logodata used.

'No hurry!' Harry said. 'I can wait.' He sat down on the hard chair and fixed his eyes on the executive.

Eleanor cut the meeting short. The poor young man, who had spiky hair and wore fashionable owl specs and a mint-green jacket with sleeves rolled up to the elbows, was growing uncomfortable under Harry's laser-beam gaze, which swept him from head to foot and penetrated the heart with a final withering blast of contempt.

In terms of Logodata's hierarchy, Eleanor knew that the young man did not rate at all, and therefore could not be allowed to occupy the firm's armchair and office space while the sales and marketing director waited. It would be as heinous an offence as asking the managing director to wait while one passed the time of day with the janitor.

This man, who was good enough at his job and provided a useful service to Logodata, was an employee of an agency which Logodata employed. He therefore, in fact, ranked rather lower than the janitor, who was at least on the Logodata staff. So Eleanor's meeting with him, which was important to her, and essential to him in order to agree on how to pursue his current project, had to be curtailed so that Harry Kusek could have his coffee with Eleanor.

'Perhaps we could finalize details over the phone?' said Eleanor smoothly. 'If I gave you a call this afternoon?'

The advertising executive, who had been hoping the meeting would extend as far as lunch, bit his lip and agreed.

'Who do you think I've just seen?' Harry demanded, hurling himself into the armchair almost before the young man had vacated it.

'Bye,' Eleanor said. 'I'll phone around two – all right? I don't know, Harry. Who have you just seen?'

'Jepson,' said Harry with satisfaction. 'You know what the impudent young devil wanted? A rise in job status, if you please, on account of taking a software salesman into his team. Walks into my office just now, as cool as you please, no appointment, with his infernal demands. Any hope of coffee, Eleanor?'

She picked up the internal phone. 'Jeannie. Could you make us two coffees, please?'

'And a couple of biscuits or some such thing,' Harry said.

'Jeannie? Sorry, love. Can you bring in some biscuits as well? No, don't go out specially. See if you can pinch some from personnel. Thanks.'

'I don't believe, either,' Harry continued, 'that he'd even broached the matter of the job to young Gee. He was very non-committal. Said he'd sounded him out in general terms and was seeing him this morning. Now what exactly does "sounding him out in general terms" mean to you, eh? Sneaky young devil wanted to sound me out first, see how the land lay with regard to his precious "status". Huh! What do you say, Eleanor, eh?'

'Come on, Harry,' Eleanor said coolly. 'You'd have done the same yourself a few years ago. Give him full marks for nerve, anyway.'

'Nerve! You're telling me, nerve!' If Harry had not so studiously reclassed himself over the years (golf lessons, country club, custom-made suits) he might have spat.

Eleanor lit herself a cigarette and pushed the packet across the desk to Harry. She resigned herself to a longish interruption to her work. With anyone else who attempted to cast her in the role of mother confessor, especially in working hours, she was ruthlessly short. It wasn't the job she was paid for and, as she frequently reflected to herself, if she'd had any taste for playing mother, she would have stayed at home. She had no

67

desire to waste whatever maternal instincts she had on executive egos so insecure that they couldn't wait till six P.M. to vent their boasts or grouches on their wives, or friends in the pub.

For Harry, however, she made a few allowances. This had less to do with his being her boss than with a vague sense of loyalty to his wives. Eleanor, usually so precise, found emotional matters occasionally defeated her logic. Was it that she felt she was somehow still minding Harry for poor rejected Biddy, his first wife, who had always worried about him and possibly still did? Or did she feel a responsibility for his present wife, Marie, who was eighteen years younger than Harry and too inexperienced, or too feminist, to pour oil on troubled waters when Harry came home full of turmoil and office politics?

Anyway, whatever her reasons for lending an ear to Harry, Eleanor's main concern now was to prevent him from feeding on his mild irritation with Ben and turning it, out of boredom, into a grievance which could hinder Ben's career. Eleanor had reason to suspect that Ben's business methods, if fully investigated, could jeopardize his career far more seriously, and she felt annoyed with him for pushing his luck still further on this occasion. But she had a soft spot for Ben, whose ruthlessness masked vulnerability and whose selfishness was so transparent that it couldn't be offensive, she thought. This again was illogical, for Eleanor had seen it cause serious offence to Sarah, who was her friend, but there it was.

She drew on her cigarette, blew smoke thoughtfully, and said, 'Isn't that "infernal nerve" of Ben's exactly what's made him such a successful salesman, Harry?'

'Possibly!' Harry spluttered. 'But let him keep it for his bloody customers! Does he think I was born yesterday?'

Eleanor smiled. 'You must admit, it had to be worth a try.' Keep it light, she thought; get him to see it as a joke.

Sarah, you'll never know what I do for Ben, your chancer of a husband. I should have been a diplomat.

'You're trying to charm me out of this, damn you!' said Harry.

Eleanor kept smiling. 'Has to be worth a try!' she repeated. 'You've employed a staff of con merchants, Harry. Could this be the secret of your success as a company director?'

Aha! She had him! It never failed to soften them up, that use of the magic word 'success' coupled with a reverent mention of the exalted job title. Harry Kusek, company director. She could see him registering the words, on a hoarding in neon lights.

'Ah well,' Harry said. 'I tried a few tricks in my day, I suppose. Was a bloody sight better at it than Jepson, as well.'

'Obviously!' Eleanor twinkled at him.

Jeannie made a well-timed entrance with the coffee and biscuits. As she was going out again, Eleanor said casually, 'No calls and no interruptions till Mr Kusek leaves, okay?' and Jeannie nodded.

'No need for that,' Harry protested. 'The show must go on, eh? Wouldn't want to interrupt your work.'

'I'm sure there'll be nothing urgent,' Eleanor said, as Jeannie hesitated. 'Nothing that can't wait ten or fifteen minutes.'

Was that pushing her luck? But Harry only laughed. 'That's my time limit, is it? All right, I'll take the hint!'

Eleanor relaxed, and mentally awarded herself two points: one for making him laugh, and one for preventing Ben from really blowing his chances by bursting in to tell her his side of the story.

'Now give me your full attention,' Harry said, 'because I've come in here with a serious offer to make . . .'

* * *

69

'It's a serious offer,' said Ben, 'and I want you to think about it seriously, because this is the kind of chance that only comes up once in a person's career.'

He couldn't avoid the sales pitch, he thought, even when he was half-hoping that John would refuse. And unfortunately, in John's case, it wasn't true. If John turned down the chance to be in Ben's sales team, he would undoubtedly be offered many other posts. The company recognized a talented fitter-in when it met one, he thought bitterly. John was shrewd with computers and naïve with people. He would actually believe all that gaff about company loyalty and 'the boss is always right'. As if anyone could be loyal to a faceless corporation that would fire you without an apology if you failed to meet their exorbitant sales targets.

'Well,' said John, 'I'm flattered, of course, that you'd want me, and that Mr Kusek thinks . . .'

He stopped. Had he said something wrong? Ben had flinched at the mention of Mr Kusek's name. He tried again.

'I'd never thought of myself as a salesman,' he said apologetically. 'Programming's my thing.'

Ben cleared his throat and looked businesslike. 'Exactly what we want,' he said. 'My sales staff are doing a great job of flogging the hardware, but they don't have the low-down on software. Oh, they can sell the programmes we produce. My team can sell ice cream to Eskimos'. He paused for the laugh. John laughed loudly.

'But what we want,' Ben continued, 'is someone who can follow up the salesman's calls – or saleslady's as the case may be, ha ha – and clinch the deal by offering a special software service. Get down to the nitty-gritty of what the customer needs. Suppose it's a specialized kind of business, or one where they have a complex accounting system? Our standard software packages might not quite fit the bill. The firm might decide against buying our computer, just because of the programs we're offering with it.

'That's where you come in. Promise them the earth. No problem that can't be solved by Logodata Inc. You know the kind of thing. Blind them with science. Sound like an expert. Then back to the office, wise up a few of the programming staff, do the tricky bits yourself, and Bob's your uncle! Impress the client with a tailor-made program, hot off the bottom line!'

'But writing programmes is a full-time job,' John objected. 'I wouldn't have time to go round and sell them as well.'

'You delegate!' Ben proclaimed. 'You use your authority over junior staff! You'll be given as many programmers as you need.' Fat chance, he thought, in this company. Be lucky to get one.

'Really?' John said. 'And they'll just do what I tell them the customer needs?'

'They'll be eating out of your hand,' Ben promised. 'Today you're their colleague; tomorrow you'll be their boss.' (If they don't thumb their noses at you, that is, he added mentally, and tell you to whistle for it because you're not as important as all their other bosses.)

John, he was amused to see, blushed.

'Oh, I didn't mean I wanted to . . .'

'You don't think you've got a taste for power?' Ben teased. 'Believe me, you'll acquire it. When you're sitting behind the wheel of your company car, tanking it up the motorway . . .' (With an angry customer at the end of it, went on Ben's silent voice, fed up to the teeth with delivery delays and broken promises, or with machines that keep breaking down and Logodata service engineers who turn up with the wrong spare parts . . .)

71

'Company car?' said John. 'Can you use it apart from work?'

'All the time,' Ben assured him. 'Petrol expenses easy enough to fiddle, too. Take the wife out on a day trip and write up the mileage as a customer call.'

'Oh, I wouldn't do that.' John was shocked.

'Course you would,' said Ben easily. 'One of the unwritten perks. Not that the written ones aren't good. And of course you'll be on the list for the sales conference. A very plushy do, let me tell you. Event of the year. One thing Logodata doesn't stint on. South of France location – Cannes or Nice. Luxury hotel – swimming pool, saunas, jacuzzi, fabulous cocktails. Wives go too.'

John's eyes widened. 'Free?'

'Sure thing, free. Got to keep the husbands occupied during the après-ski.' When John looked puzzled, he translated: 'In the evenings, when the big boys have finished work, there's lots of drinkies and lots of entertainment. Slightly naughty, some of it, but Logodata found that if the wives were left at home it got a damn sight naughtier, and none of those naughty boys could stay awake through all the presentations next day. So now it's wives too. They're taken off on shopping trips and so on during the day, and keep us all under control at nighttime. Tell Helen to start buying clothes. The women are competitive as hell. Turn the thing into a bloody fashion parade.'

John looked slightly worried. 'It's just wives, then?' he said. 'I mean, not girlfriends? For those who are single.'

'No chance,' said Ben. 'Most managing directors would allow it, but not a stern moralist like Peter Halliday. He even created stink when Harry Kusek junked his wife for his secretary. Maybe he suspects that if he allowed girlfriends on the trip, none of us married men would take our wives!'

John laughed dutifully. 'Oh, of course,' he said.

'There's another little perk as well,' Ben said, 'which maybe I shouldn't tell you about at this stage . . .' He paused for effect.

'Why not?' John asked, rising to the bait.

'Well, until I have some idea of whether you're committed. I'm not asking for a straight yes or no, of course, today, but I'd need a fairly definite idea at least . . .'

'Oh, I'm very interested,' John said. 'I think you can count on me. I mean, I'd have to talk to Helen about it . . .'

'But that's the only thing standing in your way right now, is it?'

'Well . . . yes. Yes, it is. I'm on, if she is.'

Ben could see that John had decided.

'Okay then, I'll trust you not to betray me. Strictly unofficial, this perk. A little sideline, supplying computer games to the client company's staff. You don't breathe a word of it till the machine's nicely installed and they're all happy with it. Then you casually drop it into the conversation, with one of the lads you will have got pally with, that it's a shame to be bored in their lunchtimes, with a brand-new company-financed mini computer sitting on his desk just begging to be used for one or two of those nifty little games you just happen to have in your briefcase. Cash on the nail, of course. Fifty per cent to you and fifty to me. Nice little source of income, tax free, and no one gets hurt.

'It's an optional extra, of course, but most of my sales staff are finding it goes like hot cakes. Money for jam, if you'll excuse me mixing my metaphors!'

'If it's optional,' said John, who had been looking increasingly nervous during this speech, 'I don't think I'd want to get mixed up in something like that.'

One look at Ben's face showed him he'd said the wrong thing.

'Oh, not that I've anything against it,' he said hastily. 'Nothing like that. I just mean, I'm not much of a salesman yet and it'll take all my concentration, selling the software. I don't think I could take on any extras.'

'Don't give it another thought,' said Ben smoothly. 'No obligation at all. Just a favour to you that I mentioned it. You might be glad of a bit of extra cash later on when you're moving flats or something.'

John seized on this gratefully. 'Yes, later on,' he said. 'I'm sure.'

'Well then,' said Ben, 'I won't keep you from your keyboard. Working from nine to five on a VDU? They say it makes you go blind by the time you're forty-five!' He laughed again, showing his teeth. 'Let's hope you're not glued to the screen much longer, huh?' He shook John vigorously by the hand. 'I'll look forward to working with you, John. It'll be a great laugh.'

John beamed. He was still smiling as he made his way back to the programming floor. He took the stairs two at a time. Wait until Helen heard this!

He had been relieved to hear Ben say what fun it would be to work with him. Just to start with there, he had thought that Ben seemed annoyed with him about something. He must stop imagining things. Ben was the best friend he had . . .

Ben stayed standing where John had left him. The sales pitch, he could tell, had been a success. He'd taken a bit of a risk in letting him in on the Jepson private industry in illicit computer games. Good job he hadn't mentioned the Porno-Graphics, which were going a bomb with the engineers and draughtsmen in firms which were developing computer graphics design.

Still, no harm done. John wasn't the type to talk, and it might make him feel Ben had taken him into his confidence. That would make him feel even bigger.

Ben could justifiably feel pleased with himself. Another victory won. A potential rival won over to being a colleague. A junior one, at that, taking orders from Ben. Not bad for a morning's work; it could even blot out the memory of Harry Kusek: 'Let's see how you shape up, shall we first, Ben, before we talk about rewards? You might not be up to handling a bigger team.'

The paper clip Ben was twisting in his hand snapped clean. He picked up another one, and another. He pulled them out straight and then twisted them together to make a single spike, like a slim dagger.

This gave him a certain satisfaction. It was, like everything else done by Logodata staff, an exercise in utter futility.

5
The Coffee Morning

A single minute holds infinite possibility.

All in the same minute: Harry Kusek had walked into Eleanor's office; the advertising executive had felt a stabbing pain in his heart; Ben Jepson, remembering Harry, had kicked his filing cabinet; Sarah Jepson, at home, felt a sudden rush of panic; John Gee decided his programming career was a blind alley; Polly Shaw ran round her kitchen, afraid of arriving late at Helen's, hurriedly making scones; Richard Shaw reached into his briefcase for a milk of magnesia tablet; and Helen woke up with a start.

It took her another minute or two to remember where she was. She had gone to sleep, she knew, fully dressed, on the sitting-room floor, but now here she was in the bedroom, naked, in bed.

Vague memories returned, of John waking her in the early hours of the morning, taking her by the hand, leading her to bed. Then, this morning, the alarm going off. John saying, 'Would you make us both some breakfast while I have a wash?' That's how it was. But what then? She must have just fallen asleep again, and he must have left for work. As far as Helen knew, there was nothing to eat for breakfast anyway. And heaven only knew where the plates and cups would be. Perhaps John had brought some coffee and stuff from his flat.

Coffee! Helen sat up. What time was it? Polly and Sarah would be here any minute. Exhausted by the thought, she lay down again. Coffee mornings, she thought. My second day here and I'm having a coffee

76

morning. What do you do for coffee mornings anyway? Drink coffee, obviously, and we may not even have any. They wanted to see the flat. Well, that won't take long. If I go out to buy the coffee and biscuits, they could arrive while I'm gone. Best wait till they get here.

I must get up, she told herself, but her body continued to lie there. This room is a bit depressing. Dark, even though painted white. The light switch was very high up on the wall, above the bed, impossible to reach from lying down. Helen knelt up and looked at it. She imagined a very long arm stretching up from the pillow, finger extended to reach the switch . . .

Giggling suddenly, she hopped out of bed, fetched a tube of paint and a brush from the portfolio propped against the hall wall, by the telephone, and filled the toothmug John had thoughtfully left in the bathroom.

Cadmium red. Nice and bright, slightly ghoulish for an arm. Helen had seen the picture so clearly in her mind's eye that it took her no more than a couple of minutes to transfer it to the bedroom wall. She stood back and laughed at the effect. The doorbell rang. 'Oh shit!' she said, under her breath.

It had taken Polly five minutes to get up the stairs, because she had been seized by terror in mid-flight. She stood clinging to the handrail for a full four minutes, unable to go either forwards or back. I must go, she said to herself. I said I would. I invited myself really. Why did I do it? Because I wanted to be one up on the others, to be first to know this girl, to claim her as my friend before she could decide she preferred the others? Pathetic, thought Polly fiercely. Ridiculous.

The girl – Helen – was probably regretting her casual offer, wishing that Polly wasn't coming at all. Maybe she'd even forgotten. She could have gone out, or be busy unpacking, or even still be in bed.

But Polly, you have to go on now, she told herself. You can't just run away! Like Sarah did, a little voice added, but of course that was all wrong. Sarah never ran away from anything. She just had a headache this morning, and had phoned to ask Polly to make her excuses to Helen when she went. So Polly had to go; there was even more reason now. She just had to walk up these stairs and knock on the door, or ring the doorbell, whichever it was, and say . . . No, she couldn't.

I don't know the girl. I'm fat and middle-aged. I'm boring in conversation. She's hardly more than Oriel's age. In a few weeks she'll make her own friends here, young people, designers, in clever clothes. 'First day I moved in here,' she'll tell them, 'this awful woman came round. With a bag full of home-made scones. Imagine!' Not only scones but butter, cherry jam, coffee, sugar, milk – just in case Helen hadn't had a chance to shop yet. What a cheek! Invite yourself to coffee, and turn up with a food parcel, as though afraid you'll be given nothing to eat.

Polly felt pain in her fingers and, looking down to see the cause of it, found that they had turned white from clutching the banister so hard. Take a deep breath, she admonished herself, and go and knock on the door. Then simply hand her the bag and say, 'I thought you might like a few things, but I'm sorry, I can't stay after all. I'd forgotten I'd been invited somewhere else. So silly of me. I'm sure we'll meet again some other time. Oh, and Sarah said to tell you she has a headache.'

There! Simple. The girl might feel a little hurt – both Polly and Sarah making excuses like that – but in the long run she'd be relieved. They really weren't her sort at all.

* * *

Sarah, having rung Polly to make her excuses, breathed a sigh of relief. She didn't in fact have a headache, but she felt she could easily develop one unless she had a little time to herself before she went to work this afternoon.

She would drive right out of town, she decided – Burnham Beeches, or maybe Windsor Great Park – and go for a walk. She waited until Polly would have left to go to Helen's because she had to pass Polly's house and didn't want to be seen.

As she drove past, she checked to make sure that it was safe, and noticed that Polly's car had indeed gone.

She noticed something else, another person profiting from the knowledge of Polly's absence this morning: Oriel, letting herself in the front door with her key.

Sarah applied her foot brake for a minute, then speeded up again. It was no business of hers if Oriel chose to skyve off school, she thought. Especially when she herself was skyving off a coffee morning . . .

Polly's excusatory speech stuck in her throat at the sight of Helen in the doorway, clad in a black-and-white T-shirt and yellow knickers, one wispy plait pinned to her head and the other hanging loose. There was blood on her hand.

'I just . . .' said Polly, and then dried up.

'I'm ever so sorry,' said Helen. 'I'm only just up. Come in.' And Polly was in the flat, with the door being closed behind her, before she knew how.

'Your hand,' she said. 'What have you done to it? You're bleeding.'

Helen glanced down in surprise, then rubbed the hand dry down her bare leg, where it left a streak.

'It's not blood; it's paint,' she said. 'Come and have a look.'

She led the way into the bedroom and, picking up a pair of jeans from the floor, started wriggling into them.

79

Polly hovered in the doorway, not quite sure where to look.

'It was the light switch, you see,' Helen explained. 'It seemed miles away up from the bed. You'd need a long arm to reach it.'

Polly looked. 'Did you do that?' She had never seen anything like it before. In Polly's experience, grown women did not draw on walls. 'Did you draw it first?' she asked faintly.

'No, I just painted it. Cadmium red. I thought it would brighten the room. I was getting depressed in here. It's a bit dreary.'

Helen was dressed by now. Polly felt safe to look at her.

'You need some nice bright curtains,' Polly said. 'Then it'll look all right. When you've got rid of the packing cases, the room will be quite big. You'd be surprised.'

'I hope so,' Helen said wistfully. 'Once we get it sorted out. Listen, Polly, I've got to go out and get us some coffee and stuff; I've nothing in.'

'I brought you some,' Polly said hesitantly, 'if that's all right.'

'Did you? Great. Well, I'll just get sugar and milk and something to eat . . .'

'I brought that too,' Polly sounded apologetic.

Helen turned and looked at her, properly, for the first time. 'Aren't you nice!' she exclaimed, in genuine amazement. Polly blushed. Helen started to laugh. 'Oh, sorry,' she said. 'I didn't mean to sound so surprised. As though I thought you'd be horrible or something.'

'But you did,' Polly said daringly.

'Yes, I did,' Helen replied, and this time they both laughed.

'Sarah isn't coming,' Polly remembered. 'She phoned this morning to say she's got a headache.'

'Poor thing,' said Helen automatically. 'Come in the kitchen. I'll put the kettle on. I'm starving, are you?'

Walking past the sitting-room door, Polly could not resist asking, 'Could I just have a look in?'

'Help yourself. It's the only room that's livable in.'

'Oh,' Polly said, 'this looks lovely. It's homely already. Books on the shelves and everything. You must have worked hard to do this.'

'I did,' Helen said feelingly. 'John changed it round a bit last night. Him and that Ben. The sofa was over here before. Looks all right though, doesn't it?'

Polly picked up the picture that was standing against the wall. 'Isn't this good! It's John, isn't it? You didn't paint this yourself? But you're really good!'

Helen laughed. 'Now it's your turn to sound surprised!'

'You didn't say you were an artist.' Polly shifted the blame. 'Have you done others?'

'There's a couple of portfolios full, in the hall. Sit down and have a look through, if you like, and I'll get us the coffee.'

Polly handed over the bag. 'I put in a knife and a couple of plates and cups,' she confessed. 'And tea towel. Just in case.' She was red in the face again.

'You think of everything,' Helen marvelled. 'Just as well. I was going to have everything in hand, but I slept in; I'm not even bathed. You'll have to excuse the smell. Here you are, have a look at the paintings. I won't be a tick.'

Polly untied the strings round the battered cardboard folio, and began to spread the paintings out on the floor. Looking at them, she experienced a feeling akin to relief. It had something to do with the colours, she thought, or at least with the way they were splashed on to the page. Figures and buildings and the occasional windswept tree: everything seemed alive, in motion. Faces. The faces were good, Polly thought. Helen must like drawing faces best of all. Faces and bodies. She was a little shocked by those. She knew she shouldn't be.

'D'you like them?' Helen said. She had two mugs held in one hand, a plate of scones, ready jammed and buttered, in the other, and the bag of sugar tucked under her arm.

'Oh, I do,' Polly said sincerely, 'very much. There's a kind of . . . of freedom about them.'

'D'you think so?' Helen was pleased.

'What kind of paint is it? How did you get this one to look shiny?' Really, Polly thought, she was doing quite well; asking questions that didn't sound too stupid, just like Eleanor did. She began to feel proud of herself.

'They're acrylics,' Helen told her. 'Here, have your coffee. Sugar? No?'

'I've got sweeteners. I'm dieting. Unsuccessfully.'

'Oh, I shouldn't have put jam on all these! Want me to scrape it off?'

'No, no, don't worry. Have you put them all out, Helen? They don't really keep once you've cut them.'

'I know,' Helen said.

'I'll only have one or two,' Polly said. 'You can't eat all those by yourself.'

'Watch me,' said Helen. 'I'm ravenous. I had hardly anything yesterday. Mmm, the shiny parts in this picture, and that one, see,' she said, through a mouthful of scone, 'that's done by mixing the paint with a gloss. And these rough areas, here, on the buildings – that's a bit of modelling paste mixed in. That's what's good about acrylic paint. It's, what d'you call it? Versatile, or something. Is that the word? Have another scone.'

'Yes.' Polly began to feel a little dazed. 'That one of your husband is one of the best, I think. Why don't you hang it up? Look, there's even a hook over the fireplace.'

She stood up and, stepping gingerly over the pictures on the floor, lifted the framed one up and hung it carefully on the hook that Helen had hammered into the wall for it yesterday. 'There!' she said, with satisfaction. 'Doesn't it look perfect there?'

Helen smiled. 'I reckon it does.' She began to pile up the coloured sheets, casually, on top of one another – faces and bodies and streets; shops and houses. An unfinished one of a supermarket. Polly seized it out of her hand.

'That woman,' she said. 'She reminds me of the old woman who goes round the supermarket near us. She gets a tin of something in her hand, and then she seems to get stuck. She'll stand there for ages in the aisle, or even in the checkout queue. Everyone has to go past her. You can't hurry her up. If you offer to help, she doesn't seem to hear you. She has to take her own time.'

She was talking excitedly. She didn't know what had got into her today, whether it was the paintings or Helen herself.

Helen listened intently, a frown on her face.

'How does she stand?' she asked. 'Facing the shelves or what?'

'No. Well. Kind of . . .'

'Show me,' Helen commanded. 'I couldn't get this one right; it's my second try. I couldn't get the woman to live, if you know what I mean. You do it like she does.'

She pulled a sketchpad out of the second portfolio, and a stick of charcoal. 'Okay, I'm ready. Go on.'

Feeling slightly foolish, Polly stooped and stood, clutched an imaginary tin of beans to her bosom. 'This is the aisle, say, like this, and she stands here, right in the middle, so people have to push past her with their trolleys.'

Helen's hand moved fast over the page. She scribbled

83

in shading, a hat, folds at the elbows of a tattered coat. 'Something like this?'

'She has an old basket on wheels,' Polly remembered. 'And when she's standing there her eyes just stare into space. She looks kind of lost. As if she's somewhere else.'

Polly had a sudden desire to cry. She must have seen the old woman a dozen times, never spared her a second thought, till she saw that picture. I'll talk to her next time, she thought. Take her in the café for a cup of tea or something. Never mind if she turns me down or thinks I'm silly.

She looked at Helen drawing, and at the paintings still on the floor. Plaits round her head. Naked bodies. Opens the door half-dressed. She doesn't care what she says. She's just herself and that's that.

It was a revelation to Polly. It hadn't occurred to her that to live like that was a possibility.

Sarah sat on a tree stump and drew deep breaths. Why had it never occurred to her before to escape like this? The wind was refreshingly cold with a hint of rain withheld. All around her were trees, their trunks as solid as houses, the branches and young leaves alive. They tossed and sighed restlessly. It saved her the trouble of doing it herself. It was a relief to sit here and let the world do the suffering on her behalf.

I might not go to work at all, she thought. She visualized the old people in the home. Even the bedridden were taken out of bed and propped in chairs, where they sat rigid, afraid to move. Whenever there was a break in Sarah's duties of giving drinks, changing beds and escorting to the toilet, she would sit with one of the old men or women. Just sit as they sat, looking into nothing, not saying much. Just sitting and holding their gnarled hand in her warm one. She didn't know if it made any difference, if they even noticed her really, but she did it anyway. It might help the loneliness, you never knew, and it couldn't do any harm.

Ben wanted her to get a proper job, with useful pay and proper status. Something he could tell people she did and be proud of her for it. She kept saying she'd think it over, look around for something else, but she had no wish to change. They were like babies, she thought, with their skinny, helpless limbs and their gaping, toothless mouths. They couldn't keep dentures in, the oldest ones. Complained that they hurt their mouths. The matron insisted. But Sarah let them take them out. Why should they wear them if they didn't want to? Let the visitors think the old folk looked unsightly in their gums. Better than gleaming rows of film-star teeth, regular as tombstones, anyway.

'They make use of you in that place,' Ben always said. 'You're imposed on, and you know it.' But how could babies impose on you? They wanted food, or cuddles, or the toilet, so they demanded it, or they screamed or peed on the floor. They were incapable of abusing anyone, because they didn't really know who you were. There was no malice in them. They weren't even really selfish, just natural.

They would like it out here, she thought. Trees with their sticky buds, bracken, grass, and empty grey sky, fresh air. She toyed with the possibility of bringing some of them out here. The matron would never consider it. They would probably complain of the cold and cry to go home, anyway.

Sarah looked at her watch. She would go for a walk, drive back by a different route, buy a sandwich on her way in to work. If the old people couldn't come here, to this solace of emptiness, then perhaps she would take a little bit of it back with her.

* * *

85

Oriel lay on her bed, headphones in ears, volume loud. 'Waa-waa,' she sang along. 'Waa-wah, wah-wah!' One foot waved in the air. She was still in school uniform. She rolled off the edge of the bed and started to undress, slowly, still singing.

She pouted at the paper rock stars on the wall, and waved each garment at them, provocatively. She imagined one was Elvis Simpson. She unhooked her bra (worn only on school gym days) and whirled it round her head, then clenched it between her teeth and snarled. She glanced over her shoulder into the full-length mirror, to check that she looked sexy, and was satisfied that she did, in spite of the goose pimples.

Oriel opened the wardrobe and pulled out the carrier bag she had hidden behind the shoe-rack, away from Polly's eyes and dusters. Triumphantly, clad in nothing but headphones, she drew out her secret purchase: bright yellow satin-look tights and body-top. The outfit wasn't complete yet. Oriel had her eye on a shiny black satin skirt, short as a gymslip, with a slit up the side.

She eased herself into the stretchy tights and top, tied up her long fair hair with a black bandeau headband. She wished she had the nerve to go out like that. Her friend Sonya said she'd seen a girl in the disco – but that was at night under coloured lights. If only she had the nerve . . . Elvis Simpson would never have eyes for anyone else. If only her class could see her out with him, just once. Once would be enough. 'Oh, he was all right,' she'd tell them. 'All right for one night, and then, you know how it is, I get bored.'

He wouldn't expect to sleep with her on the first date, of course, so as long as there wasn't a second, she'd be quite safe. Not that she was afraid to lose her virginity. At the tender age of fifteen, she saw it in fact as a serious handicap to her image, and felt she would be only too grateful to anyone who would relieve her of it – well, almost anyone. No, what she was afraid of was her dad. If he found out she had surrendered her childhood in some dark alleyway, she wouldn't put it past him to go out avenging her honour, or something equally old-fashioned. And that would really ruin her image. So what she was after was the appearance and reputation of being wild, without running the risks of actually putting the wildness into practice, however furtively.

It would be at least two weeks, she reflected, till she could afford the skirt, and that was assuming she worked on Mum as well as Dad, and assuming they didn't compare notes on how much they'd each given her. In the meantime, Elvis and his mates waited on street corners, with more sophisticated fare than Oriel passing daily before their eyes. Time was running out, she felt.

Endless possibilities. Marie Kusek surveyed her wardrobe. April was a tricky time of year, a no-man's-land between boots and sandals. Shoes could be so ordinary. The Ravel ones were all right, but you had to watch for puddles or they'd be ruined.

Baby Sacha was clad in her Teeny Weenies red and pink all-in-one-suit, and Sorrel wore a Junior Dash pink jogging suit and matching trainers. So Marie had chosen skintight pink jeans with a red belt, pink T-shirt and short red jacket. The red was a slight clash with Sacha's, but it was a mistake to be over fussy. But what about shoes?

'Mummeee!' said Sorrel plaintively, for the third time. 'Can we go-ooo?'

'Soon,' Marie repeated. 'Just wait a minute.'

'You said that! Come o-o-on!'

'If you don't be quiet,' Marie said, 'and behave yourself while we're out, there'll be no crisps, I'm warning you.'

The trouble was, her only clean socks were pale blue;

the pink ones were in the wash. So she really had to wear boots to cover them up. But the boots were cream, which would look okay, she supposed after all, she'd really bought them to go with the jeans. If she saw a pair of red boots . . . but no, the shops in April were full of summer sandals. The jacket was thin and the T-shirt short sleeved. If the wind didn't drop, she could freeze, but she hadn't a sweatshirt that would go.

'Maar-meeee! Pleeease!'

'All right! Don't go on!'

'I want to go naooow!'

'I'm coming! Go on down. I'm coming now.'

She pulled the cream boots on, scooped up Sacha from the bed, and followed Sorrel down the stairs.

It would have to do. They were only going to Safeway's after all.

Leon had decided to take a day off and do anything he liked, apart from paint. If he resolved not to look at a canvas, not to pick up a brush, not even to try and think of any ideas, then by tomorrow maybe he'd feel normal. He would wake up fresh; an image or a shape would suggest itself to his mind; his enthusiasm for painting would return quite naturally.

In the meantime, he would enjoy his official day off. He would leave the studio, with its bare walls, cleared by the exhibition in Chicago, which had eaten up the major part of his recent output. He would not give a single thought to the forthcoming show in New York. Four new Grszinski paintings would be included, he had been promised, as long as they were smaller than the huge ones he had been producing recently.

'Art by the centimetre now, is it?' Leon had inquired of the exhibition's director. 'How many yards of Grszinski are you willing to take?' He had known Reuben Farnheim for several years, and liked him. Otherwise he would not have teased him. Leon never risked joking with people he didn't know well. Some, in the past, had not understood his humour delivered straight faced, and had been known to take offence.

'My friend,' Reuben had replied, 'I would take a mile of your paintings, willingly. But over here it is not so much art by the centimetre, but galleries by the dollar on the rates. So there is my offer: four modest-sized paintings or one extravaganza. But I would prefer the four. It would give a better idea of the range of your talent. Besides, they are easier to sell. If you want to please me, Leon, make your paintings a size to be taken home in a station wagon, not a pick-up truck.'

Confident words, from a man used to ordering paintings from artists, to fill his gallery space on a certain date. It was not enough to be a talented artist, not enough to be inspired: the painter was expected to be inspired in a certain size, by a certain time.

Leon did not object to this. He understood that it was the SOLD stickers on framed, finished pictures that paid rates – for the gallery owners and for the artists. He was, within limits, quite prolific. He could be relied upon to produce a goodly number of paintings over a couple of months, from which the most exacting critic would have no trouble at all selecting four, or six, or eight. But now . . .

But now he would put on his coat and go out for the day, and think pleasant thoughts. Nothing to do with New York exhibitions, or unfulfilled commissions like Eleanor Farringdon's.

Today he was not an artist, but a man on holiday. Tomorrow would look after itself. If he couldn't paint tomorrow . . . but he wouldn't even consider that possibility.

6

New Beginnings

Sarah didn't go for her walk. Beset buy guilt, she drove back and called on Helen, stopping to buy her a potted plant.

'My headache's better,' she planned to say, keeping up the pretence that she had had one.

But when she rang the doorbell, there was no one in. She could hear the phone ringing, unanswered. She left the plant by the door, with a note scribbled on a page torn from her diary. 'Helen: sorry to have missed you. Called round at lunchtime. See you soon. Sarah Jepson.'

Then she drove home, and phoned Ben at work, to apologize for the bad atmosphere yesterday evening. She knew it made no sense, for her to apologize for his rudeness to her, but Sarah had been brought up to believe in the virtue of being a victim. It never occurred to her that she was not always being a martyr to goodness. Are victims created by tyrants, or tyrants created by victims? It was a question Sarah didn't ask herself.

'Mr Jepson is out for lunch. Can I take a message?'

'Just tell him his wife called, would you? Nothing urgent; no need for him to ring back.'

That would save her from feeling hurt when he didn't. He seldom phoned her from work, and had never set foot in the Laurels, the old people's home, preferring to pretend that it didn't exist.

I wonder, she said aloud, absent-mindedly watering the rubber plant, who he's having an affair with now?

By the time she arrived at the Laurels, she did have a headache.

* * *

Ben sat in his parked car in an anonymous side street, nowhere in particular, and wondered who he could possibly have an affair with.

He used affairs as other men use tonics. He had always assumed they would work, until he got too old to benefit from such pick-ups.

As well as their tonic function, affairs were, he considered, a perk of his job: it was easy enough to arrange the odd night away; not hard, when off on a genuine business trip, to combine business with pleasure.

It added to his status, as well; to the bon viveur, man-about-town image. A wife in every hotel.

The truth was, he was frightened of being alone, in a cold hotel bed in a strange town. Sarah accepted his absence so easily. Never made a scene about his having to stay away a night or two, in the furthest corners of his sales region, or further afield at times, for exhibitions or conferences.

Even at home he had always hated taking a shower without Sarah in the house. Ever since seeing *Psycho*, years ago, in the cinema. How much worse, then, in a hotel. Out of the soulless bathroom into the lonely, uninhabited room with its crisp-sheeted bed.

He would take out his briefcase and use the time to catch up on paperwork, becoming absorbed in it, then suddenly looking up, distracted by the silence. He would phone Sarah at home: 'Just checking to see you're all right there on your own.'

Sarah's voice, calm and unconcerned. 'I was just watching the documentary,' or knitting a sweater, or popping out to see Eleanor or Polly, or thinking of washing her hair. Damn her! She probably enjoyed the solitude.

He had asked once, 'You're not missing me, are you?' and she had laughed, caught off guard, then said, 'Of course I am. But it's only for one night, isn't it, Ben?'

What was it about women, that they always seemed

able to cope? How would she feel, alone in an unfamiliar hotel room, sometimes for several nights a month? But of course, she wouldn't do it, would never take that kind of job. She used to sleep in, on occasional nights, at the Laurels when they were short of regular staff, but Ben had put a stop to that. They shouldn't expect it, he said, of a married woman.

'What about you?' Sarah had laughed. 'It hasn't bothered Logodata, that you're a married man!' But it was different for men, of course; she knew it was. Anyway, all the more reason for her being home at nights. It was bad enough for him, having to be away from home at times, without having to be without her on the nights when he was allowed to sleep in his own bed.

He always felt worse, in those impersonal hotel rooms, after phoning Sarah. It was invariably after that that he would snap his briefcase shut and go down to the bar. If he could find a suitable comrade, a young rep perhaps, he would suggest a night on the town and the two would find some disco or club, and pick up a couple of girls. If not, he went alone.

It wasn't lust that drove him, but fear. Fear of loneliness, of depression, of boredom, of being faced with the emptiness of his own thoughts. A detestation of empty spaces, especially in his own mind.

He didn't count those one-night stands as affairs. Affairs were with secretaries at work or from other companies. But none of them ever wanted to have his child. He had begun to feel there was no point in sleeping with anybody unless it led to fatherhood. He could do that with his wife, if that was all he wanted.

He had become obsessed with having a child. It was essential now. He had tried all the other tonics and they had failed him, one after the other. The only one that remained, in his catalogue, was fatherhood.

Where would he find a woman who would bear him this evidence of success, completing his record of achievement, officially confirming his manhood? Beryl, Sally, Fiona – none of them had been willing to take the risk, without him first leaving Sarah. 'I'll leave her as soon as you're pregnant!' It made no sense for him to leave her before. The other girl might also be infertile. You could never be sure.

They had not believed his promise. Or had taken it as an insult. Had shown signs of bad temper and selfishness that he had never found in Sarah. That proved he was right. If he had to live with a woman who was childless, he was better off with Sarah than anyone else.

Perhaps an affair was not what he needed now, or not only that. Something else as well. A change of job? A lot to lose, if it became known at Logodata that he was looking around. It would have to be kept very quiet. Even from Sarah.

Leon ended up in the park. He came here quite often. He had even remembered to bring a packet of stale biscuits in his pocket, for the squirrels and the ducks.

It was windy today. A young mother, with a little girl walking and a baby in a buggy, had her hair blown over her face, seeming annoyed by it.

The child approached. 'What are you doing?'

He smiled at her. 'If you stand very still, the squirrel will run along the fence here. Even eat out of your hand if he's feeling brave.'

'Can I have a go?'

'Sure.' He broke off a piece of biscuit. 'See – there is one in the bushes. Keep very still.'

The child caught her breath.

'Sorrel!'

She turned. 'Mummy, there's a squillel!'

Leon smiled at the woman, conspiratorially. Not an easy word for a child to say. 'A very tame squillel,' he confirmed.

The woman ignored him. 'Sorrel. This way.'

'Oh, Mummeee! I want to stay!'

The squirrel, frightened by the noise, bolted.

'He's gone for his dinner,' Leon told the little girl. 'You'll see him another day.'

But Sorrel was upset, running after her mother and tugging at the pushchair to hold her back. The child wore a sort of pyjama suit, Leon noted – pink, with pink shoes and socks. Funny things they dressed children in nowadays, like little grown-ups. The mother wore pink as well, and had even dressed the baby in the same shade. Leon supposed she must like the colour. A little unimaginative, to have the whole family looking the same, but there, young mothers were busy. Undoubtedly, she wouldn't have time to think about such things.

Sarah rang the doorbell of Helen's flat at the same moment that John phoned to ask Helen to meet him for lunch. He was disappointed to receive no answer. He let it ring for a while, till after Sarah had written her note and climbed into her car and left. When it stopped ringing, the flat sounded empty – emptier than it was.

Polly, coming up the back stairs into the kitchen, having disposed of some rubbish in the communal bins outside, heard the final few rings but didn't get there in time.

'Your phone was ringing!' she called through the bathroom door.

'I know,' Helen called back. 'And the doorbell as well. Don't worry.' At Polly's suggestion, she was enjoying a long-awaited soak in a hot bath, and felt in no hurry to get out. 'You take your time,' Polly had said. 'I'll just potter about.'

Helen closed her eyes. She heard Polly open the front door.

'It must have been Sarah at the door,' she called. 'She's left you a plant.'

'Oh, good,' said Helen sleepily. She turned the hot tap with her toes, letting the water trickle in, topping up the temperature. Clouds of steam softened the outlines of the room.

She could hear Polly singing in the kitchen, clinking plates – washing up or something, she supposed. Perhaps, after all, this would be a place to be happy in.

Ben let his lunch run on late. When he knew Sarah would have left for work, he drove home and phoned a management agency. He started with the best one he knew. 'Aim for the top,' he always said. 'Second best is worst.'

He had only intended a preliminary call, nothing definite, just an idea of the job market. He was unprepared for the brisk and businesslike cross-examination the woman gave him. (Not a secretary; a female headhunting agent, heaven help him!)

He was disconcerted by it. Twenty questions a minute. Age? Married? Wife's name? Children – no? Wife's occupation? (What the hell did they need to know that for?) Only then was he asked about his work experience and was ruthlessly interrupted as soon as he started any kind of self-advertising sales pitch.

'Just the basic details will be adequate,' said the female voice crisply. 'And your reasons for seeking a change of employment?'

Ben hated to be caught unprepared. His palms were sweating; his heart began to race. He stammered something about ambition and status, the need to keep moving on.

'Why?' she said.

Why?

'It's obvious,' Ben said.

There was an unhelpful silence. She waited.

'I would have thought,' Ben said aggressively, 'it was well enough documented that rising young executives have frequent changes of job, for promotion and variety. It's the common situation, isn't it?'

'But why are you doing it?' she asked.

'It's not just me! Everybody does it!'

'And what,' she said, 'would your alternative be?'

He hesitated. 'I don't follow you.' He was tempted to slam the phone down. Who did she think she was? God?

'Are you in danger of losing your present employment?' she elucidated.

'No!' he said indignantly.

'So, if you didn't move, you would simply stay in your present position. Yes? I see. With eventual promotion? Probably? I see. So do you, in fact, have anything to gain by leaving?'

He tried to make fun of the situation. 'You know,' he laughed. 'you surprise me. For someone who earns her living by commission from placing people in jobs, you should be persuading me to move, not talking me out of it! At this rate your firm will be going broke!' Put this woman in her place. She was only doing a selling job, after all. Probably got paid less than him.

She wasn't impressed by his wit. 'Let's not worry about me,' she said coolly. 'I am only asking you the first question an employer is bound to ask me. Namely, are you leaving behind a bad smell at your present company?'

'No!' he almost shouted. It was a little too close to the truth. He had been very lucky, up till now, with his computer games racket. He could even justify it to himself: more fool the company for not thinking of it themselves. But every day he feared the balloon could go up. An unguarded word in the wrong place by someone incautious or naïve – someone like John Gee – and none of Ben's sales talk would save him from instant eviction from Logodata, leaving behind him a very bad smell indeed.

'Good,' the woman said. 'That's all I wanted to know. And now, your real reason for leaving is . . .?'

Thoroughly rattled now, he blurted something out about John Gee: young up-and-coming ambition joining his team; the need to keep one step ahead; he was sure she understood the kind of thing.

It seemed that she did. 'Leave me your phone number, Mr Jepson, and I will contact you if you seem suitable for any of our clients. Thank you for calling. Good afternoon.' Click.

Ben hurled a cushion round the room. Impertinent woman! Not 'If we have a job suitable for you' but 'If you seem suitable'! He didn't have to put up with that kind of treatment. Or did he?

Mrs Lorraine Gardener replaced the phone. Her colleague grinned at her from across the room.

'A bit frosty with him, weren't you? What did he do to deserve all that?'

'Just the usual thing,' she said. 'Just another poor frightened soul who's become his own God and can't live up to his status.'

Oriel heard the phone ring and decided she'd better ignore it, since she was officially not at home. She wondered where Polly was, all this time. It was boring on her own. She had counted on a row with Mum to enliven it. It could be Dad on the phone. He usually phoned home at lunchtime. She was halfway into her parents' room to answer it, but thought better of it at the last minute. She'd never get any money out of him for that black skirt if he knew she'd been skyving off school.

Richard, in agony, heard the phone ring and ring. It was unheard of for Polly to go out at lunchtime. She was always there when he called.

He had been going to ask her to pick him up from work and drive him home. If he could only lie down for half an hour, in his own quiet room, then he could be back at his desk by two o'clock, with no one any the wiser.

The thought of facing the whole afternoon ahead, without even that thirty minutes of comfort, was overwhelming. He felt as though his insides were on fire. I can't go on, he thought. It can't go on like this.

'Polly!' Helen said. 'What have you done?'

'I hope you don't mind,' Polly said. 'I unpacked a few things and put them away. All in the wrong places, I expect!'

'Couldn't be,' Helen declared. 'The packing case was the wrong place for them. Anywhere else is fine.' She opened the kitchen cupboards and saw crockery and saucepans, clean-washed and neatly stacked.

'And I hung a few clothes in the wardrobe,' Polly apologized. 'I couldn't find your iron, or I would have . . .'

'However did you do all this in the time? How long was I in the bath – a week?'

Polly laughed. 'Shall I make us another coffee, or – no, of course, I should be going home. Let you get on with things.'

'Are you pushed for time?'

'Well, no, not really,' Polly allowed.

'Tell you what, then.' Helen slipped her arm through

Polly's. 'I'll stand you fish and chips and we'll go and sit in the park. Have a picnic. What d'you reckon?'

Now that Polly was used to Helen's accent, she was finding it quite attractive. She couldn't think why she had thought it a bit – well, rough – at first.

'I reckon,' said Polly, 'that would be very nice.'

Leon was enjoying himself. He never failed to be amused by the ducks. One moment they were floating tranquilly on the rippled pond, the picture of dignity, and the next they were a flurry of squawks and wings and beaks and funny webbed feet: the whole scene transformed, by one small piece of very stale biscuit. He laughed aloud at them. Of course, he thought, the ducks would be equally entitled to laugh at him, but they were too polite or too absorbed in their own lives.

When the biscuits were all devoured, he would wander over to the playground to watch the children on the swings. Sometimes he sketched them, just for the practice, to keep his hand in; maybe as a tacit self-defence against those uninformed people who believed that abstract painters couldn't do 'proper drawings'. But he hadn't brought a sketchpad today, because it was his official day off from being an artist. (Please God, let this be the only one.) No! He would not start to think like this! Watch the children, Grszinski. Enjoy yourself.

As they were leaving the flat, the phone rang again.

'Probably John,' said Helen. 'No one else knows the number. Hello? Who? Oh – Eleanor. How are you? You what? Oh, that was good of you. I would, yes. That sounds great. Sorry? Part time? No, no, that sounds even better! Yes really; it'll give me time to paint. Didn't you? Oh well, learn something every day! Phone who? Bob Fraser. Hang on a sec, Eleanor, I'll get a pen. You got a pen, Polly? Polly's here. Came for coffee. You were right about the scones, by the way! Yeh, she's done all the unpacking as well. Here we are: fire ahead with the number. Nine-o-four-three. Okay, got it. I'll give him a buzz. Thanks ever so much. Want a word with Polly? Okay. See you. Ta-ra.

'That was Eleanor,' she told Polly, unnecessarily.

'Yes,' Polly said. Once again, she felt slightly dazed. We thought this girl was mousy and quiet, she thought. Just every now and then, without warning at all, it was like being in a whirlwind. Polly would have understood how Leon felt, about the ducks.

'She might have got me a job in the graphics department,' Helen said. 'I've got to ring up this bloke and go in for a chat. I seem to have fallen on my feet here. Right then, are you ready for the park?'

Eleanor let Harry stay and take her for lunch.

'I'll have to be back for two o'clock,' she said. 'Just a quick pub do, all right?'

Now, their shepherd's pie finished, Harry recapped on what they had been discussing.

'You're sure this is definite?' Eleanor said. 'I mean, Peter Halliday agrees?'

'Would I have suggested it to you otherwise? Of course, we've all discussed it: all the directors. This is an official – no, not the official offer; that has to come from Halliday. This is the official sounding-out.'

'The official answer,' said Eleanor, 'will have to come from Jake. And Gaby.'

Harry raised his eyebrows. 'What happened to women's lib?'

'Alive and kicking,' said Eleanor, 'along with men's lib and children's lib. Any other questions?'

'Yes,' he said. 'You haven't told me what you think about it.'

Eleanor took a deep breath. 'It's a great opportunity,' she said. 'I'm very tempted, Harry. There aren't that many women directors, and that adds to the challenge. But it does depend on what Jake says. He's had seven years of playing housewife and it hasn't been easy for him.'

'But surely, if Gaby's at school, there's no problem if both of you go out to work now?'

'He may not see it that way, Harry. For a start, it would mean no more children – definitely, rather than a "wait and see, maybe in a few years' time". And then, sending Gaby to child-minders after school hours and in the holidays; nobody at home if she was taken ill. It needs thinking about.'

'There are always ways of getting round these problems if you want to enough,' Harry told her. 'It is the chance of a lifetime: a chance that not many women would ever be offered.'

'I know that,' Eleanor said. 'But it could also mean my last chance at other things. I'll talk it over with Jake, and we'll look at the alternatives. All right?'

He shrugged. 'Can't argue with that. Like anything else to drink?'

'No, I must get back. Thanks, Harry – for the offer, I mean. I know it was you who suggested me for the directorship.'

'There were other contenders,' he admitted. 'And your sex went against you, of course. Some of these old codgers think women are permanently broody, you know!'

'Yes,' Eleanor said. She followed him out of the pub. She was thinking, he's looking old himself. How will Marie feel about the 'older man' when he's just plain old?

In the car, he said, 'Lot of details to discuss. You'd be

taking over some of the functions of the marketing department from me. I've got too heavy a workload, and it would combine quite easily with the public relations. We've drafted a few proposals on what the job should comprise. I'll let you have a look over it, back at the office.'

'I'll get extra staff, I suppose?'

'You'll just take on one of mine. Well, two initially.'

'Why two initially? And who?' Eleanor asked.

'Admin blokes. Maybe an extra secretary as well. We'll see how it goes. You'll have the two administrative staff to start with, get the younger one settled in, then let the older one go.'

Eleanor looked at him. 'You're not talking about Richard Shaw?'

Harry nodded.

'Harry, you can't mean it? Let Richard go? Redundancy?'

'Afraid so,' Harry said. 'Damn shame, but there you go.'

Eleanor swivelled round in the passenger seat to face him. 'You can't!' she said. 'Harry!'

'The man's become a bit of a passenger, frankly,' Harry said. 'Richard's a good bloke, thorough at his work, but abominably slow. The assistant's shaping up nicely – should step into Richard's shoes soon after the move. You'll have no trouble there.'

'No trouble!' Eleanor said. 'Telling one of our oldest friends – yours too, Harry – that he's being made redundant! No thank you!'

Harry's face was stern. 'This is business, my dear,' he said. 'Friendships are strictly for outside working hours.'

'Harry, you can't just ignore the fact that you and Richard have been at each other's dinner parties for years. Polly was one of Biddy's oldest friends, and now

102

she's a friend of Marie's. They stood by you through the divorce; they never took sides . . .'

'If you go on like this,' said Harry, 'you'll have me tempted to agree with my colleagues who said a woman would be too emotional for the job. One function of directors, unfortunately, is not to shirk the responsibility of hiring and firing wherever necessary. Economics before emotions, d'you understand me?

'In fact,' he added, 'some of them could view the handling of this Richard business as an acid test of how you'd shape up to a directorship. A kind of – huh – initiation rite. Come on,' he said, seeing that Eleanor had turned white. 'Could be worse, eh? Could have been the ducking pond!'

'You mean,' said Eleanor tightly, 'that the directorship depends on my agreeing to fire one of my friends' husbands? No axing Richard, no directorship?'

'I'm afraid,' Harry said, 'that in the present plan, those are the alternatives.'

'I'll have to be going,' Polly said. 'I left all this morning's dishes in the sink, and Oriel will be home in half an hour.'

Helen couldn't see why either of those should be a reason for going home, but she just nodded. 'Thanks for everything, Polly,' she said. 'You're a good friend.'

'Oh,' said Polly, 'it was nothing. Are you going too?'

'No, I'll stay here a bit. Make the most of the sunshine.'

'Perhaps I'll see you tomorrow,' said Polly casually. 'Or after the weekend.'

'You never know,' agreed Helen. 'I've got to see a man about a job sometime though!'

'Oh, yes. Well, thanks for the day.'

'Thank you. For all the scones and the work and everything – as well as the company.' They laughed.

'See you, Helen.'

'See you.'

Polly walked firmly towards the gates. I mustn't be a nuisance, she thought. Mustn't take it for granted I'll always be wanted, just because she was glad of a hand today. But the words rang in her ears, 'You're a good friend.'

It was possibly the nicest thing anyone had ever said to her.

Helen took out her sketchpad and began to draw the children on the swings: little blurred scribbles showing movement, legs outstretched, head back. Free as a bird.

'Excuse me,' said a voice. 'You are an artist?'

'Not really,' she said, only half looking up.

'A student?'

'I was.' This time she looked at him properly. A man, fortyish, with fluffy light brown hair, thinning a bit. A pleasant face. A bit nervous perhaps. 'I was at art college up north,' she elaborated. 'I left a year ago. I work as a graphic designer.'

'Ah? For an agency?'

'I did,' she said. 'I only just moved down here yester-day, so I'm about to get another job – I hope. Part time.'

He was interested. 'Do you mind if I . . .?'

'No, sit down. Plenty of room,' said Helen generously.

'Part time,' Leon said. 'To leave time for painting?'

'I didn't plan it that way,' Helen explained. 'But it sounds good. I thought I wouldn't have any time to paint, once I moved down here.'

'Oh – why is that?' Leon inquired.

'I was living on my own for a while up in York,' Helen said. 'Well, a friend had a room in the flat, but he led his own life really. I'd been sharing the flat with my boy-friend, you see – John – but his firm moved him down

104

here at short notice, so I had to stay on till the flat was sold. It took three months in the end.'

'And now? Now you are both living here, and you thought your life would leave you no time to paint?'

'Yes,' Helen agreed. 'But if the job's only part time then that'll solve it. I thought I'd miss it – the painting – because I got used to doing a lot, those three months on my own. I used to get up in the night and that, if I got an idea on something to paint.'

'Ah, yes,' Leon said, as if remembering. 'But then the light is often a problem, no? If you start a painting in daylight and want to finish it at night, the artificial light changes the colours so.'

Helen looked at him. 'Do you paint?'

He nodded his head, ironically. 'For a living. But unfortunately now I seem to have – how would you put it – struck a block? Has that ever happened to you?'

'Frequently,' said Helen, with feeling. 'It doesn't matter if you're painting just as a hobby – except that it drives you up the wall – but it always used to happen to me at college when there was some deadline for work to be in. Just knowing that it had got to be done by a certain time and no excuse . . . it freezes you.'

'Exactly,' Leon said. 'I have an exhibition in New York – not my own, but one I am contributing to – in six weeks' time. And frozen is the word for it. I find I can't paint at all.'

Helen sucked in her breath sympathetically. 'How many paintings do they want?'

'Four,' said Leon. 'Small ones,' he added, grinning. 'Some of mine take the whole wall. I have instructions to limit the size.'

'That could be why you've dried up – d'you think? If you haven't got a free hand to do what you want?'

Leon shook his head slowly. 'It wouldn't be a problem

105

to limit the size. To earn one's living in painting, one gets accustomed to being a little – what is it – flexible? I think this . . . this block had been coming on for some time. I don't know why this is.'

The man was looking at her, Helen noticed, with real misery in his eyes. Painting must be his whole life, she thought.

'There must be a reason for it,' she said. 'Has it happened to you before?'

'Once. A few years ago. But I knew what that was. I had been painting in oils, you see, for most of my life – you use oils?'

'Acrylics mainly.'

'Ah, you will understand, then! I had been going to exhibitions of new young artists, and much of their work was in acrylics, and I found I envied them. The medium had a certain fluid quality, a lightness of touch you couldn't get with oils. In the end I felt such dissatisfaction with the work that I was doing that I couldn't paint at all. Complete block, like now!'

'So what did you do, that time?' Helen asked him.

He shrugged. 'What could I do? I threw away the oils and started to experiment with acrylics. For six months, I sold nothing, because I was painting rubbish – like a child learning to paint for the first time! I was so used to oils, and this acrylic paint was so different to me. I thought a number of times, I give up! I will go back to what I know. But I found then I couldn't paint in oil any more! For those six months, I was not a painter at all.'

'Hang on a minute,' Helen said. 'That rings a bell. Were you quite well known as an oil painter when you did that, and you gave it all up? I remember reading something in a gallery catalogue. Would that have been you?'

Leon laughed. 'I don't know. Maybe there is some other painter as foolish as I was!'

'It was brave to take the risk,' Helen said bluntly. 'I remember thinking that when I read it. That's why it came back to me. What's your name?'

'Grszinski,' said Leon apologetically. 'Leon Grszinski. And yours?'

'Helen Soley, but you wouldn't have heard of me!'

'I'm sure that everyone will,' said Leon gravely. 'You are very good.' He had picked up her sketchbook and was looking through it, carefully.

'I don't recognize the name,' Helen said, 'but I think I must have seen some of your work. Have you exhibited in the north? It must have been York, or Durham maybe, or – I don't know. It could have been one of the exhibitions I came to in London. Tell me what your paintings are like. I might remember then.'

'If you liked,' Leon said, 'you could come to my studio and see. I have very few there now, but I have photos of the ones I have sold in the past. If you're interested.'

Helen's eyes lit up. 'I'd love to! Now?'

He smiled at her. 'Why not? It's a little way from here, but there is a bus. Your boyfriend would not mind?'

'Why should he?' Helen asked.

She tucked her sketchpad and crayons into her bag and they set off.

'You went off with some stranger you met in the park?' said John incredulously.

'Well, he wasn't a stranger by then, was he? And John, d'you know, as soon as I saw that first painting, I knew who he was. *Jonah in the Whale!* Did you ever see it? They've made it into posters and cards and such. It's semi-abstract, but there's this frightened little face, and

107

hands clinging on to lumps of gristle and that, and it's very dark, and all these swirls of red and . . .'

'No, I've never seen it,' John said sulkily.

'And he's got this amazing studio, John, you should see it. It's all skylights, and it's huge. He knocked two rooms into one, in this attic flat, so there's just a little bedroom and bathroom and a tiny kitchenette that used to be a cupboard, and the rest is studio. It's fantastic.'

'Oh,' said John, 'so you saw his bedroom too?'

'Don't be daft,' Helen said. 'He showed me round the flat.'

'I can imagine.'

'You've been watching too much *Dallas*,' Helen teased him. 'No, he said he'd like to meet you; to give him a ring one night this week and go round for a drink. And John – guess what – the best? He says I can use the studio to do my painting in, any time I like!'

'You'll have no time for that,' John said. 'And anyway, you can paint here.'

'The light's not too great in the flat,' Helen explained. 'I noticed that . . .'

'Oh, the flat's not good enough now?'

Helen stared at him. 'What's got into you?'

'Oh nothing, nothing at all. Except we've been planning this for so long, and when you finally arrived, I thought we'd have some time on our own. Now all you can talk about is things you're going to do without me, and people you've met while I've not been here.'

Helen put her arms around him and hugged him. 'We'll have all the time in the world together,' she said. 'I thought you'd be pleased with me, making friends and settling in. You wanted me to fit in, didn't you?'

'Yes, well, I am pleased,' he said, mollified. 'I'm glad you got on with the women. I told you you would, didn't I?'

'Yes, and John, Eleanor rang, and d'you know what she said?'

'Sit down,' John said, 'and I'll make us a cup of tea. Tell me later on. I've got some news for you first, about my job.'

Oriel was back in school uniform, walking down the road as though she had come from school and was on her way home.

On the corner, as usual, Elvis Simpson and the crowd whistled and called at the girls.

Oriel approached, her heart beating loud. If you think I'm all right now, she thought, in my school gear, then just wait till I'm in that yellow, with the black skirt when I get it.

She had just drawn close to where they stood and they were turning to her, when their attention was caught by a girl across the street.

'Wow-ow!' they chanted. 'Whoo-whee!'

The girl was curly-blonde, wore a clingy, curvy skirt and cut-off top. In April, Oriel thought; she must be freezing!

The girl turned and waved, cheekily, at Elvis. Oriel was past them now. They hadn't noticed her at all.

I'll show them, she thought. If that girl can go out like that, I can come down here in my yellow. I won't wait for the skirt. Then they'll notice me. I'll stop their traffic, all right!

7

Compromises

Sarah finished work at five o'clock. Only three hours today. Since Ben had insisted on her refusing to take her turn at sleeping in at the home, she was no longer considered regular staff. This meant that her hours fitted in with other people's convenience; often she didn't know how many hours she was expected to work until she arrived that day.

'Can you stay on and do teas?' the duty matron would ask, just as Sarah was leaving. Or, 'You can come in and help with the coffee morning tomorrow, can't you? Didn't anyone tell you about it?'

She was not required to go to staff meetings any more, since becoming 'casual', and this meant that she lost touch with what was going on. Last week she had been feeding one of the residents her lunch when another assistant told her, 'Don't give her that! She's been put on a special diet. Didn't you know?'

Sarah had felt like a criminal, giving a defenceless old woman food that was bad for her. 'Nobody told me she was diabetic,' she said.

'Doctor's report only came through last week,' the assistant replied. 'It came up at the staff meeting. Not your fault; someone should have told you.'

This job is important, Sarah told Ben in her head. It's people's lives. It's not like selling computers.

Oh dear! Another attack of resentment. I'd better calm myself down, she thought. She liked to face Ben with a smile when he came home from work. Recently, for some reason, she had been finding this increasingly difficult.

* * *

People tended to sneak off work early on Friday afternoons. Ben used to do it when he was a rep. Now that he was a manager, he told the reps off for it. To prevent them from disappearing 'on a sales call' at four o'clock, he scheduled their weekly meeting for that time, and made sure it never finished before five. Often it went on later.

Ben liked meetings in which all the reps were surreptitiously looking at their watches. It meant that no one talked too much. They listened to him and agreed with all his suggestions, because they wanted to get home.

Today, they had been a little late starting. Ben had been so unsettled after his phone call to the management bureau that he couldn't go straight back to work. On impulse, he had called in for a cup of tea with Marie. He couldn't, of course, tell her what was upsetting him, but he had gone on about his staff and their inefficiency, and she had been warm and sympathetic.

He made sure she knew – as an alibi, in case she told Harry he'd called during working hours – that he was not skyving off work but had twenty minutes to wait before picking up his company car from the garage.

Marie had been looking very good. Tight pink jeans, red top. Too good to waste on an old ruin like Harry, Ben thought. He toyed with the idea of having an affair with Marie, weighing the satisfaction of spiting Harry against the probability that Sarah would find out. Bit close to home, he decided reluctantly. Women are hopeless at keeping secrets from one another. It would all come out at one of their damn Gossips.

Still, the sight of a pretty face and a dose of female sympathy cheered him up. He fetched his car from the garage, returned the one he had been using to the hire firm, and made it back to the office by ten past four, to start the meeting.

It was the first actual work he had done all day. The rest had all been scheming and politics. He would have to spend Sunday catching up on paperwork. On the whole, Ben considered it worth it. 'Got to keep one step ahead,' as he always said.

Sarah sat at the back of the one church she knew that was left unlocked during the day.

It's not that I really believe in you, I'm afraid, she apologized to no one in particular. It's just that I needed somewhere quiet. I can't drive out to the woods twice in one day.

The need to be alone was imperative. Sarah knew to her cost that it was no good ignoring it. After two operations for lumps in the breast – the second time suspected of being malignant, but both times thankfully not – Sarah had been told to pay more attention to her needs. 'The body is a barometer,' the doctor had said. 'It reflects the way you are living. Don't fight it! Listen to it. It knows where the need is.'

He asked what had caused her to develop the lumps. 'Don't ask me,' Sarah had said. How should she know? He was the doctor. 'It's your body,' he had said imperturbably. 'Attached to your soul. Registering your fear and resentment.'

Sarah had been annoyed with him at the time. Her soul was none of his business. He wasn't even a psychiatrist.

Still, she had taken notice because, ridiculous though it was, when he had asked that question her first impulse had been to say, 'Well actually, my breast is staging a protest. It's shouting "Keep off!" at my husband who, whenever he fondles it, is thinking of his secretary.'

She mustn't think things like that in church. Strange, she thought, how decently everybody behaves in churches – all prim expressions and hushed voices. As though God were something respectable and polite. Conveniently forgetting the Christ who confronted demons, was cuddled by prostitutes, hugged lepers, was branded a dangerous subversive, challenged the established church, and died bloodily, splayed naked, in front of a jeering public.

Which still doesn't answer the question, Sarah thought, of what I am doing here and what I expect to get before I leave. Peace, of course. Ben and I are not very good at peace. Even when the television's off, and the stereo, and the radio, the silence is still full of undercurrents. Too many things don't get said, for fear of saying too much.

Saying what? Sarah rehearsed it in her head. 'Ben,' she would say. 'Here's what we're going to do. You are going to sit down, and I will gag you while you listen to me.

'For a start, I am not going back to that clinic. The fact that I put up with you poking me around several nights a week, while wishing I was somebody unfamiliar, does not entitle you to persuade me back to that place where men in white coats insert instruments into me as though this was what the body was intended for. Let me tell you something surprising. I am sensitive about my body and about who gets invited into it. I do not wish you to bring your secretary with you in your mind, nor anybody else's secretary, nor the woman who lies across the centre pages of this month's *Playboy*. I consider this an abuse of my hospitality.

'Neither do I wish to invite a team of specialists-in-women-below-the-waist to share in the clinical details of our love life. It may be old-fashioned of me, but I was brought up on boy-meets-girl and I can't quite make the transition to sperm-meets-egg. Especially when this blind date seems to have such trouble in working out.

'Furthermore, Ben, about my job. It may not involve dashing around the motorways in a car that's paid for by somebody else, persuading people to buy things that you want to sell, but it is important to me. And if you tell one more of your friends, so-called, that Sarah works as a bum-wiper in the local old folks' place, I will do something nasty to yours.

'And I also never want to hear you again agreeing with your mother that I'm using those old people as substitute children. She may believe, if she wants to, that childless women are pathetic, but those old people are real, not some kind of cuddle-dummy. They may be my only children, but they are not substitutes. If we had our own family, I might not have time to love old men and women, but we haven't, and I do. Okay?

'And while we are on the subject, Ben, not only can you not stand the sight of the old and helpless – which you will be one day, yourself – but you're not so keen on the young and helpless either. In short, you can't stand other people's children, not even when their nappies are freshly changed and they haven't got runny noses or sticky fingers. And I think you're afraid that you have stopped believing the magic formula of "Everybody feels different towards their own". What makes you think they're bound to resemble their father? What makes you think you'd like them if they did?'

Oh dear, Sarah thought sadly. Am I being very rude? If I am, she told the naked man on the cross, then that's all right. I'd hate you to tell me I'm just being honest.

'Sales conference is ten weeks away,' said Ben briskly. 'Which leaves you two months to ensure that this region busts all targets, breaks all records, including mine, and walks off with all the prizes. Because if one of us doesn't win the free week's sunshine in St Tropez, I will personally suntan all your backsides for you – right?'

* * *

'And there's another thing as well,' Sarah continued to address Ben mentally. 'Your work. You don't tell me much about it. Oh, I know about the hassles and the which-stupid-fool-said-what, but what about you? Do you ever think it's useless, silly? Do you really care if someone else's region sells more machines than yours? Does it touch your heart?

'Or does it ever seem to you like kindergarten school? Red team beats blue team, another gold star on the chart, and a chance to be ink monitor for the term?

'Are you forced to pretend it's important, because it's not what you planned? Because no little muddy schoolboy climbing trees ever wove blissful dreams about growing up to be a computer salesman?

'I don't mind, Ben, if you're pretending. We could keep it secret, make it a private joke between ourselves. I don't mind if you tell me you can't take it seriously, all this state-of-the-art, exciting innovation, you're-nobody-without-a-word-processor gambit.

'Just tell me that you're doing it all tongue in cheek, Ben; that you haven't convinced yourself that the world revolves around prestige customers and rival companies and multi-dollar contracts.

'I'll pretend along with you that it's the major purpose in life. Just tell me you haven't talked yourself into believing it.'

Sarah picked up her handbag beside her on the pew, cast a glance round the dim and unresponsive church, and went home.

'John,' said Helen. 'This job. Is it what you really want, or just what Ben does?'

'You think I'm under his thumb, don't you?' said John, amused. 'I've changed, you know, in the time I've been living down here on my own. I've grown up a lot.'

'Well, you can't have learnt that from Ben,' Helen allowed.

'You know,' John said, 'sometimes you can be a bitch.'

'Just honest,' said Helen. 'He does think he's king of the castle, doesn't he? Coming here and telling us how to arrange our flat.'

'Oh, so that's it!' John jeered. 'You're sore because he didn't like your picture!'

'No,' said Helen. 'I'm sore because you didn't think about whether you did. You just accepted his decision.'

'I don't have to think every picture you paint is perfect, do I?'

Helen rounded on him, tears in her eyes. 'You don't have to look at it like he did! He made himself a critic, looking at an object for sale. I expected you to see a gift, that I'd spent a lot of time on because I love you.'

'I'm sorry.' He was across the room to her in an instant. 'Honest, I am. You're right, love, I didn't see it properly. Look – are you hungry?'

'Not particularly. Why?'

'Nor am I. What d'you say we put bed before supper tonight, instead of the other way round?'

'John,' said Helen later.

'Mmm?'

'Everyone here keeps referring to you as my husband. How come they all think we're married?'

He mumbled something.

'What?' She propped herself up on one elbow and looked at him.

'I said, we're as good as, aren't we?'

'Yeah, I think so,' she agreed. 'What we've got is just as good. Who needs the certificate?'

'I didn't mean that exactly,' he said. 'I meant, we almost are. Just a question of setting a date.'

Helen sat up and stretched for the light.

'Ow!' he complained, shielding his eyes from the glare.

'Say that again,' she demanded.

'Ow!'

She giggled. 'Not that! About getting married. I thought we'd both always said we wouldn't.'

'Yes, but, well, it was a foregone conclusion we would eventually.'

'Not by me, flower,' Helen said. 'I like the relationship as it is. It feels freer.'

'Well, love, as time goes on you need the security. It's natural. All women do.'

Helen snorted. 'Who says that? Chairman Ben?'

'Don't be silly,' said John uncomfortably. 'No, seriously, Helen, it was all right where we were before, and while we were students and young, but down here it just wouldn't be accepted.'

'Who by?' she said. 'Us?'

'No – everybody. I've got a position of responsibility now, and everyone else is married, and it's just the natural thing to do, isn't it? After a certain age.'

'Well, I haven't reached it yet,' said Helen, 'because it seems as natural to me as lemmings jumping off a cliff.'

'Helen! Listen to my point of view.'

She closed her eyes and lay back. 'What is it?' she said idly. 'That we've got to get married because you've told everyone I'm your wife?'

John made a strangled noise.

She opened her eyes and stared at him, a straight blue gaze. 'Oh John, you didn't, did you? Have I hit on the truth? It wasn't just everyone jumping to conclusions: you *told* them we were married! Eh?'

He swung his legs over the edge of the bed and grabbed his clothes, angrily. 'You want everything your own way!' he blurted out.

117

'Yes,' said Helen evenly, 'or no? Did you lie to them about me?'

'Yes!'

'Oh why?' she wailed. 'Didn't you think I was good enough as I am?'

'*I* do!' he shouted. 'I was only protecting you, because *they* won't!'

'Then let them think what they like, John. It isn't protecting me to present me as something else. It's pretending that they're right: that people who don't live like them are no good.'

'I know!' he said. 'I know all that. But it's what I want too. It'd be much better to be married – better for us. You see, you don't understand what the life's like down here, and I do. In these big companies, there's a lot laid on for the wives. They're really taken care of.'

'What do you mean?'

'Well, for example – this is just one example, right? Don't go twisting my words and saying it's my only reason for wanting to be married, because it's not. Just one example, okay?'

'Yes, okay. Go on.'

'Well, Ben was telling me that wives of the sales staff – and I will be sales staff if . . . well, I will be, I've decided – get invited to the sales conference.' Seeing the expression on Helen's face, he went on hastily. 'Now, that's not what you think. They have a free holiday, staying in the same place. Cannes or Nice, he says. Luxury hotel, swimming pool and all that, and the wives get taken out on shopping trips.'

'Good God,' said Helen faintly.

'You see? And not only that, but the top salesmen from all the different parts of the company get a free extra week in St Tropez as a prize.'

'By themselves?'

'Sure! All the top people, and their wives.'

'Together, though? Staying with the other salesmen and wives, in the same hotel?'

'All the winners together, yes! A two-week party, virtually! First the conference week – about two hundred people – and then, if you're one of the lucky ones . . .'

'Girlfriends as well? If you're not married, are you expected to take your girlfriend along instead?'

'No. Ben says Peter Halliday says . . .'

'Phew!' Helen exclaimed. 'Well that's clinched it. I stay as the girlfriend. I couldn't face all that.'

John was startled. 'It's one of the biggest perks of the job! Ben says the women love it; they all buy sexy new clothes for the occasion. Don't you think it sounds great, truly? Don't pull my leg.'

Helen started getting up. 'It sounds like hell, if you ask me. A holiday with two hundred salesmen, all pissed as newts, and their wives in a beat-that-for-a-cleavage competition? No, thank you. You want to know what I think?'

'I don't know if I do, but you'll tell me anyway, I expect,' he said.

'I think,' she said soberly, 'you'd be better sticking to what you're good at. You've got this talent for writing computer programs, and you've said before that the projects get more interesting as you go on. And maybe there aren't all these perks that the salesmen have, but you're using your own gift, and you do get quite a free hand.

'Now, Ben couldn't do your job, and I don't know if you could do his. Maybe you could. But so could a lot of other people that don't have your kind of gift. All you'll be using it for is tinkering about with ready-made programs, making little alterations. The rest of the time you'll be on the road.'

'So?' John asked.

'You've always enjoyed the programming, that's all I'm saying. Never had any taste for selling, until Ben started this bit about "My way's the only way", did you?'

'Why can't you just back me in what I want to do?' he argued. 'Why have I got to stay the same? I've told you, I've changed.'

'Yes,' she said. 'Maybe you have.'

'Helen,' he said, as she reached the door. 'Don't be so set in your ways. You've got to compromise, you know.'

She stopped and faced him. 'All right,' she said, 'I will. I've told you how I see it, that this job's not your own choice, but Ben's. But if you think it is what you want to do, then I'll back you all the way. Fair enough?'

'Well it is what I want to do.'

'Okay. Well, I'll do nothing to stand in your way. You tell him you'll take his job, if that's what you want. It's your life. But I have mine too, and this thing about being a company wife – I can't see it suiting me. I'll love you, whatever you do and whoever you want to work with, but that has to be enough. No lifetime vows, and as far as the company you work for is concerned, I'm staying in the background.'

'It's a question of compromising,' Polly said.

'No!' said Richard. 'No one in Logodata is to know about this.'

He was lying, white-faced and sweating, on their bed.

'You're destroying yourself, Richard,' Polly pleaded. 'It isn't heroic, it's destructive.'

'I've got my job to do!' he shouted. 'Can't you understand that?'

'I can understand what it's doing to you,' said Polly, 'when I see you come home in this state. Why don't you have a quiet word with Harry? See if it's possible to cut your hours down?'

'Part-time work?' said Richard. 'Men don't work part time!'

'Men with ulcers do. Or they find themselves in hospital, and then they can't work at all.'

'No! I'm not going to listen to this! And you're not to say anything to anybody, you hear me, Polly?'

'I won't, if you don't want me to. But Harry would understand, if you talked to him, I'm sure. He's been your friend a long time.'

'Polly, you don't understand! This is business, not a social club!'

She was hurt. 'I might not understand business,' she said, 'but I understand what friendship is about.'

He patted her hand. 'I'm sorry, love. I know you do. But the point is, Harry doesn't.'

'I could do it for you. I could have a word with Marie and she could talk to him.'

'Polly, I'm telling you, stay out of it. Please.'

'All right, I've said I will. Or – listen, Richard – how about Eleanor? If I just said to Eleanor, in confidence between the two of us, "Look, what are the chances of Richard working less? Do you think the firm could manage, now that he's got that young assistant?" I'm sure she'd try and find some compromise, Richard. I know Eleanor. She's tough, but she's kind.'

'Look, Polly,' he said. 'We have a very good standard of living, and I've worked for it. There is no possibility of continuing to enjoy this kind of life unless I work full time.'

'I could get a job,' Polly said. 'It wouldn't pay much, probably, but we could cut down. There isn't a huge mortgage to pay off, and I've often thought I might enjoy a job. Nothing clever, of course, like yours, but still . . .'

'I have my principles, Polly,' said Richard. 'And one of them is that my wife does not work.'

'Oh Richard, that isn't principles; it's pride! I wouldn't mind.'

'Well then, I have my pride,' said Richard stiffly. 'And I will not send my wife out to work.'

She tried to smile. 'I could always send myself!'

Richard hit the bed with his fist. 'Over my dead body!'

'Yes,' said Polly sadly. 'That's what I'm afraid of. All for pride.'

'Leave me alone,' he said. 'I'll try and get some rest. Tomorrow I'm going to have to mow that lawn.'

'Helen, you're unbelievable!' John said, choking over a mouthful of take-away sweet and sour prawns. 'All that rubbish about not wanting anything to do with the company, and now you tell me you might have a job there! Why didn't you say so before?'

'I just said I wouldn't be a professional company wife. This is a separate issue, my own job. It's different.'

'When's the interview?'

'I've got to ring the man. I'll do it on Monday.'

'What's the salary?'

'Don't know. I don't even know what the hours are yet.'

'Nine to five,' said John. 'It's the same for the whole company.'

'No, it's part time. I don't know if I'll have any choice in the hours.'

'That's no good!' John said. 'You'll need a full-time job.'

'I'd never thought of anything but full time,' Helen admitted. 'But this sounded good. I'd have some time to paint.'

'That's not fair!' John said. 'I have to work full time. We won't have nearly the income I'd counted on.'

'The new job you're taking pays more,' Helen pointed out, 'so we should be able to manage.'

'It's not a question of managing,' John said. 'We'll want to buy things for the flat – new furniture, and that stereo's rubbish, and you'd be glad of a microwave if we're both out at work. Helen!'

Helen, growing bored with the conversation, was reading the paper.

'Yes?'

'Anyhow,' John said, changing tack, 'I don't know if it's a good thing to both work for the same company.'

'I shouldn't think it'd make much difference, honey, in a place that size. We'd never see each other. You could give me a lift to work, which would be handy, and we could make our own way home. Besides,' she said, giving him a playful punch on the shoulder, 'when you're a man of the road I doubt you'll be travelling to the graphics department, will you?'

'That's not the point . . .'

'Who will I see, then? Which people would I be working with?'

'I don't know anyone in graphics. You might have a fair bit to do with Eleanor's department.'

'Oh, that's okay. I took to Eleanor, I must say.'

'Not Eleanor personally!' John was shocked. 'You wouldn't work with her; just her staff.'

'Is she a big noise then, at her work?'

'A senior manager,' John told her. 'But you liked her, did you? She can be brisk.'

'Can she? I thought she was all right when I met her. Of course,' Helen added mischievously, 'I didn't know she was a senior manager then, did I?'

The doorbell rang. John leaped up and threw the tinfoil dishes into a heap. 'You get the door,' he said, 'and I'll take these down to the bin.' He rushed out to the back door.

'What the . . .?' Helen began, then she understood. The caller might be someone from Logodata, and they could not be caught eating Chinese take-aways straight from the pans. She heaved a deep sigh, and went to answer the door.

'Oh, come in!' Talk of angels, Helen thought, and they come flapping in.

'I'm just on my way home from work,' Eleanor said, 'and I thought I'd call in and see how you got on with Bob Fraser. Did you ring him?'

'Didn't have a chance,' Helen said. 'Come in, have a seat.'

'I can see why,' Eleanor said. 'You've been busy unpacking. This room's cosy. Helen, that picture's very striking. I've been trying to get one done for Jake's birthday, but the painter's dried up on me. Who did this – someone you know?'

Helen laughed, and Eleanor looked at her sharply. 'Oh, it's yours,' she said. 'You said on the phone that you painted, didn't you? This is very good indeed. Would you do one for me – for Jake?'

'Sure!' Helen was delighted. 'But what about the other painter?'

'I should think he'd be relieved,' Eleanor said. 'Poor old . . . hello, John. I hope you don't mind me calling in.'

'Oh no, of course not. I mean, we're very pleased.' Helen was touched to see him blush. He hasn't got too sophisticated in some ways, anyhow, she thought. 'I don't know what we can offer you to drink,' he said flustered.

'No, please,' Eleanor said. 'I'm on my way home; can't stay. Listen, Helen, I tell you what I could do if you like. I'm going in slightly late on Monday, because I'm seeing an agency exec at home first, in the hope of getting an uninterrupted meeting, so I could take you in to Logodata to meet Bob Fraser then. It's up to you, if you'd rather phone first, but they're pretty informal in that department so I'm sure he wouldn't mind. I could come in and introduce you and then leave you to have a chat.'

'That'd be great! Thanks a lot.'

'Good. About ten then, maybe quarter past. Okay? I must fly. Lovely flat, John. Is the rest visible, or would you rather I didn't ask?'

'It's a bit of a mess,' John started, but Helen said, 'No, have a look. This is the kitchen – all neat, because Polly did the lot, today.'

'Isn't she good! Do you like her?'

'Yes,' Helen said, surprised at the direct question. 'Very much.'

'Good,' said Eleanor. 'Bathroom – that's a good size, isn't it? Bedroom in here? Oh my goodness, what's that? Did you paint that too – that arm? It's very effective. I'd hate to wake up to it though!'

'It was a joke,' John said. 'We'll be painting over it.'

'Oh, don't do that!' Eleanor exclaimed. 'It's a talking point. I'll see you on Monday then, Helen. Have a nice weekend.'

'There now!' said Helen mischievously, when Eleanor had left. 'It's a talking point. Does that give it the Logodata seal of approval, I wonder, or should we wait and see what the managing director says when he comes round?'

'Helen, if you . . .'

'All right!' she said. 'I get the message. I'll make the coffee.'

Eleanor had been going to go straight home, but as she drove past the Jepsons' house, Ben was just getting out of his car. She braked. She didn't relish what she had been

125

turning over in her mind to say to him, but now seemed as good a time as any to get it over with. One problem less, she thought wryly.

'Ben!' she called out of the car window. He looked momentarily annoyed, then came over.

'Eleanor!' he said warmly. 'On your way home? You finished late tonight too, did you? We dedicated workers, we keep the company going!' He laughed, but stopped, seeing her face. 'Anything the matter?'

'I'll come straight to the point, Ben,' said Eleanor. 'I called in to your office a few weeks back. You weren't in, but just as I was leaving, your phone rang, so I answered it. The caller obviously assumed I was your secretary and asked me to give you a message – in strict confidentiality, he said; no leaving notes on the desk – to the effect that he couldn't supply your present demand for certain computer games and should he send some alternatives?'

'Oh, yes,' said Ben easily. 'They're a hobby of mine, these games, and . . .'

'Spare me the bullshit,' Eleanor interrupted. 'I asked him about the quantities he was considering sending, and they were astronomical. This is serious business, Ben! You're making a packet out of this sideline, on the company's time, with the company's clients . . .'

'I'm just the middleman,' said Ben quickly. 'They're not for our clients. I'm selling to salesmen in other companies. They find their own clients.'

'Yes,' Eleanor agreed. 'That would account for the enormous quantities. There's too much for just our own clients. You're wholesaling to Logodata's rivals, in addition to retailing to the company's clients.'

'Our own clients aren't involved! I told you!' he protested.

'Do you think I'm stupid?' demanded Eleanor furiously. 'Just don't try to con me, Ben, as well as the

126

company! Harry Kusek's already pretty pissed off with you, and I'm not covering up for you any more. After I'd spoken to this man, I called your secretary in and told her I knew all about this racket, and she confirmed it.'

'Oh shit!' he groaned.

'Yes, and you're in it. Involving your secretary in this kind of deception! The girl could lose her job! It's not just your own that's at risk. And all those young reps in your team! What about them? You're dragging a lot of people down with you, Ben.'

He stood for a moment, impassive. Then he said, 'You haven't mentioned it to anyone except the girl? Not the reps? Or Harry Kusek?'

'Only the secretary,' she said. 'And now you. What are you going to do about this, Ben?'

He looked at her. 'You're right about one thing,' he said. 'I am making a packet. You can't be finding it too cushy, with Jake not earning. Your salary's good, but there are always extras, aren't there? If you want in on this, I'll cut you in sixty-forty. Forty per cent to you, sixty to me,' he elucidated, lest there be any mistake.

She sat so still and silent that for a moment he thought she was giving the offer her consideration. Then she said, with deadly calm, 'I've got your supplier's name and phone number, Ben. If this whole thing isn't called off by Monday morning, I'm not going to Harry Kusek; I'm going straight to Peter Halliday.' She turned the ignition key and started the car.

'You wouldn't report me to the MD!' he said, incredulous. 'Eleanor, you're a friend! What about Sarah? She knows nothing about this, you know.'

'You should have thought of her before,' said Eleanor bluntly. 'Monday morning, Ben – and I'm perfectly capable of checking up; don't think I won't.'

'That doesn't give me time to . . .!'

'Monday morning,' she said, slipping the gear into first. 'That's my final word.'

As she drove off, she saw him the rearview mirror, still standing on the kerb, motionless.

'So you wouldn't give a friend the sack, Eleanor Farringdon?' she said aloud. 'But this is different from Richard's case,' she assured herself. 'Richard never earned it; he's as honest as daylight, if not more so. No one could say that of Ben.'

Ironic really, she thought. Emotions, as Harry had said, had nothing to do with business – and nor had they anything to with unethical business practice, of course. Right was right and wrong was wrong, and friendship had nothing to do with it. Richard was an honest, hardworking man, and Ben a small-time crook.

Then why, Eleanor asked herself with perplexity, were her feelings so much less clear-cut than her ethics? For she was quite indifferent to Richard, while, despite all her perception of his faults, she loved Ben.

8
The Weekend

Ben was a restless sleeper, apt to drag all the bedclothes with him when he turned over, and prone to sudden starts, kicks, and jabs in Sarah's ribs. He slept aggressively, she thought. Sometimes the tension disturbed her so much that she got up and tiptoed downstairs and spent several hours on the settee, before creeping back to join him in bed. He never woke, so it was an easy way of obtaining the solitude she seemed to need.

This morning, Saturday, he rose early as usual, put on his Adidas jogging suit and Nike training shoes, and went out round the park. Then he returned, had a shower, poured both of them a glass of orange juice, and got back into bed to make love to her.

Sarah made up her mind to enjoy it, and was surprised to find that she did. She stroked his back, and his shoulders felt vulnerable. She wondered if someone had put him down at work, or perhaps if some girl had resisted his advances, and she felt hurt on his behalf. He buried his face in the side of her neck.

He's only a child, she thought. It's no good expecting too much of him.

On Saturday mornings all the Shaws slept in, and Richard, regular as clockwork, made love to Polly, because this was the most sensible time for it. They would always finish by ten o'clock and Polly would go down to make the breakfast while Richard shaved.

They had a cooked breakfast on Saturdays – bacon and eggs and toast – because Richard had been brought up to believe that sexual intercourse sapped a man's energy. So Polly worked, frying bacon and cracking eggs, even buttering his toast, to restore his stamina and repair any damage she might have wrought.

'Why do we always have to have bacon and egg on Saturdays?' Oriel asked, wandering into the kitchen in a brief Pink Panther nightshirt.

'You don't,' Polly said. 'You can just have toast if you want. Put a dressing gown on; your father's coming down.'

'Did you get any Rice Krispies?'

'No, you didn't ask me to, Oriel.'

'Frosties then?'

'No.'

'Shreddies? Cornflakes? Mum!'

'Oriel, don't start, please. Go and get dressed, or put a dressing gown on at least.'

'Why? He's only my father, isn't he?'

'He doesn't like you wandering round half-dressed; you know he doesn't. Go on.'

'Why do we always have to do what he wants?'

Polly raised an eyebrow at her. 'I hadn't noticed that you did.' She was surprised to find herself answering Oriel back like this. She was talking like Helen, she realized; saying what she thought.

Oriel sat down at the table and started to leaf through the colour supplement.

'He woke me up this morning,' she said. 'Grunting. Why does he always grunt?'

'Mind your own business,' Polly said. She could feel herself starting to blush, so she kept her back turned to Oriel and firmly buttered toast. You wouldn't catch Helen getting embarrassed about a remark like that, she told herself.

'How can I mind my own business,' Oriel demanded,

'when I can hear you both through the wall, every Saturday morning?'

What would Helen say to that one?

'Put your headphones on,' said Polly, inspired. 'Listen to that new cassette I bought you. That's mainly grunting as well, I thought.'

'Oh Mum! You're pathetic. And Dad's disgusting. He's too old for it anyway.'

'You think he's too old and he thinks you're too young, and you're probably both wrong, aren't you?' Polly was aghast at herself. What had she said? Oriel *was* far too young. She shouldn't even be mentioning the subject.

Oriel was silent. This was so unusual that Polly turned to see why. Oriel was blushing. Good Lord, Polly thought.

'I don't know what you mean,' Oriel muttered.

Polly was on the point of apologizing, but bit her tongue. There must be a good reason why I said that, she thought. It isn't like me to come out with such things.

So she sat down opposite Oriel and looked at her and said softly, 'I think you do know what I mean. I know you're a very good girl and you don't mean to flaunt yourself, but to some boys the way you behave and the way you dress yourself are a kind of sign language.'

Oriel folded the paper noisily.

'Don't know *what* you mean!' she repeated. 'It's all rubbish.'

'I mean that you're playing a game, and someone is going to take you seriously,' Polly said. 'More seriously than you do.'

'See you, Mummy sweetie,' Oriel said, getting to her feet. 'I'm just going off to dress my seductive body, so's not to flaunt it in front of poor old Dad.' She went out and slammed the kitchen door.

Polly poured herself a cup of tea. Well, Polly, she thought, that was a waste of time, wasn't it?

'You awake?' Helen said.

'Mmmm.'

'Want a cup of tea? I'm making one.'

'I'd rather have you.'

'Okay. John?'

'Mmmm?'

'Not like last time though, eh?'

'What's wrong?'

'I told you, I don't like it like that, on my hands and knees.'

'I thought it was great. A real turn-on.'

'I felt like a sheep. And it hurt.'

'Don't be silly! It was okay.'

'For you.'

'Well, I'm sorry, Helen, but you shouldn't have asked me to stop. A man can't, just like that. It's easier for the woman.'

'Not when she's the sheep.'

'Helen! We've done nothing but argue since you got here! You never used to be like this.'

She sat up. 'I'll make the tea.'

'No. No, lie down, come on. It's only because you're not used to it, that's all.'

'Where did you get the idea from anyhow? *Farmers' Weekly?*'

John began to laugh.

'Not *Farmers' Weekly*,' he said. 'It was this magazine Ben lent me. It said . . .'

'Oh no!' Helen shouted. 'I'm not having Ben in the bedroom as well, John!'

She shot out of bed, grabbed a nightdress off the hook on the back of the door, and went out to the kitchen,

132

furious. John heard her making tea, with quite unnecessary noise.

Leon lay in bed and thought he might as well get up. Then again, he might as well stay in bed. He had an idea for Eleanor's painting. It was completely uninspired, but safe.

The paintings he had done for the Chicago exhibition were violent abstracts. Not suitable for a birthday present. Eleanor would want something nice for Jake. Something expressing love, not a shock of explosive colour.

His dreams were violent recently, as well. They disturbed him. He was a peaceful man, or so he had always thought.

He needed to paint. Painting was what kept him balanced. It had kept his sanity seven years ago when Carly left him. He had no great confidence in his mental stability. What would happen if he couldn't paint?

Perhaps Eleanor's commission should not be seen as a burden but a godsend. It could be just what he needed. A safe, ordinary painting of a pleasant subject. He would listen to those who said modern art was rubbish. He would do a portrait, as detailed and realistic as a photograph. It would be a good therapy, and Eleanor would be pleased.

Leon got up, cleaned his teeth and washed, then picked up the phone and dialled Eleanor's number.

Jake had been up for two hours already. He and Eleanor had started making love and been interrupted by Gaby, howling because the arm had come off her teddy.

'I'll get up,' Eleanor said.

'No, I'll do it.'

'Sure? I will if you like,' she said, and fell asleep.

133

He woke her up later, with a cup of coffee. She was very white, with dark rings under her eyes.

'Aren't you well?'

'I'm fine. Is there any shopping or anything to do?'

'We're taking Gaby out for the day. Had you forgotten? Thorpe Park.'

'Oh heck, yes I had. Sorry. I'll get up. Do you want to go now?'

'No, she's quite happy. Have your breakfast.'

'Yes. Thanks for the coffee, Jake.'

I am not going to think about work, she decided, all weekend. Not about Harry or Ben. It's impossible for me to accept Harry's offer. That's all there is to it. I will think about how to tell him on Monday morning. Till then, nothing. Weekend. Gaby and Jake. Thorpe Park. She got dressed, in jeans and sweatshirt, then sat in the kitchen, sipping coffee and examining the teddy.

'Bring me the work basket, Gaby, and I'll sew it together again.'

Gaby returned. 'Sew it blue,' she suggested, holding the cotton reel out to Eleanor. 'I like that one.'

'I'll have to sew it the same colour as your teddy,' Eleanor said, 'or the stitches will show.'

'I want them showing,' Gaby said. 'So we'll know.'

'Oh, all right.' As always with Gaby she felt helpless. She doesn't look at things in the same way I do, Eleanor thought. I can't predict her way of thinking.

She bit off a length of blue cotton, threaded the needle and started to sew. Gaby let out a scream of sheer agony. Eleanor dropped the teddy.

'Oh God!' she gasped. 'What is it? Tell me, Gaby!'

She was down on her knees by the little girl. Jake ran in. Gaby went on screaming.

'What's happening?' Jake scooped Gaby out of

134

Eleanor's arms. 'Safe now, precious. Daddy's got you. What is it? Where's the pain?'

'Teddy!' Gaby howled.

'Eleanor, give me the teddy, quick.'

Eleanor handed it over. She was shaking.

'Oh, is that it?' Jake asked Gaby. 'Poor old teddy got hurt, yes?'

'Yes!'

'Naughty old Mummy stuck a needle in teddy's arm, without giving him a sweetie first to take away the pain?'

'Yes!' Already, the tears were dry, the problem solved.

'Well, no trouble, precious. We give him an extra sweetie now from the jar – okay? And one for Gaby and one for Daddy as well.'

'Two!' Gaby bargained.

'One for Gaby and two for Daddy?' Jake exclaimed. He raised his eyebrows comically. Gaby laughed. He carried her next door. Eleanor heard them debating over teddy's favourite sweetie. She went into the downstairs toilet and locked the door. Her knees were shaking and she felt weak. She sat down on the seat, put her head in her hands and burst into tears.

In the hall, the phone began to ring.

'Eleanor, can you get that?' Jake shouted.

'Okay!' She tore off a length of toilet paper, blotted her eyes and nose, forced an expression of brightness, and went to answer the phone.

'Hello – who? Oh Leon, yes. Oh good. Fine. Good. Yes, I'll try and come round later on. Not today. I'll try and make it this evening, or tomorrow sometime. All right. Bye.'

Damn she thought. Just when she'd asked Helen to do her a painting instead. Still, they could afford two, and really she had wanted a Grszinski. A portrait of her and

135

Gaby would be a good present for Jake. She hadn't known that Leon did portraits.

She went upstairs to start looking out some photographs of Gaby and herself. Leon had said he would sketch her from life, if she could do just one sitting, but the photographs would help him.

The thing was, how could she find an excuse to go out for a couple of hours without Jake knowing what was going on? It would be even more difficult to arrange to take Gaby along, so that Leon could at least see the child once.

She would have to think of something. Meanwhile, there was the day out. All three of them, as a family. She selected a dozen of the best photographs quickly – Eleanor was used to making quick decisions – and ran downstairs.

'Come on, slowcoaches!' she said gaily. 'Are we ready to go? I'm really looking forward to this!'

Harry had a lie-in on Saturday mornings and let Marie have her turn on Sundays.

This was a major change in his routine, since the old days. Biddy had recognized that a hard-working man needed a good rest and extra cosseting at weekends. Marie also understood this, of course, but the fact remained that two small children woke both of them early every morning, with no allowances made for Saurdays or Sundays.

Harry had forgotten that young children did this. His son and daughter from his first marriage were grown up and had left home. They had not condemned him, over the break-up, but hardly ever saw him now. He didn't know whether this was the way that grown-up children normally treated their father or not.

On Harry's lie-in morning, Marie was not always

scrupulously careful about keeping the children away from him. This morning, Sorrel climbed into bed with him.

'Where's Mummy?' he asked, in protest.

'Changing Sacha's nappy. Can we go to the squillies, Dad?'

'To the what?'

'To see the squillies,' she repeated.

'What are the squillies?' he asked in bewilderment.

'Squillies!' she shouted, annoyed. She thumped him, through the bedclothes, smiting him in the groin.

'Ow! Sorrel, Sorrel, go and get your mother. Ask her – tell her – to come in here.'

'No, I won't.' She continued to hit him.

'Marie!' he yelled. 'Marie!'

She appeared in the doorway, with Sacha balanced on one hip.

'What is it?'

'Take Sorrel,' he said plaintively.

'Come on, Sorrel.'

'No!'

'She won't go,' Marie said, giving up. She plonked Sacha down on the bed, next to Harry. The baby started to chew Harry's ear, dribbling on the pillow.

'Marie!'

She shrugged her shoulders. 'They're your kids as well. I have them all week. Harry, did you find me a job yet?'

'No, but as soon as one of the secretaries leaves, I will suggest you to personnel.'

'Ben said there was a new girl started the other week. You never let me know there was a vacancy.'

'I don't know everything that goes on, my dear.'

'You mean, you don't want me to work.'

'No, it's not that, I promise. You do whatever makes you happy.'

'It would make me happy to go back to my old job,' she said, 'instead of spending all day talking babytalk.'

'Marie, I can't fire my secretary just to give you back your old job. Besides . . .'

'Besides, you'd get sick of me.'

'Not at all. How can you say such a thing? You're the light of my life.'

'And you're an old fraud,' she said, softening. She sat down at the dressing table and started applying make-up.

Sorrel started hitting Harry again.

'Don't do that to Daddy,' he said.

'Squillies!' she shouted.

'Marie! Marie take her away from me. Now. And what are the squillies?'

'Squirrels,' Marie said. 'She saw some bloke in the park feeding them yesterday. She's talked about nothing else ever since. All right, Sorrel, that's enough. We might go later. We'll see.'

'Is that what you did yesterday?' he asked jealously. 'Went to the park.'

'We just walked home that way, from Safeway's. Fantastically exciting. See what you miss, being at work? Lucky thing.'

'What else did you do?' he asked. He didn't like feeling left out of things. It was as though they all forgot he existed, during the day.

'Watched afternoon telly and cleared out the toy box. Ben dropped in for a cup of tea.'

'Ben Jepson? What for?'

'Does there have to be a reason? Oh yes, he was waiting to pick up his car or something. The garage hadn't finished with it.'

'How long did he stay here?'

'Not long. Why?'

'I don't like young men calling in on my wife when I'm not around.'

'I do. Why do you think I want to go back to work? All I see all day is babies and children and other mothers. It isn't natural. Come on, kiddies, let's go and leave Daddy to his rest.'

'Bring me a coffee,' he begged. 'And an ashtray.'

'Waitress as well as nanny, am I today?' She kissed him on the forehead. 'Coffee then, but no ashtray. You're not smoking in the bedroom. Come on, Sorrel. Good girl. We'll go and see the squirrels later. Say bye-bye to Daddy, Sacha. Wave! Don't lie in too late, Harry, I want you to do those shelves. Bye!'

Harry closed his eyes. He felt drained. It used to enchant him when his pretty young secretary felt familiar enough with him to boss him about. It was a stimulating game, enjoyed by both. Now that she was his wife, it meant business.

He gave an involuntary sigh. Squillies! Afternoon TV, and walks in the park. She probably had no time to think of him. At the office, nowadays, he felt as though cast adrift. In the old days, with Biddy, home had seemed to anchor him. She seemed to carry his interest in her heart during the day, buying him a new shirt or socks, preparing his favourite meal, shopping for his special drink and pouring him one as soon as she heard his car in the driveway.

All quite unnecessary, of course. He didn't need security in such ways. He must remember, too, the deception behind this cosy lifestyle. Four years, drinking like that, in the daytime! Gin and whisky. Some weeks, not so bad, hardly anything, she said. Other times, much worse. And he'd never noticed! Never knew anything about it, till it all came out about him and Marie. Then all these other matters came out too.

'Who knew about this drinking of yours?' he had asked. He was very shocked. He told her so.

'That's why I never told you! I was ashamed of myself, but not half as ashamed as I knew you'd be of me.'

'I'd have every right.'

'You've every right to be proud of me for giving it up. I hope you'll never know what a hard thing that is.'

'Who knew? Who did you tell about this?'

'Sarah. Polly. Eleanor. That's all. Nobody else, Harry, I swear it.'

'Good God, woman! All people connected with work! Haven't you got a single shred of loyalty or respect for me?'

'They're my friends!' she had sobbed, uncontrollably. 'They helped me through it, when you couldn't care less.'

'I didn't know!'

That was the part that hurt. It made him look such a fool. They must have all known. Had they come round to visit on bad days, made her black coffee, helped with the housework? Discussed her, behind her back? Synpathetically not offered her too many refills of her glass at parties? How could she have done such a thing to him? (And that other voice asked him, on sleepless nights – 'How could you have been ignorant of such suffering? Where were you when she had such empty-heartedness that she drank to fill the void?')

Oh, he was better off now, no doubt of it. And Biddy was all right, living at her sister's. Marie was the beautiful wife he had never expected to earn, and he the lucky husband envied by younger men. Two lovely little girls, cute as an advert. A well-appointed house, company car, renewed every two years, six weeks' annual leave, a prestigious job with a major company, with commensurate salary.

What more could the heart desire? Apart from the departure of these niggly little chest pains, attributable to indigestion, as Marie sensibly said. She had, quite rightly, put him on a diet. All wholegrain stuff, very healthy. It took a younger wife to know about things like that. Poor old Biddy had done her best, but she'd never understood him as Marie did.

He waited for his coffee for half an hour, then gave up and went back to sleep.

'See?' said John. 'Now you can't tell me I hurt you that time, can you?'

'No.'

'I told you it was just a question of getting used to it!' He hugged her. She pulled the bedclothes higher over her shoulders.

'What are we doing today?' she asked.

'We'll have to get some shopping in. Then I said I'd go in to the office with Ben for a while, so he can show me the ropes: explain the procedure, take me through some of the customer files and that.'

'At the weekend?' Helen said.

'Well, I won't be starting the job for a couple of weeks, and then it would be a while longer before I got the hang of it, so he said to save time we'd get through the preliminaries now. Then I can get right down to work as soon as I start.' His eyes shone.

'And when's this thing – this salesmen's party in France?'

'Sales conference, dumbo! Get it right! Just a couple of months away. I don't know the exact date. Think it over, Helen. I'd really want you with me on that, you know.'

'I wouldn't enjoy it, John, and that wouldn't help you. You could enter into the spirit of it more on your own.'

'No! You'd love it when you were there. It wouldn't be

like you think. I bet when we came back you'd say you'd had a great time.'

Helen put her head under the bedclothes.

'I'm taking John into the office this afternoon, to give him an informal briefing,' Ben said.

'All right, love.' Sarah was relieved. I'll wash my hair, she thought, and read my library book, with Placido Domingo on the tape deck.

'I might bring John back here afterwards for a drink.'

'All right. Why don't you ask Helen too?'

'She doesn't like me,' Ben said.

Sarah was surprised. 'She hardly knows you.'

'Enough for instant dislike.'

'Oh dear,' Sarah said. 'That's awkward for you. You'll be seeing a lot of John, when he's working for you, won't you?'

'Tell you what,' he said. 'You work on her for me. Have her round while we're out. I don't want her stirring up trouble with John. He's got to be a hundred per cent company man.'

'I will if you like, but to be honest, Ben, I can't find much to talk to her about. It might be better to leave it to the others, at the Gossips. They'll draw her in.'

He frowned. 'Who's having next week's?'

'It's Polly's turn.'

'Well, Helen's hardly going to have much in common with Polly, is she? I think you should have another try. Maybe get Marie in as well; she's nearer Helen's age.'

'I'll ask,' Sarah said doubtfully, 'but it is the weekend.'

'Okay – look, give Marie a ring first and see if she's free to come round, and if she is, ring Helen then. Yes?'

'All right.' There goes my free afternoon, Sarah thought. Oh well, never mind.

* * *

142

'If you're going out,' said Helen, 'I might go over to Leon's and do some painting.'

'This afternoon?'

'Yes, while you and Ben are working.'

'You could do the shopping then,' he suggested.

'We'd best do that together, John,' she said. 'There's a lot to get in.'

'Yes, but I want to get some paint as well, to do up the sitting room. If I went and bought that this morning, you could even make a start on it this afternoon.'

'We've only got that room straight! We must have one room we can live in, John. Can't you start with the bedroom? It's more in need of it, anyhow.'

'That's not the room people see. We want to get started on this place straight away. Make it fit to have people in.'

Helen remembered her resolve to fit in with John. 'Whatever you like,' she said. The picture of the old woman in the supermarket would have to wait.

'Harry, aren't you up yet?' Marie said. She lay down beside him on the bed. 'Sarah phoned. She wants me to go round this afternoon.'

'With the kids?'

'I suppose so.'

'What about me?'

'She said you're welcome if you want to come too, but Ben won't be there. He and John are going to the office to work out his new job.'

'Good. Good. No, I won't go, if it's just women and babies. I'll do those shelves. What about Sorrel and those squirrels she wanted to see?'

'She'll have to wait. Unless you want to take her?'

'Not really,' he said. He yawned. 'It's been a long week. I'm tired.'

'So am I,' Marie admitted.

'Are you?' He was alarmed. He didn't expect this, from a wife so much younger than himself. 'Why? You're always so full of go.'

'I'm tired all the time just now,' she said. 'Or bored. I don't know which it is.'

Bored, he thought. Don't let her start drinking, like Biddy did. 'You should have some more of your friends round,' he said. 'Or go out and buy some new clothes. No expense spared,' he said generously. 'Have what you like, eh?'

'I do,' she said. 'I think it's the kids make me tired, though. If I could get out of the house in the daytimes, if I had a job, that would make all the difference.'

'Does it have to be Logodata?' Harry asked. 'You know, if you can't have your old job back, you might get nothing so good. Secretary to some junior manager, something like that. Bit of a come-down from being my personal assistant. You could do better in another company.'

'I know,' she said, getting up. 'I'll think about it.' She sounded dispirited.

'I'll get up,' Harry said. 'I'll come down and have a coffee with you.'

Leon cleared a corner of the studio, and set up a spare easel in it, in case the young girl came round. He hoped she would. It might give him some inspiration, to have Helen there painting. A studio that wasn't used acquired an atmosphere of uncreative staleness. He set out a tray of tubes of acrylic paint, and a palette. A couple of sable brushes too. They were not much use to him at the moment, and Helen probably couldn't afford the best.

The mechanical actions soothed him. He longed for Eleanor to bring the photographs round so he could start sketching. He began to sketch out a background for a

144

possible portrait. He could do the two faces, mother and child, appearing through swirls of multi-coloured mist.

He chose a colour at random and began to paint, very carefully, with controlled movements, quite unlike his usual passionate intensity. After a few minutes he experienced such panic that he could not see or breathe. For no reason at all, he felt close to death.

Polly had gone up the road to visit a neighbour who was just out of hospital. Richard was in the sitting room reading the paper.

'I'm going out!' Oriel shouted.

'What? Where?'

'Bye!' she cried, slamming the door.

She was wearing an old raincoat, covering her yellow body-top and tights, with no socks and flat black pumps. She would have been freezing cold, on this April day, if she had not been in such a state of terror and exhilaration. She was burning up nervous energy at a rate that must have been draining the power reserves of half the city's population. She imagined old ladies fainting as she passed them, absorbing their small resources of energy for her greater need. Middle-aged men would suffer panic attacks, supplying her with their last vestiges of steadiness. Lights would dim all over London as her electric yellow body outshone their glare. Reservoirs evaporated as she sweated excitement and fear.

Oriel was going to meet Elvis Simpson.

Elvis was unaware of Oriel's intention, which was to accost him in the street, flinging raincoat and convention to the winds, and parade him through the shopping centre, arms entwined, in view of her friends who had Saturday jobs in Chelsea Girl and Etam's.

In return for this favour from him, Oriel was prepared

145

to make the supreme sacrifice, defying a lifetime's tuition in morality and energy conservation.

If Elvis had known about this, he would certainly have been at his street-corner post, keeping vigil with his mates.

As it was, he had succumbed to a greater opponent in an annual battle, and had gone to the dentist, with his mum.

Sarah poured tea for Marie and orange squash for Sorrel, who poured it on the carpet and paddled in it. She had spent the morning shouting about the squillies, and was all set to spend the afternoon the same way.

After an hour and a half of attempted conversation, Marie slapped Sorrel, who kicked her, ran away, and bit the baby on the wrist, leaving toothmarks. Sacha screamed hysterically.

Ben and John returned.

Ben and Sarah met in the kitchen.

'What's going on?' he demanded.

'I did as you suggested,' Sarah said, 'and invited Marie first, before I phoned Helen.'

'Where's Helen then?'

'She said she was spending the afternoon decorating their sitting room.'

'Why didn't you put Marie off, then?'

'How could I?' Sarah asked. 'Phone back and say "Don't bother to come; I only invited you to fill in the gaps in the conversation with Helen"?'

'I'm taking John up to my study, till the pub opens,' said Ben. 'You'd better get rid of them, Sarah. I can't stand the noise.'

Helen had finished the first coat of paint, and felt she had earned a rest, so she went for a stroll round the park, buying herself a chocolate bar on the way. She felt virtuous, having sacrificed her afternoon's painting for John's sake. Once she'd done a fair share of the only kind of painting John was interested in just now – rolling layers of emulsion on the walls – she would feel justified in claiming her spare time as her own. Then she would take that nice bloke up on his offer to use his studio, and the painting of the woman in the supermarket, being so hard-earned, would surely turn out to be a masterpiece.

The wind was cold, and Helen soon turned to go home again. She almost bumped into a girl in bright yellow tights, clutching a raincoat round her and crying.

'Sorry,' Helen said first, then, 'Are you all right?' then finally, 'Oh – it's Polly's daughter, isn't it?'

Oriel broke into sobs and ran away. Her raincoat flapped in the wind, and mud splashed up the backs of her yellow legs, as she ran through the puddles, soaking her shoes.

I wonder if I should go after her. Helen mused. She decided against it. The girl would probably rather get over whatever it was by herself.

Marie walked back through the park, feeling depressed. Sorrel was getting unmanageable, she thought. If it went on like this, she would get looked after by a child-minder, job or no job. The child had run far ahead, looking for squirrels. The wind was cold, and there was a fine drizzle. Marie wished she had stayed at home this afternoon, or persuaded Harry to come to the park with them all.

She had been pinning her hopes on his getting her a job, remembering her days as his PA. Happiness was something she took for granted then. She knew it would not be the same now, working at Logodata in some less prestigious capacity, returning home to tired babies and a cold house, with supper to cook. And yet – it must be better than this.

She didn't want to work for another company. She couldn't admit it to Harry, with his fear of human weakness, but she felt she had lost her nerve about working among unfamiliar people. Logodata would feel more like family, with Harry there, Ben, Richard, Eleanor, John Gee. She knew lots of the salesmen, and they were always good for a laugh and a flirt. If she made mistakes in her work, she would be protected from being criticized too severely by her status as the wife of Harry Kusek.

She suspected that Harry didn't want her back there, partly because it diminished his status to have a wife working as a low-ranking employee – secretarial grade – and partly because it would rekindle memories. The managing director had taken a jaundiced view of her liaison with Harry, at the time. He was old-fashioned in his views, Marie thought, and prejudiced in favour of Biddy, who got on well with his wife.

Damn Biddy! Every now and again, her name would come up, even now. She was part of Harry's past, but people would keep bringing her into the present. Even at the Gossips, Polly or Sarah or Eleanor would sometimes refer to her. They had all treated Marie kindly, and allowed her to take Biddy's place without a murmur. Marie had believed she had Harry to thank for this, and had been scandalized to learn from an accidental remark of Polly's that it was Biddy herself who had asked them not to make Marie an outcast, for the sake of Harry's happiness.

Three years after Marie had fought for Harry – fought Biddy's stronger claims on his loyalty, the hostility of his parents and his own fears for his reputation at work – she was still occasionally haunted by nightmares of Biddy, pale and anguished, screaming Harry's name and bleeding from hidden wounds.

At the time, buoyed up with desire to win, Marie had survived both the time of crisis and the long-drawn-out legal wrangling that followed it. She had weathered the gradual easing of the cold war with the in-laws – with the final truce secured only by the arrival of the legitimately conceived grandchild, Sacha.

Biddy stopped phoning up to plead with Harry, once Marie suggested having the phone number changed and going ex-directory. She left the area, went to live respectably with a widowed sister. She did the decent thing and disappeared. She even forgave Marie, to whom she bequeathed not only her husband and her home and her friends, but all her house-plants as well. She took the budgie, but left a note apologizing for this.

Marie had never been so thoroughly forgiven for anything. Nor had she ever felt so unforgiving. She wished that Biddy had not only disappeared but evaporated totally, ceased to exist. She believed privately that it was neither boredom nor child-minding that was making her feel so tired now, nor even delayed reaction from all the battling in the past, but the terrible and never-diminishing burden of Biddy's forgiveness.

9

Outings and Homecomings

Helen couldn't get Leon out of her mind. His face haunted her, his eyes dark with misery. Could such anguish possibly be caused by an inability to paint? Or was the artistic drought just a symptom of some deeper cause?

John phoned, to say he was at the pub with Ben. Sarah had stayed at home, saying she had to clear up after Marie's children left. 'Come and join us,' John said. Helen declined. He argued. She said she wanted to paint. 'You're not going round to that man's place,' John said. 'I forbid it.'

Helen wondered how many hours he had spent listening to Ben, to come out with a heavy-husband remark like that. It sounded silly. She said simply, 'I'm not going anywhere.' She refused to argue with him when he wasn't himself. She had no desire to argue with a replica of Ben.

She put the phone down and went into the kitchen, where she had already laid out her few half-used tubes of paint. She found it helped, to have too few colours to choose from. It gave her limits to exceed.

The painting of the supermarket woman had become simplified in her mind. Somehow, she pictured a face emerging from a mist of confusion, in which all the different products – packets and tins – faded and swirled. It would symbolize the woman's bewilderment and inability to cope with all the unlimited choices facing her, Helen thought.

She began with the swirling mists, in passionate colours – reds and oranges. She was surprised at the violent effect this produced. The poor woman, she thought involuntarily. All the turmoil going on behind the blank stare and drooping lids. She started to paint the face. She painted the eyes a little blurred, vague with age and tears, then, dissatisfied with this, deepened the colours of the iris, made the pupils more opaque.

She stood back to judge the effect. What she saw startled her. Out of a blood-red whirlwind emerged two eyes of terrifying intensity. Terrifying, she thought – or terrified?

They were not the eyes of an old woman. They were Leon's eyes.

John wished that Helen had come to the pub with them. He was feeling uncomfortable. It was not that Ben wasn't excellent company, as usual – lively and witty – but some of the jokes made him slightly uneasy. So did the way Ben kept looking at the women, staring at their bosoms or their legs, making loudly voiced comments about them which were obviously intended to be overheard.

Some of the women appeared to like this, and giggled, and eyed him up in the same compartmental way, like a butcher eyeing a carcass to decide where the rump should end and the sirloin begin. Other girls clicked their tongues, raised their eyebrows at one another and turned their backs on him.

John could imagine how Helen would react. He wondered if Ben had ever looked at Helen in that way, or if she somehow knew that he regarded women like this, like goods on a supermarket shelf.

Perhaps the trouble with Ben was that he was offered too much choice. John had spent nights out with Ben, in his pseudo-bachelor time while Helen had stayed in York, and had seen the ease with which Ben's flattery could persuade a girl that he admired and cherished her. John had also, once or twice, seen Ben at breakfast next day behaving as though nothing had happened. Having spent the night with the girl in a hotel, he would send her home without breakfast, kissing her briefly goodbye while she smiled and held back tears, and John could tell that Ben had trouble in remembering her name.

It was not, of course, that John blamed Ben for any of this. He wasn't narrow-minded or anything like that. It was the way of the world and Ben was very much one of the world's men. John had not, himself, been beyond reproach in Helen's absence. But it was different now Helen was here, living with him. He hoped that Ben would realize this. For the first time, it occurred to him that Ben might not see things in quite the same way that he did.

Helen gave up the attempt at drawing the supermarket woman. It no longer seemed important.

She laid the picture of the eyes to one side, on the draining board. The light was poor in here. She was trying to paint on the kitchen worktop, and the light – what there was of it – came from behind her, so that her shadow fell across the page.

She painted Leon's shadow, a long grey streak stretching across the park, with small children in its path. Was he dangerous, then? Some kind of threat to children? For a moment, she felt frightened by what she was doing, but she made herself go on. She seemed to be letting her paintbrush do the thinking. If I go on, she thought, I may get to the bottom of this. There wasn't anything frightening in him when I met him. I can recognize a good man. A kind man at heart. She took another sheet of paper.

Next, she painted a heart, exposed beneath a winter overcoat, topped by Leon's face. She painted the man seated, on a park bench. The private soul exposed in a public place? Don't analyse it, she told herself. It's not your field, philosophy and all that. Just paint.

She painted an open gash in the heart with, inside it, a small dead unborn baby. Something died in him, she thought. I wonder what that was? His gift for painting? No, that had come to birth; was merely asleep now.

She placed that picture on top of the first one, of the intensely staring eyes, and took a fourth sheet.

Leon opened his eyes and found that the room was not spinning round any more. He was not dead. Good. He looked at the picture he'd started, with its coloured mists enshrouding mother and child, tore it into shreds and threw it away.

I mustn't paint like this just now, he thought. There is a reason why I must stop painting abstracts. I don't know what this is, but I will follow my instincts.

He began to paint again, very slowly, a perfectly formal setting for a portrait: a homely living room with chintz curtains drawn, a pink-shaded lamp, a sagging sofa. He began to feel comforted. He added a blazing fire, a hearth-rug with a cat lying on it. Things will sort themselves out, he thought.

Elvis Simpson sat morosely on his own in a corner of the pub, nursing a pint of bitter and a sore gum. What was the point of going to dentists? They only made things worse, poking about your mouth, sticking their nasty sharp instruments into sensitive places.

For no reason, his mind jumped to Annie, the girl he had had in the alleyway last night. The experience had rattled him. Everyone had told him Annie was good for a laugh. You could tell she was. She dressed very come-on; she had a body that wasn't made to be ignored; she giggled a lot and hung on to blokes' arms while she was talking to them.

Everyone had had Annie, or everyone said they had. Some of the girls in her class called her a slag, which was a sure sign the boys weren't just boasting. Girls didn't get that jealous of someone if it was all just talk.

And she'd shown no opposition when he'd walked her home down the alley, and parked her in the dark patch between two street lamps. He'd only done what anyone would have done. He had never tried anything kinky, nothing like that. He had just gone ahead and done it, the way he always did. So why had she started crying and screaming like that? Scared the life out of him.

'What did I do?' he said. 'I never done nothing!' Nothing to set her off crying and sobbing, tears streaming down her face, all woebegone, standing there against the fence with her skirt hitched up and her tights around her knees. She looked like a child that had been abused. But she was sixteen, over the age of consent, and she had consented, hadn't she? So how could it be his fault if she cried like that?

He sipped his beer and flinched. Bloody dentists. You agree to let them have a gentle look at your mouth and while you're sat in the chair and can't escape they go and torture you.

Sarah sat back on the sofa and opened her library book. Placido Domingo sang. She had washed her fine fair hair and was leaving it to dry naturally. Peace. Poor Marie, she thought. And poor little Sorrel, trapped here all afternoon. She'd have been happier in the park, chasing her squirrels. Poor baby Sacha, bitten so hard on her soft little wrist. And poor little me, come to that. Why do I listen to Ben telling me who to invite to fill my free afternoon?

He would be down the pub now, she thought, swigging pints or Scotch, cracking jokes for anyone who would listen. His voice would get louder, taking in an even wider audience. Smiles would appear on people's faces. 'Get you another drink, squire?' some man would offer.

He was good company, Ben. Sarah wished that she was. He put people at their ease. Not her, of course, but then that was her own fault, because she was awkward. Ben told her so. 'Standing there with a silly smile on your face,' he'd say. 'Like a cow. Dressed in your mimsy silk skirt and prissy blouse, like a goody-two-shoes. Goody-two-flat-feet. The only contribution you make to a conversation is to put your foot in it.' He was right, too. She did always seem to say the wrong thing. Once or twice she had spoiled his jokes by saying something too soon, thinking he had finished, or by making it obvious she hadn't seen the punchline. She didn't do that now. She kept quiet and let him talk, or she sat on the edge of the crowd and talked to one of the women, or to Eleanor's husband Jake, who also seemed to stay clear of the throng.

Still, she was on her own for now, probably for the whole evening. He might even go back to John and Helen's when the pub closed. He might even phone to say he was spending the night there, if that was all right with her? And she would say oh, of course. Of course it is. And she would pretend he was telling the truth about who he was staying with, and he would pretend she didn't know he was lying.

They had had lots of practice at this. The reason she had never called his bluff, never made a scene, was because she so fiercely needed his absence. She was relieved not to have him with her all the time, beside her every night, fighting the whole world even in his sleep.

'Sarah's a saint!' people said. 'How does she put up with his infidelity? Doesn't she suspect anything?'

But it's worse than that, she thought. I don't suspect. I

know. By saying nothing, I encourage him. I don't know what that makes me. An accessory to the act? Not a saint. Certainly not that.

Ben leaned on the bar and called for more drinks. 'And one for yourself, squire!'

The barman thanked him.

'I must be going home, after this,' John said.

'What? Skipping your round? Can't have that!'

'I said no to this one,' John pointed out.

'Never make a salesman if you're always watching the clock,' Ben said. 'Got to let the customer think you've got all the time in the world. That's the trick.' His words were slightly slurred.

The pub had filled up. Two young girls were playing the fruit machine. Both had upswept lacquered hair, one streaked with mauve and pink, one dusted with glitter, and both wore short black leather-look skirts over fluorescent tights – one lime green, one pink and purple diagonal striped.

'Let's find ourselves a seat,' Ben suggested. He passed behind the girls, and slid a casual hand across the back of their skirts. They wheeled round and stared at him in contempt. John expected obscenities, but the taller one simply said 'Wally!' quite mildly. The other girl had already turned back to the machine.

They sat down at a table nearby.

'Bit rough for my liking,' Ben said, indicating the girls, but John noticed that he kept his voice down.

The girls attracted attention, John thought; people's eyes were inevitably drawn to them by the way they looked. It seemed strange that they should be acting as though they wanted to be ignored. But of course, he realized, it's just that we're not their type.

Ben was telling him a story about how he had caught

156

out a salesman in some fiddle. 'I said to him, we all do it, mate, but the moral is don't get caught! Right?'

'Right,' John said. His head was beginning to swim. Must be the drink, he thought. He hadn't eaten since having two sausage rolls for lunch, with Helen.

Ben continued to talk. A young lad approached the girls at the fruit machine and began to talk to them. He's more their type, John thought. He had backbrushed gelled black hair and wore jeans interwoven with glitter thread, with cream toecap boots. One side of his face looked slightly swollen. On the back of his jacket was embroidered – slightly wonky, as though his girlfriend or his mum had done it – the single word 'Elvis'. I didn't know they still worshipped the King of Rock 'n' Roll, John thought. Maybe his mother did, and named her son after him. He suppressed a laugh. Ben hadn't got to the punchline yet.

'Got to catch 'em while they're young, that's the only way,' Ben said. 'Agree?'

'Agree,' said John. He looked to see if Ben was talking about the young trio by the fruit machine, but Ben wasn't watching them. He went on with his story.

The taller girl – obviously the spokesman for both – suddenly interrupted what Elvis was saying and raised her voice. 'Guys like you,' she declared, 'have got one idea in their heads – to do it wiv a girl and to get it over wiv quick as possible so you can get to the best bit. And d'ju know what the best bit is, for you lot? Telling your mates!'

The crowd at that end of the pub had fallen silent when she started to speak in that strident voice. Now a ripple of laughter began to spread.

Ben looked up. 'What's going on?' he said.

John was giggling into his pint. He couldn't answer.

Ben looked at his watch. 'Let's be off,' he said. 'This place gets boring later on.'

* * *

Elvis was overcome with embarrassment. He thought, why does everyone have to pick on me? He aimed a kick at a Coke can, resentfully, but it rolled mildly into the gutter.

Ben and John came out of the pub behind him, heading for the car, parked in a side street. Ben slapped Elvis jovially on the shoulder. 'Can't win 'em all, son,' he said.

Elvis spat at him. 'Don't s'pose you win many – dad,' he returned. The retort eased his feelings. He swung off down the street.

The girl's remarks bothered him, especially after that episode last night. What was so wrong with getting it over with quickly? It happened quickly, didn't it? What else were you meant to do? And of course he told his mates. He had a reputation to keep up.

'It's a question of status with these young kids,' Ben told John. 'See how many birds they can knock off.' He unlocked the driver's door and got into the car.

His slang is getting outdated, John thought. He slid into the passenger seat, stretched and yawned. 'Oh well,' he said. 'I'm glad I've outgrown that.'

Ben shot him a suspicious look. He started the engine, and the car moved off.

Now Helen was painting a head alive with fire. Flames leaped from eyes, ears, mouth, hair. Around the edges of the page were faces, all with the same haunted eyes. Old people, children, unborn babies. Her brush dabbed itself in the black paint. Across the bottom of the page it inscribed the word 'Holocaust'.

Dear God, she thought, help me. What have we got here?

'Sorry I'm late,' John said, coming in the back door. 'Ben kept me.'

'Hi,' she said absently.

He put his arms round her. 'Kiss,' he said.

She kissed the air to the left of his face.

'Something funny happened in the pub,' he said. 'These two girls . . .' He could tell she was not really listening.

'Sorry, if I'm interrupting something,' he said sarcastically.

'Oh, that's okay,' she said.

'I'll get myself something to eat,' he mentioned.

'Fine.' She was holding a piece of paper out at arm's length and making a face at it, as though she didn't like what she saw.

'What is it?' John asked. He looked at it, then at the other sheets on the draining board. 'Very good,' he said. 'What's this one meant to be? It looks like somebody's shadow.'

'It is,' Helen said. 'John?'

'Yes?'

'What dates were the Second World War?'

'Thirty-nine to forty-five, why?'

'What age would somebody be now if they'd survived a concentration camp and been old enough to remember it?'

'Depends, doesn't it? Mid-fifties?'

Helen frowned. That was no good. He obviously wasn't anywhere near that age. More like forty, or a little over, she thought.

'Has there been anything else since, that you could describe as a holocaust?' she asked.

He came and looked over her shoulder at the final painting again. He shrugged. 'Fire in a house? Plane crash?'

'No.' She put the paintings aside. 'Scrambled eggs?'

'Great.' He kissed her again. 'You're a good little almost-wife,' he said, tempting fate, but she didn't seem to hear him.

* * *

159

Ben found Sarah asleep on the sofa, some classical music playing softly, a coffee mug empty by her side. Her hair, newly washed, was soft in the lamplight.

I love you, he thought, with an unexpected ache. Even if everybody does think you're perfect. I forgive you for being the only goodness I've got.

He was about to wake her up to come to bed, then thought better of it. She couldn't be more peaceful than where she was. He brought down the single duvet from the spare room and laid it gently over her. She stirred, then seemed to decide not to wake up. Even in sleep, he thought, the decision was a conscious one. She had such control of herself.

He turned out the light and stood for a moment beside her in the dark. I know you don't always want me, he told her silently. I can't blame you for that. I don't always want myself.

He went upstairs to bed alone.

'She's settled at last,' Jake said, coming into the sitting room where Eleanor sat with her feet up, in front of the gas fire. Her eyes were closed.

'Good,' she said, without opening them.

'It was all the excitement, I expect,' he said. 'She doesn't usually wet the bed.' He sounded slightly anxious, as though this was a failure for which Eleanor might hold him responsible.

'Poor Gaby,' Eleanor said. 'It offended her dignity. Are all children as self-possessed as she is? They don't seem to be.'

Jake looked at her. 'She's just a baby,' he said. 'A Daddy's girl.'

'Don't rub it in.' Eleanor grimaced.

Jake moved to switch the television on. 'Want to see *The Week's News?*'

'Yes. No, hold on. You watch it. I've remembered I've got to pop out for half an hour.'

He kept his back turned to her. 'Okay.'

She waited for him to ask what for, but he didn't. Odd, she thought. Oh well, it saves me using the excuse about collecting papers from the reception desk at work.

'Won't be long,' she said. She picked up her handbag from the hall table and checked that her car keys were in it. The envelope of photographs was already tucked into the capacious side pocket, which locked.

In the car, she wondered what had suddenly reminded her to go to Leon's. It was quite late. If he was an early-to-bedder he might not still be up. She could just slip the envelope under the door, or leave it under the mat and drop a note through the letterbox letting him know it was there. It had been comfortable sitting by the fire and she had had no desire to go out again in the cold, but Leon's face had suddenly come into her head and it seemed important to go now.

His flat was not far from the Logodata offices, on the top floor of an old house. The stairs were carpeted. She knocked softly on Leon's door and he opened it almost immediately, in his dressing gown.

'Oh, I am sorry,' Eleanor said. 'I didn't mean to get you up. I was just going to leave these.'

'No, I was not in bed,' Leon said. 'I had just had a bath. Come in for a minute.'

She made a half-hearted refusal, but went in anyway. The truth was, she couldn't resist this place. She loved the studio atmosphere, its spaciousness, the skylights, the half-finished canvases and the faint smell of paint. To her, there was something sacred about being an artist, and she loved to be associated with it.

Leon was already making her a coffee. He didn't risk her refusal by asking if she wanted one. He needed the company, and he knew that Eleanor sensed this and didn't resent it.

'So the block lifted then?' Eleanor said. 'I'm glad of that.'

He didn't deny it, merely said, 'I thought I would do a very conventional portrait. Would that disappoint you?'

'Of course not,' she said. 'I was just intrigued that you suggested it. I didn't think it was your field.'

He smiled but looked sad. 'It isn't really, I confess. But have a look at this. See what you think of something like this, for a background.' He indicated the painting of the sitting room.

'But Leon, that's beautiful!' she exclaimed. 'It's perfect as it is.'

'No, no,' he protested. 'Just a setting for the portrait of you and your daughter.'

'Leave it as it is!' she said. 'I'd love to have that on my wall, and Jake would love it as well. It's peaceful and cosy. Don't add a thing to it.'

'No, please,' he said. His hands were trembling. He needed to do this painting. It was the only thing he felt safe with. She must not take it away from him.

She sensed the tension in him and said, unconsciously making her voice sound soothing, 'You do exactly what you want, Leon. You're the artist. I'm delighted to have a painting by you, that's all. I still don't think you're charging me what you're worth, but I won't argue with that because I'm sure I couldn't afford it if you did!' She smiled at him. He relaxed.

'I wonder though,' Eleanor said, 'if I could ask a favour of you.'

'Yes,' he said, with difficulty. 'Anything you wish.'

'Could I possibly have another look through those photos of your past paintings? You showed me them before, so I could just get a general idea of what you did, but I would like to understand them better, the abstracts in particular. I'm very ignorant about art.'

Oh no, he thought. Don't make me go through what I can't do any more, what I'm too afraid to paint now.

Aloud, he simply said, 'Of course,' and fetched the album to show her. Even in his present state of terror, it was inconceivable to him to refuse a request.

Richard had mown half the lawn in the afternoon, had been stopped by pain from his ulcer and had to lie down for an hour, with Polly rubbing his stomach to ease the soreness, and bringing him sweetened hot milk.

After that, he went back and mowed the other half of the lawn, coming in grey and exhausted. Over a cup of tea, he had had a row with Oriel. He called her idle and vain, and she called him fussy, middle-aged and petty-minded. She had slammed up to her room, and Richard had complained to Polly about her for another hour.

Polly cooked toad-in-the-hole for supper, Richard's favourite, to put him in a good mood, but Richard had read somewhere that greasy food was no good for ulcers (like having a pet, Polly thought, that needed special food) so he refused to eat it. Oriel, finally enticed down from her room and persuaded to sit at the same table with Richard, refused to eat it too, saying she was on a diet.

This was the cue for Richard to call Oriel a young hussy, and Oriel to call Richard an old woman. Both slammed their way out of the kitchen, returning independently five and ten minutes later to ask Polly to cook them something else. Polly, uncharacteristically, refused, saying she was going out to take the convalescent neighbour a plateful of toad-in-the-hole which was, she said, delicious.

This removed Richard and Oriel's second contingency plan, which was to give in ungracefully and condescend to eat the supper Polly had cooked, as long as they could eat in solitude.

United for once, both accused Polly of starving her nearest and dearest to feed all the strangers in the neighbourhood, but Polly was unmoved by this terrible accusation.

'You know I can't cook for myself!' Richard thundered.

Polly took a fiver out of her purse and told Oriel to go out and buy them both a Kentucky Fried Chicken.

'I can't eat fried stuff!' Richard yelled. 'You don't care about my ulcer, do you?'

'I do,' Polly said. 'I think you should treat the cause, which is tension. Now, do you want me to leave you a portion of this or don't you?'

They both said yes, sulkily, and retired to eat in separate rooms.

Polly returned later to find Richard sawing the legs off the coffee table, red in the face with exertion. 'It had to be done,' he panted. 'Couldn't be left like this a moment longer. I'll have to replace them with ones that don't wobble.'

'Darling,' Polly said, 'we'll buy a new coffee table. Don't strain your tummy again.'

'You think I am made of money!' he shouted. 'You and your "Why don't you work part time?" You've no sense of financial management at all.'

'All right,' she said pacifically. 'Where's Oriel?'

'Gone out.'

'Out where ?'

'She didn't say, just said she was going out. She doesn't tell me anything.'

'Oh Richard, didn't you ask? It's past ten o'clock.'

Seeing him draw breath for another tirade, Polly said hastily, 'Never mind, I expect she'll be home soon. Like an Ovaltine, love?'

'When I've finished this. Put the milk on to heat. I'll be six or seven minutes.'

'All right. Biscuit?'

'No. Yes. One of those coconut ones. Not the chocolate coated, just the plain coconut, know the ones I like?'

'Yes,' Polly said. 'I know what you like, love.'

'Now this one, for instance,' said Eleanor. 'Is it a mood, or does it symbolize something?'

'What I saw in it,' said Leon, 'was a balance. You see, here – as though each of these lines and shapes is only just held up by another. A precarious balance. But what the painter expresses in an abstract and what the viewer sees may be very different. It's not that the viewer is wrong. It's that looking at a picture is also creative.'

Eleanor thought about this. She nodded. 'I see. So the painter puts something of himself into the painting, but so does the person looking at it?'

'That's what I believe,' said Leon.

'And sometimes the viewer doesn't like what he sees?' Eleanor said. 'Does that mean he doesn't like the painting or he doesn't like himself?' They both laughed.

'These two, for example,' said Leon, pointing, 'received very good reviews, but the gallery had actually hung them sideways. So there, obviously, the viewer had less chance of seeing what I saw!'

Eleanor stared at him. 'They hung them the wrong way up? Couldn't you tell them?'

'I did,' he said, 'but they didn't rectify it at first. I did mention it again later on, but by that time several critics had visited the exhibition, and the gallery staff felt it was unnecessary to change it. I suppose they would have looked foolish.'

'Why didn't you insist?' Eleanor asked. She was astounded to hear this. 'It was your painting!'

'Yes. I suppose I didn't like to make a fuss,' he said.

'But Leon,' she said aghast, 'this is your soul!' She tapped the photographs. 'You let people walk all over your soul like that? If anyone did that to me, there would be a holocaust!'

His eyes went opaque. 'A holocaust,' he said.

'I would have torn them to shreds,' said Eleanor robustly. She noticed he had gone very still, very tense again. She turned the page of the album. 'Tell me about this one,' she said. He was silent, far away. She put her hand gently on his arm. He jumped.

'Yes? I am sorry.'

'This one,' Eleanor said, 'is lovely. How did you come to paint this?'

He talked again, normally. She offered him a cigarette. He relaxed. Sitting there with him in his dressing gown, turning the pages of the book, looking at the pictures, she felt like a mother reading a bedtime story, helping the child unwind after its day. Perhaps I'm not such a bad mother after all, she thought. Perhaps I let Jake relieve me of too much of the motherhood.

Jake turned the lights off and went to bed. She's having an affair, he thought. I knew it. He would not let this worry him, but would deal with it in an adult and civilized manner. It did not threaten him, just as Eleanor's other ways of expressing her independence had never put any pressure on him, as a man.

They discussed everything, that was the secret. They would discuss this too, when it was over. He would tell her he had known all along, but had trusted her to control the situation, and she would admire his confidence and fortitude.

He brushed his teeth and put on the nightshirt Eleanor had bought him on her business trip to Miami in December.

He realized he had turned the light off in the hall, so he returned downstairs barefoot, to switch it on again. This would show Eleanor how considerate he was, in spite of her minor transgression which really, in this day and age, meant nothing at all.

Eleanor was driving home, with the windscreen wipers going and the street-lamp glare hurting her eyes, when her attention was caught by an outburst of shouting and screaming in the street behind her. Peering into the driving mirror, she saw a young girl running into the road, pursued by five boys. Two of them grabbed her and she fell down, screaming hysterically.

Now, Eleanor wondered, are they just fooling or what? She pulled in to the kerb, reversed round the corner of a side street, and drove back the same way. The group had moved out of the road now and were clustered round the girl, who was on her knees, with her head down almost to the ground. If this was fooling, Eleanor thought, it looked as though the game had gone far enough. She let the car slow down almost to zero. Do I interfere or don't I?

As she was hesitating, a couple of the lads hitched the girl to her feet, and Eleanor caught sight of her face. She braked, flung open the car door and jumped out.

'Oriel!' she bawled.

Everyone looked in her direction, then one of the boys shouted, 'Shit, it's her mum!' and they ran off, theatrically ducking and weaving, as though she had a machine gun. What do they think I am, Eleanor thought irritably; the A-Team?

'Get in the car,' she said.

Oriel got in, not looking at her. She was wearing an open raincoat with nothing underneath it, as far as Eleanor could see, apart from a kind of leotard and tights. The girl wrapped the raincoat over these, defensively.

167

'I thought flashers were usually old men,' said Eleanor drily.

'It's not funny,' Oriel sobbed. 'There was a whole gang of them. They set on me.'

'While you were quietly minding your own business?'

'No! I was out looking . . . looking for a friend, that's all.'

'Was he one of those boys there?' Eleanor demanded.

'No. I didn't find him.' Oriel sniffed noisily. Eleanor handed her a tissue.

'Does Polly know you're out?'

Oriel blew her nose and didn't answer.

'Does she?' Eleanor repeated.

'Just drive me home,' said Oriel sullenly.

'Not yet,' Eleanor said.

Oriel reached over to turn the ignition key. 'Start the engine,' she said.

Eleanor looked at her coolly. Oriel took her hand away, and looked out of the window at the rainy street.

'It strikes me,' said Eleanor, 'that you're not out looking for a friend; you're looking for trouble, and that's exactly what you found. Are you pleased with yourself?'

'Oh, shut up,' muttered Oriel.

'In a minute,' said Eleanor imperturbably. She sat and waited. Oriel turned her head slightly and looked at her out of the corner of her eye. 'How old are you, Oriel?' Eleanor inquired.

'Fifteen,' she said. 'Old enough to be out. Nearly the age of consent!' She sneered.

'Of course,' said Eleanor pleasantly, 'so it wouldn't count, if you were raped, would it? No one would mind.'

Oriel shot her a furious glance.

'Are you staying on at school after next year?' Eleanor asked.

'No, I'm not!'

'What then? Sixth-form college?'

'No. I'm leaving. I'm fed up with school, thank you.'

'What are you going to do?' Eleanor persisted.

'Don't know.'

'What kind of job would you like?'

'Don't know. Something.'

'Do you have any interests, Oriel? Apart from . . .' No, she wouldn't say it. Keep it sweet, Eleanor, she told herself. She's only a kid. 'Any hobbies?'

'Don't know. Not really.'

'Is there anything – anything at all – that takes your interest, that you'd like to do or be?'

Oriel thought. 'I wouldn't mind being a rock star,' she said.

'Can you sing? Play an instrument?'

'Not really.'

'Is there anything else you want to do with your life?'

'Go to New York,' Oriel said.

'Really?' Eleanor said. 'Why's that?'

'Don't know.'

Eleanor suppressed a sigh. 'Something you are good at,' she recalled, 'is looking after small children. Sorrel loves you, doesn't she?'

'Don't know,' Oriel said, but she looked at her.

'I have some friends,' Eleanor said, 'in business with an American company. They live in London and spend the summer months in New York – not the city, but New York State. They have two little girls – about two and eight, they must be now – and they take on an au pair every summer holiday. Would you fancy doing that job?'

'Yes,' Oriel said.

Alleluia, thought Eleanor. Not a 'don't know' but a 'yes'. 'It would be for a whole two months,' she said, 'and it would be quite a responsibility, but they'd look after

169

you. I wouldn't recommend you to them unless you were prepared to work hard, consistently, the whole time.'

'I would,' Oriel said.

'And do as they told you?'

'Yes.'

'Like you do with your parents?'

'Oh,' Oriel said. 'That's different.'

'Not very,' said Eleanor. 'And your parents would have to agree to it, of course.'

'Yes.'

'All right, then,' Eleanor said. 'You talk to them and see what they say, and if they're in favour – and only if – I'll talk to my friends.' She started the engine. They drove home in silence.

The lights were all on in the Shaw's house.

'I expect they're worried sick,' said Eleanor. 'Go in and make your peace with them.'

'Will you come in with me?' Oriel asked, subdued.

'No,' Eleanor said.

Oriel hesitated a moment. 'Okay,' she said. She got out of the car, then leant in and said, 'Thanks,' and shut the door quickly.

Jake had left the hall light on for her, Eleanor noticed, and gone to bed. She realized how tired she was. She went up and undressed quickly and slid into bed beside him. He was asleep, lying on his stomach with his head turned away from her side of the bed. At least he wasn't worried about where I was, Eleanor thought. She wondered if she should feel resentful about this, but went to sleep instead.

10
The Hand of God

'There's something about Sunday mornings,' John said. 'You can tell it's Sunday the minute you open your eyes.'

'What time is it?' Helen asked.

'Ten to eleven.'

'It's not, is it?' She started getting up.

'What's the hurry? It's Sunday!' he said.

'I know, but I want to go over to Leon's. Will you come too?'

'Oh, not today! I thought we'd get on with painting the sitting room. If we put in a whole day at it we could have it finished by tonight.'

'There's no hurry for that,' Helen said. 'We could spare an hour or two to go, couldn't we?'

'Helen, you are dead selfish!' he exclaimed. 'All you think about is what you want to do! I don't want to go over there to watch you paint pictures, do I?'

She sat down on the edge of the bed. 'I'm not going there to paint. I think Leon might be in some kind of trouble, John. Maybe we could do something.'

'What kind of trouble?'

'I don't know,' she confessed. 'Some kind of distress.'

'What does that have to do with us?'

'It seems to have,' she said, wrinkling up her nose in puzzlement. 'I mean, those pictures I did last night; they all seemed to have something to do with him. They were like clues to what's going on in him. I've never known anything like that before. If he was nothing to do with us, I reckon it wouldn't have happened to me.'

'I don't know what you're talking about,' John said.

'But one thing I do know, and that's that you can leave me out of it.'

'I can't just leave him in that state, John! I'll have to go.'

'Well, you go on your own, then,' he said furiously. 'I think you're crazy. It sounds dangerous to me. He's a stranger you met in the park. He could be a maniac!'

'I don't think he is,' Helen said, 'but if you think it's dangerous for me to go, then come with me.'

'No, I won't! You're not ruining my Sunday with your stupid ideas.'

She continued dressing, in silence, then went out to the kitchen and made toast and tea. She looked at the pictures again. Holocausts, she thought, and long shadows, and terrified, staring eyes. Whatever it all means, I'm sure it's not meant to be ignored. It's too strong for that. But why me? What could I do, a stranger to him? John's right; it's not my business. But a voice inside her said, 'What if no one else can reach him because no one else has seen him this way?'

'Helen,' John said, coming in and taking the pictures out of her hand, 'I want you to listen to me. Okay?'

'I'm listening,' she agreed. She stood the toast in the toast rack and turned to face him.

'How long,' he asked rhetorically, 'have I been waiting for us to be together like this?'

'Three months,' she answered.

'Three months,' he confirmed. 'Three whole months of living alone, while you stayed up in York in that bloody flat!'

'It was your decision, for me to stay and get a high price for it,' she reminded him. 'I would have sold it quick and cheap and come down here with you.'

'Oh, so you're blaming me for that now, are you?' he demanded.

172

'Not blaming, no; just saying you had a choice.'

'That's beside the point! Stop twisting everything I say! All I'm saying is, I waited three months for you – which is longer than either of us thought it would take; don't say it wasn't. And when you finally get here, what do you do? Go chasing off on your own crazy projects, and never think of me!'

'I've only been here a couple of days,' she said. 'And in that time I've done what you wanted – got to know some of the people you know, painted the sitting room under-coat, heard about a job. That's not bad, is it? Selfish?'

'You never even asked me about the job,' he grumbled. 'I might not want you working in the same place as me.'

'Don't you?'

'I didn't say I didn't; I just said you might have asked.'

Helen started spreading margarine on the toast.

'Anyhow,' he continued, 'you may have done all those other things, but your heart's not in it. You were just waiting till you could get to your painting.'

'True,' she said equably. 'But then you can't really put your soul into undercoating walls, can you? It's just something to be done.' She put the tea and toast on to a tray and carried it into the sitting room. John followed her.

'Helen,' he said loudly. 'I do not want you going to that man's studio.'

'I know,' she said. She took a bite of toast.

'So you won't go?' he pursued.

She shook her head. 'I'm going.'

'I won't come with you!'

'Okay.'

'Don't come crying to me if you get into trouble,' he warned.

'I won't, then.'

'You can be as hard as nails, did you know?'

173

She shrugged. 'Eat your toast,' she said. 'I've sugared your tea.'

'We won't paint the sitting room, okay? I know you can't put your soul into it, as you say. We'll go out for the day. Find a pub by the river, go for a walk. Eh?'

'Sure. After I get back.'

He tried sarcasm. 'So nature isn't good enough for your soul? You have to play ministering angel as well! Is that the kind of soul you have?'

Helen dusted crumbs from her hands. 'No,' she said briefly, 'but at least it's still my own.'

She collected the pictures from the kitchen, dropped them into a portfolio which she tucked under her arm, took her jacket from the hall cupboard, and went out by the back door.

'I am delighted to see you,' said Leon gravely.

'How are you?' Helen asked. She stood and looked at him, awaiting an answer.

'I feel better,' he said. 'Sit down; let me make you a coffee. A lady who commissioned a painting for her husband's birthday called last night with some photographs for me to work from, and I have made a start on the portrait.'

Bells rang in Helen's mind. 'That lady wouldn't be called Eleanor, would she?'

'Yes – how do you know?'

'I know her; she works at the same company as John. She mentioned that she'd commissioned an artist. I didn't know it was you!' Helen refrained from adding, 'She asked me to do it instead, as you'd got stuck.' Bang goes my first commission, Helen thought. Oh well, all in a good cause, I suppose. She thought Leon looked happier.

'Do you take sugar?'

'Two please. Ta.' I won't show him my pictures, she decided. No point in upsetting things if he's all right now.

'John hasn't come with you,' he commented, 'so that means you've come to paint today – yes?'

'Yes,' she said. 'That's what I've come for. If it's okay with you?'

'Of course.' He showed her the easel set up for her at one end of the studio. 'Move it about till the light falls as you want it. Help yourself to these, and anything else you need.' He gestured towards the tray of paints and brushes.

'Oh no,' she protested, 'I wouldn't use your materials! By rights, I should be paying you for the use of the studio space. This'd be more like you paying me!'

It was near the truth, he realized. He would willingly have paid her to fill up the vacant space of the studio and the empty void of days in which he was unable to work, or to think straight. But he didn't wish to burden her with his desperation, so he simply said lightly, 'It is a traditional privilege for older artists to subsidize younger ones a little. I can say I invested in you, when you become famous.'

'Some hopes of that!' Helen said. She hung her jacket on a hook on the wall and set a fresh sheet of paper on the easel. She found she was slightly nervous, painting in company. He might think the results were rubbish.

That's all she was nervous about, she told herself. Nothing to do with John saying the man might be dangerous. She started to paint quickly, mechanically. Leon returned to his sketches for the portrait.

After ten minutes, Helen crushed the painting into a ball and threw it on the floor. She went back to the picture of the old woman in the supermarket. At least, I can paint that without thinking about it now, she thought. A nice safe subject. She didn't want any more pictures of Leon.

175

She blobbed in a rough outline of supermarket shelves, the aisle, the trolley, the woman's body, the face. Even as an outline, before she added the detail, the face was Leon's face. No, no, no, no, no! She reversed the sheet and began to paint on the back. This is useless, she thought. I'm in a flat panic or something. What's this about? She sat down on the floor, and gazed at the blank sheet. Think, Helen, she told herself. If you don't want to repeat last night's performance of painting your subconscious thoughts – or his subconscious thoughts, whichever way it was – then plan ahead.

Leon grew increasingly nervous as Helen discarded her efforts. I am having a bad effect on her, he thought. He said, 'I hope I am not infecting you with my own inability to paint.'

'No, no,' she said quickly. 'Anyhow, you are working again now aren't you? Can I have a look?'

'Yes, of course.'

She stood in front of the easel where he had placed the room scene, and looked at it for a long time, puzzled.

'So?' he asked.

'It's very good,' she said slowly, 'but it doesn't seem like your style.'

'No,' he said. 'It is not.'

There was a silence.

'Would you say,' he asked finally, 'that my usual style was violent?'

Helen jumped. Leon noticed it, and backed away. She knows, he thought. My fears are correct; the violence in my dreams reveals the person I really am.

They stared at one another. Helen was aware of nothing except the sheer force of unhappiness coming from him, and the fear. But she knew the fear was his now, not hers. She took a deep breath.

'Leon,' she said, 'I did some paintings last night. That's why I really came. There's something in them . . .'

The doorbell rang. He froze, looking at her helplessly.

'Shall I get it?' she suggested.

'No, I'll go.' He came to life, shook his head as if to clear it, and went to the door.

'We've only popped in for a minute,' Eleanor said, 'so that you could see Gaby. Jake thinks we're at the park. Helen! What are you doing here?'

'Painting.' Helen said.

'This is amazing!' Eleanor exclaimed. 'I didn't realize you knew each other! How come?'

'We met over artists' shop-talk,' said Leon. Helen thought, he doesn't want to say, 'We met in the park,' in case Eleanor thinks it's odd. She didn't resent this as she resented John covering up for the sake of appearances.

'Well!' said Eleanor. 'And I've gone and commissioned both of you for the same painting! Isn't this embarrassing?'

Her frankness made them both laugh, breaking the ice. Gaby stood very still, holding her mother's hand – as if protecting her, Helen thought.

'But I do still want both,' Eleanor said. 'Really. One for Jake's birthday present and one for sheer self-indulgence.'

Both Leon and Helen protested, insisting that the other did the painting.

'You'd neither of you be any good in business,' Eleanor joked. 'You're meant to fight to *win* contracts, not lose them! No, seriously, if you can paint again now, Leon, I'm delighted, because Jake loves your work, but I would like one of your pictures as well, Helen, birthday or no birthday. You're very good. So that's settled. Two pictures. Right?'

Helen was tempted to pull out the pictures of Leon and

say to Eleanor, 'What shall I do about this?' But it seemed unfair to Leon to invoke someone else's support – like ganging up on him, two against one. Besides, Eleanor, so cool and businesslike, seemed anxious this morning and even a little lost. Being with her child seemed to bring out the child in her. That was strange. Most mothers adopted an I-can-cope, I'm-the-boss attitude with their own children, and shrank back to being individuals only when the children were not there.

The child was very solemn, self-possessed, standing close to Eleanor like one who takes her role seriously. A born mother. Eleanor deferred to the child's opinion. 'What do you think of the studio, Gaby? What do you think of the picture?'

Gaby studied the living room picture. 'Who lives there?' she asked.

'Leon's going to paint you and me sitting in that room,' Eleanor told her.

'And Daddy?'

'No, it's a picture for Daddy to look at. A picture of us, as a present for him.'

Gaby said nothing.

'Do you like the cat?' asked Leon, pointing to the creature on the hearthrug.

'We haven't got a cat,' Gaby said.

Eleanor coughed. 'It's a pretty room, isn't it, Gaby?' she said. 'Don't you think it looks cosy?'

Gaby gave the picture another examination, then turned to Leon. 'Our house doesn't look like that,' she said simply.

The child's realism defeated them. Gaby looked through the photographs Eleanor had given Leon, and picked out the one she thought best of herself – in her best dress, unsmiling – and one of Eleanor, taken when

178

Eleanor was offguard, looking out of thw window, chin cupped in hand, deep in thought.

Leon did few brief sketches of Eleanor and Gaby together, which Gaby approved of, though some of the pencil lines were, she found, 'a bit messy'. She inquired whether Leon had an eraser, and was relieved when he said that he had. She refused his invitation to do a painting herself, reminding Eleanor after an hour and a half that Daddy would be waiting for his lunch. Eleanor, duly chastised, made her goodbyes and they left, hand in hand again.

Helen and Leon looked at each other and laughed.

Richard had got up at half-past eight, saying he must make an early start, and had driven to the DIY warehouse, which stayed open on Sundays, to buy some wood. Now he was busy fashioning new legs for the coffee table, in a flurry of swearing and sawdust.

Oriel, after last night's row, stayed in bed, and turned her face to the wall when Polly took her in a tray of breakfast. 'I bought you some Rice Krispies, Oriel,' she coaxed. 'The Indian shop was open this morning. You said you wanted some.'

'I've gone off them,' Oriel said.

Polly went and peeled the potatoes for dinner, then sat at the kitchen table and read the Sunday paper, without taking anything in. Fury emanated from Richard in the sitting room, hacking timber on the carpet, and resentment seeped down the stairs from Oriel, in self-immured isolation in her room.

Polly wondered why it was that she spent all week looking forward to the family weekend, and then spent all weekend longing for Monday. I must be very hard to please, she thought. On Monday she would phone Helen and ask her round for a coffee. She could make a few

179

scones for her to take home, or maybe a Victoria sponge. Polly began to feel better.

Oriel came down the stairs, in her raincoat. 'I'm going out,' she challenged.

'Oh, darling, where?'

'Out.'

'For a walk? I'll come with you, shall I?'

'No. See you.'

'Oriel, what are you wearing under that coat? Oriel . . .'

Oriel was gone, slamming the door fiercely. Polly caught a glimpse of shimmering yellow legs.

Richard came out of the sitting room. 'I told that girl she was not to go out again this weekend!' he shouted.

'Oh, dear,' Polly said sadly.

Elvis's mother was having her regular Sunday battle with him.

'You're to come to church, do you hear me?' she shouted. 'I'm not having people think my son is a heathen!'

'You never give up, do you?' he shouted back.

His mother began to sob, with one eye watching his reactions over the top of her hankie.

'Spare a thought for your mother, once in a while!' she begged. 'You're a cruel, wicked son to me, so you are!'

Elvis blew his top. 'Then there's no point in me going to church, is there? That's for good people!'

He pulled on his scuffed cream boots.

'Where are you going?' Mrs Simpson roared.

'Out!' he roared back. 'Away from you!'

After he had gone, she sat with her head on the table. 'I don't understand it,' she told herself. 'He was such a good little boy.'

She's such an old witch, Elvis raged, as he went down the street. I went to the dentist for her, didn't I? She can't

180

expect me to go to church as well. I don't believe in God. I believe in science.

It wasn't science, however, that he worshipped, craved and pursued day and night, but sex. Since discovering sex, he had been seized with a devotion to it, bordering on obsession. It was his religion, his only god, and it soon became like the God he had imagined as a child: stern, self-seeking, tyrannical, endlessly demanding. The god created by Elvis Simpson's image and likeness devoured him, body and soul. It drove him out on the streets on cold, windy nights. It tormented him in his warm bed, with insatiable discontent and unquenchable heat.

And yet he regarded himself as free, and free-thinking. He would have nothing to do with a God who believed in peace. Elvis was bold, wild, independent – and enslaved to a human god which was easily pleased but never satisfied.

Sarah cast a discreet look around the church while the vicar was giving his sermon and mused on how few young people there were here, in fact how few people at all. In ten years' time, she calculated, about ninety per cent of this congregation will have died, and this building could be empty on Sunday mornings.

Not surprising, either, she thought irritably. The readings had been full of archaic words: 'unto thee' and 'thou biddest' and 'thus spake'. What did that mean to anyone these days? And the intonation of the vicar's voice was beginning to grate on her nerves. Nobody spoke like that naturally. Did the vicar go home and drone at his wife, in that silly artificial singsong, 'Oh, makest thou me a cup of finest Nescafé, dearest beloved companion of my loins'? If he did, Sarah thought bitchily, that might account for the rising clerical divorce rate.

She fixed her mind on the cross above the altar. This

church had a plain bronze cross. It had abolished the uncomfortably human naked figure. Perhaps that was to convey the fact that he was now risen, but it seemed to Sarah in her present frame of mind, typical of the church to have kept the cross and abandoned the person.

Sarah rose quietly, avoiding the eye of the vicar, and left the church. I'm sorry, God, she said inwardly, but that place was making me feel unholy.

Oriel saw Elvis before Elvis saw her. He was mooching along, scuffing his feet, kicking at bits of litter – sweet wrappers, cigarette ends, anything. He stopped in front of the Super-Sonic shop and gazed hungrily through the window at the black and silver stacks of sound systems – amplifiers, double tape decks, rows of gleaming unfathomable controls. Scientific. Powerful. Turn a few knobs and out comes sound – loud, soft, treble, bass, vary the balance as you wish. That was the kind of god Elvis could covet: a god you could tell what to do; a god with an On/Off knob. Let his nagging mother sing 'Lead kindly light' in church. He would settle for this lot!

'Hi, Elvis,' said Oriel.

He looked round. 'Hi.'

'What you doing?' she said.

He shrugged. 'Nothing.'

'Oh,' she said lamely.

His eyes returned to the shop window. 'Six speakers,' he said reverently. 'Double tape deck, self-reversing disc deck, Dolby, VHF radio, compact disc, add-on video.'

Oriel followed his gaze. 'Wild!' she agreed. She had only a sketchy idea of what he was talking about. 'Where are you going?' she asked.

He shrugged again. 'Don't know. Around.'

'You meeting your mates?'

'No.'

'Oh.' She nearly said, 'Oh good,' but stopped herself in time. Shame it was Sunday, though. No one would see her with him. Unless he took her into the pub for a drink. But he probably had no money. She didn't mind about that. Some girls would, but she didn't.

'I'm not going anywhere either,' Oriel said. 'I'll walk around with you if you like.'

'Suit yourself,' he agreed.

Leon went out to the delicatessen for salami sandwiches and Coke.

Helen leafed through the photographs of Eleanor and Gaby. She picked up Leon's sketchbook and began to draw. She worked fast. At art school, she had always managed five drawings in the Life class, to most people's one or two.

She could see that her idea would work. Becoming excited, she flipped the sheet and began to draw a more careful version, filling in some details – expression in the eyes, a necklace, a teddy bear. She picked up a few crayons, added colour here and there.

'Leon!' she called, as he came in. 'Come and see what you think!'

He laid down his purchases and went over to her. She has forgotten her fear of me, he thought.

Helen had drawn Gaby sitting in an armchair like a throne, looking straight ahead with total composure. She wore make-up, a formal dress – as in her chosen photo – and was not smiling. Around her neck was an expensive-looking necklace, not the kind of jewellery a child would wear, and on her wrist was a watch, severely plain.

In the background sat Eleanor, on a hard chair. She wore no make-up, was dressed in a bright red tracksuit, and held Gaby's teddy bear – also copied faithfully from one of the photographs.

'Helen,' Leon said, 'that's perfect.'

She was laughing, excited with what she had done.

'Gaby as the grown-up and Eleanor as the child,' Leon said. 'I wouldn't have thought of that, but now I see it, it is exactly right. You have a good vision of people.'

Her face dropped. All the elation went out of her.

'What have I said?' he asked, concerned. 'Have I upset you?'

'Oh Leon,' Helen said, 'I came here today because I did some paintings of you last night and I thought you might be in trouble or something.'

'I?' he said, astonished.

'I'll show you,' she said, 'before I lose my nerve. You can think what you like. Here. Here they are. Have a look.'

She handed him the paintings one by one, in the order in which she had painted them, starting with the one of the staring eyes.

'But this is an amazing coincidence,' Leon said slowly. 'I started to do a painting very like this one, only yesterday. I had intended painting Eleanor and Gaby's faces emerging from a dark-coloured mist – exactly like this. For some reason, it frightened me, so much that I felt ill, I lost my balance, I thought I was dying. Why is this, Helen, do you know?'

'I don't know,' Helen said, 'but it seemed to me that the face in this was yours. I hadn't a doubt of it. Shall I show you the next one?'

'Please.'

This was the picture of the long grey shadow of a man, with children in its path.

Leon studied it in silence for a long time. Finally he said, 'I once painted my father like this. From a different angle, with the figure at the top of the page and the shadow falling – so – with my brother and myself overshadowed by him. I painted the sky red, to show his anger.'

'Your father?' Helen asked. 'Was he often angry with you and your brother?'

'Always angry,' Leon said softly. 'Angry with everybody: with his children, his elderly parents, his wife. He attacked my mother,' he added, and his voice now was almost a whisper, 'while she was six months pregnant. My mother was hoping for a girl. She thought a daughter might be a gentle influence on my father. It would have been her third child.'

'Oh no,' Helen said. 'He didn't . . .'

Leon nodded. 'My mother wasn't hurt, only bruised, but she lost the child.'

'I think,' Helen said, 'that you've just explained the third painting, and maybe the fourth as well.' She handed him the one of the man with the unborn child lying curled up in his broken heart.

'Yes,' Leon agreed. 'It even looks like my father. I don't think he ever forgave himself. He became very – what is the word? Sober? No – withdrawn – after that.'

'Are they still living, your parents?' Helen asked.

'My mother is still alive. She is living in Cracow. My father died, just two months ago. My brother and his family live in New York.'

Helen frowned. 'Do you think that your trouble with painting has anything to do with your father's death, Leon?'

He spread his hands expressively. 'I wasn't aware of any effect. It's possible, I suppose, but we were not close. I had not seen my parents for – oh, two years. I am ashamed to say I felt no grief.'

'Well . . .' Helen said. 'I don't know much about it, but I'd say there would be more than one way of grieving. I knew this lad at art college – the one who moved into the

185

flat for a while. You remember I told you about him –
Oliver?'

'Yes. The one who parted from his girlfriend and had
nowhere to live?'

'That's him. Well, his father died last year, and Oliver
and him had always hated each other, you know? But
after his father died, for a good few months Oliver said
he felt like him all the time. He found himself talking like
his father; he started smoking the same cigarettes as his
dad used to; he dreamed of him nearly every night, and
do you know, he even got all the chest pains and panic
attacks his father had had for the year before he died. He
was terrified at first, because he thought he must have
inherited his heart condition himself, but the doctor said
it was just a way of grieving. Oliver said he felt it was,
like, a way of getting to know his father at last, from the
inside. He said, "The old bugger finally dropped his guard
and let me inside his skin."'

Leon listened intently. Then he said, very slowly, as
though the words hurt him, 'I have been having dreams
of terrible violence. It is not violence done to me, but by
me. A terrible compulsion to damage and destroy. A
need to reduce human beings to bones and blood. I have
been very afraid. Afraid to paint abstracts – which my
father hated – in case I put this violence on to the canvas
for everyone to see and be afraid of me. I have become
afraid of myself.' He put his head in his hands and cried,
crouching forward to hide his face.

Helen sat perfectly still, staring at the final painting she
had to show him, the one she had labelled 'Holocaust'.
Dear God, she prayed, give us a short-cut to the end of
this; he's had enough. Give me the words – no, don't; just
give me the love, because it isn't the words that count, I
know.

Leon stopped. He pulled a handkerchief out of his

pocket and blew his nose. 'You are kind to come today to tell me this,' he said. 'You too, you must have felt afraid, when you saw what you had painted, and yet you came here, on your own.'

'I was a bit afraid,' Helen admitted, 'but not of you. You're a good man.'

'Thank you,' he said humbly. 'My father too – I believe he was a good man. He was of the generation of Jews who suffered the concentration camps, you know. His family, in generations before, had travelled all over eastern Europe, always escaping persecutions, pogroms, by the narrowest margin. Always the hunted victims, always on the run. My father, I think, developed an instinct for trouble. He escaped the camps, but I think he suffered for all those who did not.

'He too had dreams. He slept always with the light on. He always had the same kind of dreams: old people murdered, babies battered to death. His grief, I think, turned to bitterness, and his bitterness became violence. In the end, the victim of all those generations became the family tyrant. In his rage against the tyrants who killed his people, he created a new generation of victims.'

Helen nodded. 'So he dreamt about the experiences other people had – things he hadn't seen himself?'

'Yes, he dreamt about the camps as though, as soon as he slept, he was there himself. My mother used to say, "The Jews are one people. What can you expect? They have one heart. One bleeds, they all bleed; one dies, they all die inside." She told my father, "Don't blame yourself, that you escaped while they did not. In your heart, you never left. You are still there, long after they have all died. Perhaps they are the ones who escaped. Don't torment yourself so." I think she was right.'

'It sounds right,' Helen agreed. 'But look, Leon, I'm not good at putting things but, well . . . I remember

Oliver said he felt like he'd given his dad permission to die by, kind of, agreeing to finish his lifetime for him. You know what I mean? Like, Oliver would take on what his dad couldn't manage to stay and cope with.'

'Yes? What kind of things?'

'Well, the one thing his dad couldn't take was what he called "nancy boys". He had really narrow ideas about what a "real man" was – silly things, you know, like drinking bitter and having hairs on his chest and never being seen pushing a pram. You know the kind of thing. Well, the reason he couldn't stick Oliver was that by his standards Oliver turned out all wrong; he didn't play sport, didn't drink, cried if he got hurt – or if anyone else did.

'Oliver reckons that, once he began to feel the way his dad did, he could see why his dad couldn't stand him. He said, "When I came along, it was like the unmanly side of himself – the gentle side he kept hidden – came on show. It was like seeing a reflection of himself, and not liking it, and everyone else being able to see it too." '

'Yes,' Leon said, 'I can see that.'

'So the thing his dad couldn't do,' Helen said carefully, 'was forgive his son for being like himself and not covering it up by pretending to be all tough and macho. See?'

'Yes, I see,' Leon agreed.

'Then what Oliver did was, kind of, become his father, with his way of talking and his way of thinking, even. He kind of . . . sorry, I keep saying "kind of", don't I?'

Leon put his hand over hers. 'You are doing very well,' he said gently. 'Please go on. Or would you like a rest? Some lunch first, or a coffee?'

'No, I'm fine. Thanks. What I'm saying, I think, is that Oliver let his father move in with him, if you like, after he died, and the two of them fought it out for a bit, which gave Oliver a rough time. Then they kind of – sorry – came to terms, and Oliver realized they'd always been one and the same, but they'd found different ways to be it, probably just because they were brought up in different generations.'

'Yes. I can see that. And you think it is the same in my family? My father and myself – both gentle and both violent?'

'No, I don't mean that – except that I suppose everyone's both of those. You know – anyone could be the victim or the tyrant, depending on the circumstances. And maybe all tyrants are victims, or . . . oh, I don't know. No, what I meant was that maybe your father shared the feelings of the people in the concentration camps – the victims, that is – but the thing he couldn't do was forgive the tyrants.'

'Ah,' Leon said. 'So he became the tyrant and couldn't forgive himself?'

'Something like that, yes.'

'And I? I have let him . . . move in with me, you said, with his violence and his hatred of abstract paintings and his fears. Is that it? And through him the tyrants are also understood and their trouble is shared?'

It was Helen's turn to put her head in her hands. 'I can't think any more,' she said. 'My brain isn't used to this!'

Leon was contrite. 'I have made you exhausted,' he said. 'Rest yourself for a moment; I will bring you a sandwich.'

'Oh no, I must go home,' Helen said. 'I never meant to stay so long!'

'A sandwich and coffee first,' Leon said gently but firmly. 'And then I will take you home myself, in a taxi. It is the least I owe you.'

Helen gave in easily. 'Okay,' she said, with relief.

While he was in the kitchenette, putting on the kettle, she folded up the fourth painting – the Holocaust, with all the faces of adults and children and unborn babies – folded it very small and hid it away in the zip pocket of her jacket. There would be no need to let Leon see it now. He had seen through to the root of the trouble himself and this final shock was unnecessary.

'Ta, God,' Helen said. 'I'll owe you a favour – okay?'

11
Disclosures

When Ben, in answer to John's phone call, went over to see him, Sarah expected to feel relieved at being awarded another brief spell of peace, but she did not. His restlessness is infecting me, she thought. I can't sit still; can't settle at anything.

She felt tired and hyperactive at the same time. In the end, she went into the kitchen and looked out her mother's old cookery book and started to bake.

I can't keep rushing off to parks and churches, she told herself. Surely I should be able to think clearly at home, without continually feeling that Ben is in the room with me, irritated by every movement of my mind?

She reached for the food processor in the back of one of the deep kitchen cupboards. Ben was very proud of this kitchen. It was his first port of call when he showed people round the house. 'How lovely!' everyone said, 'How unusual!' And not infrequently: 'It must have cost you and arm and a leg!' It was a strain on the arms and legs to keep it clean, even with the help of Mrs Mackie for three hours a week.

It was a kitchen designed with machine-like precision, full of machines – all built in, including the microwave – and the whole effect of it resembled a machine, with its silver-grey and black fascia, and smooth grey acrylic-coated draining board and sink with black taps. All the machines – washer-tumbler, dishwasher, cooker hob and two ovens, microwave, deep-fryer, toaster, kettle, and even the sandwich grill – were either black or grey. The flooring was black and grey ceramic tiles, and the venetian blind grey.

It had been designed to gleam, so for maximum effect it had to be kept clinically clean. Sarah, remembering the kitchens of her childhood, found this one about as homely as an operating theatre or an aeroplane cockpit, but it had been a source of delight to Ben.

Sarah had become an avid cleaner and polisher of the kitchen (even polishing the taps after every washing-up) not because she was proud of it, but because she was afraid that if it started to show the least sign of wear Ben might rip it all out and start again, with a new design and new colour scheme.

She was not prepared to let him do that while he was still a focus of hatred for the sales reps of half a dozen kitchen-fitting firms. Salesmen were such terrible customers, Sarah thought, and Ben was surely one of the worst: positively paranoid about being 'ripped off' or overlooking some better deal from another company. At one time, he had purposely arranged for reps from three rival firms to call at the same time, without forewarning any of them, and had let them fight for his attention, each one pushing the merits of his own ideas. Finally, two of them had stormed out of the house, leaving Ben to order Sarah to make tea for the victor.

For months, the kitchen had been a battleground, with different generals planning strategies. Sarah, who had always felt that a kitchen was an intimate, personal place, had come to regard the planners with the same wary deference, growing into hostility, with which she viewed the medical team at the clinic, who stood around discussing what to do next with her womb.

Sarah put the food processor back into the cupboard. I'll mix the cake by hand, she thought. Somehow, she had gone right off technology.

* * *

'You'll have to ring the police if she's not back tonight,' Ben said with relish. It was the third time he had made this observation, and he was up to his fifth time of saying 'You must have been off your rocker to let her go'. John was on his fifteenth time of wondering why on earth he had asked Ben to come round for moral support. Ben appeared to be taking a positive delight in Helen's disappearance.

'She's been gone more than six hours,' John fretted.

'Has she behaved like this before?' Ben inquired solicitously.

'Oh, I don't know – yes, I suppose she comes home late from things, but this . . . I don't even know the man's name, or where he lives.'

Ben clicked his tongue, enjoying the drama of the situation. 'Far be it for me to judge,' he intoned, 'but if she was my wife . . .'

'Well, she's not,' John snapped, 'and if you must know, she's not mine either.' This was the one thing he had not wanted Ben to know, and as soon as it was out he regretted it, but Ben was irritating him, with his inference that a man should keep his wife under proper control.

'Oh-oh!' said Ben, For once, he seemed lost for words. Afterwards, John was not sure whether he was glad or sorry that Helen chose this moment to come home.

As she left Leon, in the taxi, Helen said, 'Do you reckon you'll be able to paint now, in your own style?'

He nodded, soberly. 'I think so. Thank you for everything, Helen.'

'You never know,' she said 'your painting could actually be better for all that fear. I remember that *Jonah in the Whale* picture you did. You're good at painting fear.'

He laughed. 'Is that a good thing?'

'Well, I guess it's something everyone can recognize. I'd better go, Leon.'

He leaned forward as she went to close the door. 'Will you do me one more favour, Helen?'

'Sure. What is it?'

'Paint the portrait of Eleanor and Gaby. It will be very good, the way you saw it.'

'But what will you do?'

He grinned at her. 'Maybe I will paint her a Grszinski after all!'

Helen's homecoming was a real anticlimax, Ben thought, after all John's build-up of suspense. It lacked dramatic conviction, failing either as a row or as a reconciliation. No blows, curses or tears. Just a prosaic 'I've been worried sick about you,' from John, and an even more prosaic 'Yes, I was longer than I thought I'd be; sorry. Anybody want a cup of tea?' from Helen.

Ben made no effort to hide his disappointment but Helen, tired now, resisted the temptation to bait him about it. She sat cross-legged on the floor, sipping tea, and made polite, noncommittal responses to John and Ben's attempts at conversation. Even when Ben referred purposely to 'your husband – oh no, of course he's not; excuse me,' she only raised an eyebrow and said nothing. Regarding this as a challenge, Ben repeated himself before long: 'As I was saying to your husband . . . no, your – what do you call him, in these situations?' Helen smiled sweetly at him and replied, 'I call him John,' whereupon John, flustered by this reopening of hostilities, launched into an account of what he planned to buy for the flat, and Helen started reading the arts review in the Sunday paper.

'Helen is bored with our company, John,' Ben said

loudly, to provoke them both. He was in a destructive mood.

'I'm just tired,' Helen said, 'that's all.'

'Oh, by the way, Helen,' John said hastily, 'Oliver phoned. He said would you ring him back after ten tonight.'

'Did he leave a number?'

'Yes. He's staying at a friend's flat for a couple of weeks.'

'Okay.'

'And who,' said Ben curiously, 'is Oliver?'

'A friend of ours,' Helen said shortly.

'Friend of yours,' John corrected her.

'Oh?' said Ben, smiling. 'Like that, is it?'

Helen looked him in the eye. 'He's from my old art college, he's permanently broke, and he had the spare room in our flat in York.' Make something of that if you want to, her tone said.

Ben did want to. 'And of course he moved out the minute John left to come down here,' he said.

'No,' Helen said.

'Don't get the wrong impression, Ben,' John said, laughing loudly. 'Oliver's perfectly safe. He's gay.'

Helen stared at him. 'He's not!'

It was Ben's turn for the laughter and he indulged in it theatrically, while John and Helen continued to debate the subject.

'Whatever made you think he was?' Helen asked.

'He wears pink satin jeans, for fuck's sake!'

'So what?'

'He is gay! It's obvious! The way he talks, the way he stands . . .'

'John, he had a girlfriend! It's because they broke up that he had nowhere to live.'

'That doesn't prove anything! It's probably why they split up.'

'After two years?'

'Okay – one girlfriend! That proves nothing.'

'And now he has another girlfriend, if you must know.'

'And in between, he had Helen,' contributed Ben.

'You love this kind of thing, don't you?' Helen accused, turning on him. 'Gossip? Scandal? It's what you really live for, isn't it?'

'Helen, calm down,' said John authoritively, but Helen was already out of the room. They heard her shutting herself in the bedroom.

'Ah well,' said Ben, hoisting himself to his feet. 'Must go. I'll leave you to your cosy domestic bliss.' He noted with amusement that John's face was like thunder. Helen's in for a rough ride when I leave, he thought. For once, he thought complacently of Sarah. Their marriage had something going for it, after all.

John gripped his arm when they reached the front door. 'I've changed my mind,' he said, 'about that job.'

Ben's amusement faded. 'Oh come on,' he protested. 'It's all arranged.' The last thing he needed was more complications at work.

'No, I don't mean the job,' John said. 'I mean the sideline – the unofficial bit.'

'The computer games?'

'That's it, yes. I'll do it.'

Ben reviewed alternative answers. He could simply tell John the truth about the racket being called off. He rejected this option as soon as he thought of it. 'Look,' he said instead. 'Don't go back on your own decision just to get back at your missus – or whatever she is.'

John's colour deepened. 'I'm not!' he asserted.

'Yes, you are,' said Ben coolly. 'Now, I've had my bit of fun, winding Helen up, and I make no apologies; you both asked for it. But you're not going to use me as a pawn to score points off her.'

'I thought you wanted me to do this selling thing!' John said, but some of the heat died out of his voice.

Ben looked at him for a moment, then put his hand on John's shoulder and said, with a depth of feeling that surprised himself, 'I've changed my mind, old mate. Don't start on the fiddles at this stage, eh? Could land you in schtook before long. With Helen as well. And you need her on your side, you know. She'll stand by you as long as you're straight with her.'

He left John staring after him. And will Sarah stand by you, asked a voice in his head as he ran down the stairs, if she ever suspects what you've been up to? Maybe she does already suspect, answered another voice, infinitely tireder.God knows she's turned a blind eye to enough other things. How long is she going to go on pretending she doesn't know me as I am?

John, storming into the bedroom, full of fury and righteous indignation, found Helen sobbing on the bed.

'Oh look,' he said uncomfortably. 'Don't take on.' He sat on the edge of the bed and patted her tentatively on the knee.

'It's no good,' she cried. 'It isn't working out. We don't have the same ways any more. We'd be better apart.'

'Nonsense,' he said. He curled round behind her on the bed.

'We would! You know it as well as I do!' she said.

He hugged her more tightly. 'You're tired,' he said, 'and so am I. Now, you promised you'd have a go at fitting in with this kind of life, didn't you? You haven't given it a fair trial yet! Don't go back on your own decision, eh?' He was quite unconscious of quoting Ben.

197

'I can see it's not going to work out,' she said. 'I've had time to see that.'

'All right,' said John soothingly. 'We'll talk about it tomorrow. But now I'm going to make us something to eat, and we'll watch telly – okay?'

But when he returned to say that the tea was ready, he found her fast asleep.

'Oriel,' said Elvis.

Oriel jumped. She had been trailing round behind him, or beside him whenever he was not zigzagging down the street kicking tin cans, for hours. It seemed like hours, anyway. It was so long since he had taken any notice of her that she thought he had forgotten she was there. By the time he spoke her name, she had almost forgotten he was there, too.

'What?' she said.

'Have you ever done it?' he asked.

'What?' she said again, stupidly.

'Have you ever done it? With a bloke?'

'Oh that,' said Oriel. ''Course I have.'

She crossed the fingers of her left hand, under the raincoat she was carrying. It wasn't easy to cross them, because they were almost frozen. Her lips had turned blue and she had been shivering for so long that she had ceased to notice it.

'Well, how long,' Elvis demanded, 'does it take you?'

Oriel gulped. She opened her mouth to speak, but no sound came out.

Elvis confronted her, standing still in the middle of the pavement, between British Home Stores and The Pizza Feasta, and adjacent to an overflowing litter bin.

'How long,' Elvis repeated, 'from when the bloke starts till when he finishes with you?'

Oriel tried to remember all she had learnt at school,

from Annie's playground seminars on her experiences. She took a deep breath. 'About an hour,' she said.

'An hour?' Elvis was shocked and outraged. 'What does he do for a whole effing *hour?*'

Oriel had a rethink. Maybe I got it wrong, she thought. But I'm sure Annie said she and Dave were in the back of his car for an hour before that copper came along, who turned out to be his dad. I must be right. Annie knows. Oriel decided to bluff it out. She sneered at Elvis, or came the nearest she could to sneering with a frozen mouth and ice-cold cheekbones. 'You mean you don't know?' she said.

Elvis seemed untroubled by her scorn. 'No!' he said impatiently. 'I mean, how long to do it *once?*'

'I've just said,' said Oriel haughtily.

'An hour? A whole hour though?' Elvis repeated. He was very upset. He considered himself an expert on sex, if nothing else, and here he had been missing something all this time. About fifty-seven minutes of it, by the sound of this.

'Well . . .' Oriel was on shaky ground. Her knowledge seemed to have reached its limits. She had thought she was pretty well briefed on the theory. She racked her brains and was rewarded by sudden inspiration. 'Of course,' she said, 'that includes all the foreplay.'

Elvis stared at her. 'And what the hell,' he said furiously, 'is foreplay?'

'Warming up,' Oriel replied. She was beginning to feel a burning desire for him to leave her alone.

'Getting warmed up,' said Elvis, between gritted teeth, 'takes about half a minute, don't it? And your actual nitty-gritty takes about two minutes – right? So what do you and this guy of yours do for the rest of the time, eh?'

It was Oriel's turn to be shocked. Two and a half minutes, she thought! I was going to sacrifice my everything to him, or somebody else like him, and risk getting pregnant or getting a dose of something – all for two and a half minutes? If I sneezed at the wrong moment I'd miss the whole thing, and there he'd be kicking Pepsi cans at cars again, and it would all be over bar the itchy rash a few days later, if Annie could be believed about that as well.

Fury rose in Oriel's thinly clad yellow bosom. 'You're rubbish!' she yelled.

Elvis was wounded. 'And you're sick!' he retaliated. 'You must go with old men of thirty who can't even get it up!'

'Sod off!' Oriel shouted.

'Up yours!' Elvis returned.

A silence fell. Tension relieved, they waited for each other to make the next move.

Elvis shrugged. 'Want to go round the back of the multi-storey?' he asked, to show that he bore no grudge.

'Not with you,' Oriel said. She envisaged the long walk home, with despair. She had never felt so cold in her life.

'Only asking,' Elvis said. He hadn't really fancied her anyway. Not for an hour. Three minutes, maybe. Even five. What did girls expect these days? He felt old and tired. He wondered if his Mum had made any cake. She sometimes did on Sundays if she was feeling bored. 'See you around,' he said, turning away.

'Elvis,' Oriel said.

'Yeh?'

'Got 30p for bus fare?'

He fished in his back pocket, and handed her three tenpence pieces. 'Here,' he said. Then he ran off down the street.

Oriel stood looking after him, turning over the coins in her cold hand. For the first time, she felt something akin to love.

* * *

Eleanor wondered what she could have done to upset Jake. 'Anything wrong?' she asked, as he brushed past her in the kitchen, fetching tomato ketchup for Gaby's fish fingers and peas.

'I'll talk to you later,' he said. 'There we are, darling,' he crooned at Gaby. 'Don't forget Teddy likes lots and lots.'

This is getting ridiculous, Eleanor thought. She was startled to catch Gaby looking across at her as Jake spoke. The child raised her eyebrows. Her expression was one of patient resignation. A sudden bubble of laughter rose in Eleanor's throat, but Gaby was already directing her concentration towards her plate.

Well I never, Eleanor thought. A woman-to-woman glance from a seven-year-old. Eleanor had hoped that her failure to feel besotted and motherly towards her own child might be something she could outgrow. She had looked forward to having an adult relationship with a grown-up daughter – provided that the daughter could forgive her the disinterest during her infancy. Now she wondered if that adult mother-and-daughter relationship depended on the child's age at all. Perhaps we could have that kind of relationship now, Eleanor thought. Perhaps I should just treat Gaby as an interesting person and get to know her. Perhaps she might even prefer that to my hopeless efforts at games and babytalk.

She poured herself a coffee and sat down at the table with Jake and Gaby. 'How would you feel if I gave up work?' she said bluntly.

Gaby stopped eating and stared at her. Jake looked furious. Eleanor waited.

'Gaby,' Jake said, 'have you got enough ketchup, bunnykins?'

Gaby ignored him. 'What?' she asked Eleanor. 'Now?'

'No,' Eleanor said. 'In a couple of months' time.'

Gaby considered. 'What will you do all day,' she asked, 'if you don't go to work?'

'I don't know yet,' Eleanor admitted. 'Cook, I suppose, and go shopping and clean the house.'

'Daddy does that,' said Gaby simply. 'And you cook at weekends. You don't have to give up work.'

'Eat your tea, Gaby,' Jake said. 'We'll discuss this later, Eleanor.'

'It affects all of us,' Eleanor said. 'I want to know what you both think. No, I don't have to give up work, Gaby, but I'm tired of it.'

'Eleanor,' Jake said.

'Why are you tired of it?' Gaby inquired.

'Gaby!' said Jake.

'Because,' said Eleanor, 'some of the things people are expected to do at work are not very nice.'

'What things?' asked Gaby.

'Eleanor,' Jake interrupted, 'this is way above the child's head.'

'She seems to be understanding perfectly,' said Eleanor drily. Gaby smiled at her with sudden radiance. 'You see,' Eleanor told her, 'there are people called directors, who tell everyone else what to do and how they should work. Sometimes they tell someone they're not wanted any more, and that person loses their job.'

'Did they do that to you?' Gaby asked.

'No. They want me to be a director. But if I agree, I will have to tell somebody else he's lost his job. Do you see?'

Gaby nodded. 'And that would make you tired,' she said.

Eleanor was puzzled for a minute. Jake shot her a triumphant glance: see, I told you the child couldn't understand all this.

'Make me tired?' Eleanor repeated.

202

'You said you were tired of going to work,' said Gaby patiently.

Eleanor laughed. 'That's right. Yes, that is what would make me tired. And sad. I wouldn't like to do it.'

'You'd rather stay at home and clean the floors,' said Gaby understandingly. Eleanor smiled at her. 'That's a very good way of putting it, Gaby,' she said.

'Well, apply for the janitor's job if you want to clean floors!' said Jake bitingly. 'For heaven's sake, Eleanor – turning down a directorship?'

'In return for sacking Richard Shaw,' Eleanor informed him. 'The terms were made very clear to me.'

'By Harry? Yes? Well, that's easy enough to remedy,' Jake told her. 'Get Harry to do it himself. He eats out of your hand, doesn't he?'

Eleanor pushed her coffee away, feeling sick. 'Jake,' she said, 'you're not thinking. Sack Richard Shaw? Whether Harry does it or I do, the man still loses his job. I don't want to be part of that.'

'They must have a reason for doing it,' Jake argued.

'Several reasons,' Eleanor agreed. 'None of them good enough to deprive a man of his livelihood, knowing that at his age he could well find it hard to get another job. The official reason is that he's slow at his work, which is true, but he's not all that slow; the work gets done, and I've never known him to make a mistake.'

'What's the unofficial reason?' Jake asked.

'Well, I'm guessing,' Eleanor admitted, 'but I've been with Logodata enough years now and seen enough people come and go to recognize the pattern. Richard doesn't fit the image of a go-ahead modern technology industry. He's a plodder – reliable, unexciting, reluctant to move with the times. The sales reps have a grudge against him; he's fussy over the paperwork being done correctly and handed in on time. He's a nagger, but then that's part of his job. Granted, he makes a bit of a meal of it and enjoys ticking the reps off like schoolkids. But his real drawback – I think – is that he's scrupulously honest.'

'That's a drawback?' said Jake incredulously. Gaby had given up all pretence of eating her fish fingers, and was staring at her parents, looking from one to the other like a spectator at a tennis match. 'I would have thought,' Jake continued, 'that the managers would be delighted to have someone clamping down on the sales reps' fiddles. Surely it's in their interests to employ somebody honest?'

'Somebody selectively honest,' Eleanor corrected him. 'Richard is honest across the board. He won't turn a blind eye to managers' fiddles either. Nothing they can do about it, of course. But a lot of important people in the company – including some directors – have long memories, and Richard has done a number of people out of some very juicy perks. He's saved the company a fortune, but the company is made up of people who put their own fortune first, and some of them are now in a position to get back at him.'

'But surely,' Jake protested, 'the man can't be made redundant because of some top bods' personal grievances? It's against the law, for a start!'

'It is,' Eleanor conceded, 'which is one of the reasons Logodata has its own team of legal experts. They know every loophole and how to exploit it. And even if the company gets sued and loses the case – which has happened, on occasions – so what? It's a wealthy multinational company. It pays up without a murmur.'

'It's bad publicity, though, surely?' Jake pointed out.

'One paragraph on an inside page in the national press? Not even a one-day wonder. If it was some scandal about the products – oh yes, that would damage the company's reputation all right. But unethical redundancies for minor personnel? Nobody gets indignant about that. It goes on all the time, in every company, the bigger ones especially. Believe me, Jake; they're a law unto themselves. I've seen this happen so many times. But I've never been involved this closely, and I don't want to be. I want out.' Her eyes were filling with tears. She hadn't realized how strongly she felt about this.

Gaby leaned forward suddenly and patted her mother on the hand. 'It's all right,' she said. 'You can stay at home with us. Can't she, Dad?'

'And who,' Jake said, 'is going to earn the money for the three of us to live on?'

'That's what I'm asking you,' said Eleanor slowly. 'I'm not pushing you back out to work if you don't want to go. But if I changed to another kind of job, I would have to retrain, and that could take a few years – depending on what kind of job it is.'

Jake was silent. Then he said, 'All this is because of Clifford, isn't it?'

Eleanor looked blank. 'Clifford who?'

'Don't play the innocent!' Jake accused. 'You've got this all worked out and you know all the answers and you know you'll get what you want, as usual!'

'Jake,' said Eleanor. 'I don't know what you're talking about!'

'Then I'll spell it out for you,' he said. 'Ever since Clifford phoned three weeks ago to say my old job at the college was being advertised, you've been brewing this and you've made up your mind for me – never mind what I want!'

'Your old job?' Eleanor said. 'Do you mean McCarthy has left?'

'I told you!' Jake said.

'No, you didn't,' Eleanor asserted. 'Sure, I knew Clifford had phoned – I answered it, if you remember. But all he said to me was that he and Jasmine were having a party on the seventh which I told him we wouldn't be free for because of going to your mother's. Then I handed him over to you, and I went straight out because I was late for something or other. Can't remember what. I never asked if he'd phoned for anything else. Was that what it was?'

Jake shook his head, pondering. 'I must have told you when you came back.'

'This is the first I've heard of it,' said Eleanor positively. 'If I'd known, we would have discussed it – wouldn't we?'

'You didn't discuss this directorship thing with me,' said Jake sullenly. 'When did you know about it?'

'Friday lunchtime. Today's only Sunday. I wanted a chance to think.'

'So do I,' he said. 'I'm going to give Gaby her bath now. We'll talk over supper. There's something else more important I've got to say, too.'

'What is it?' Gaby asked.

'Bathtime!' Jake replied. 'I want to discuss with you whether Ferdie the frog will jump into the bath first or . . .'

'No!' Gaby yelled. 'I want to know too! Tell me what you're going to tell Mummy!'

'That was it!' Jake said. 'Promise! Come along.'

'Gaby,' said Eleanor, as Gaby opened her mouth for further yelling, 'we'll be talking for hours. We'll tell you in the morning. I promise you. Go with Daddy now.'

To her surprise, the child went. Eleanor heard her say, as she went up the stairs, 'You'll tell me all the important things, won't you, Daddy? Don't forget.'

Eleanor giggled. That's my daughter, she thought. Perhaps we should just let Gaby take on the directorship at Logodata.

* * *

206

'Oriel,' said Polly. 'It's time we had a chat.'

'Spare me,' Oriel sneered.

'I'm trying to,' said Polly seriously. 'I've run you a hot bath, so go and have that and thaw yourself out a bit and I'll come and talk to you. Don't lock the door.'

Oriel looked at her sideways. 'You're very bossy lately,' she said. 'Something's got into you.' But she went upstairs anyway.

Polly made Oriel a cup of hot chocolate and carried it up to the bathroom. The door was unlocked. Oriel lay passively in the warm bathwater, skinny and blue with cold.

'Here,' Polly said. 'Drink this.'

'Where's Dad?' Oriel said.

'In bed. His stomach's bad.'

'He can't blame that on me,' said Oriel defensively.

'Oh, he can,' Polly assured her. 'But what caused it was himself, getting angry.'

Oriel thought about this. 'Are you angry with me as well?'

'No,' Polly said calmly.

'Well, anyway,' Oriel said, 'I'm not having you lecturing me on how to be a good little girl, so forget it.' She sat up cautiously and sipped her hot chocolate.

'I can't tell you how to be that, because I never was one myself!' Polly said.

Oriel looked at her scornfully. 'Don't tell me you were a little raver in your day, 'cos I won't believe it,' she promised.

'I'm not saying that,' Polly said. 'But it was what I wanted to be, with all my heart.'

Oriel choked. 'You what?'

'Yes,' Polly continued dreamily. 'I was never any trouble to my mother, you see. None at all. I was the kind of daughter mothers approve of: never out late at night, never mixed with unsuitable boys. Nor suitable ones either, come to that. I went to school, came home, did my homework, went to bed. And when I went to bed, I changed. I became wild and beautiful and uninhibited and every man in the world threw himself at me, swearing undying devotion, and when they were nearly dead I gave in to them. One after another. Gracefully, but with unbridled passion.'

'What?' Oriel said again.

'All in my head, of course,' Polly conceded. 'But you see, I wasn't a good little girl. It was just that nobody wanted me. You can't call that virtue, can you?'

'Didn't you ever go out with anyone, before Dad?' Oriel asked.

'Oh, I did. A few boys. One of them wanted to go to bed with me.'

'And did you?' Oriel demanded.

'No.'

'Thought you said you weren't a goody-goody?'

'I wasn't,' Polly confirmed. 'I was afraid he'd go off me if he saw how fat I looked without my clothes, and then I'd have nobody.'

Mixed emotions struggled in Oriel's rapidly thawing bosom. 'Why are you telling me this?' she said finally.

'I don't know really,' Polly admitted. 'I suppose just to let you know that I wasn't so different from you at the same age, except on the outside. In my mind I was a fallen woman – and a great success as one. It was only my body that kept me out of trouble, or at least my dislike of it. You don't have that safeguard.'

Oriel coloured, and hunched her knees up to her chin. 'Mum!' she protested.

'On the other hand,' Polly went on, 'you don't have to prove anything. You're pretty, and you should feel confident that you're attractive.'

'I do,' said Oriel defiantly.

'I'm glad of that,' Polly said. 'That means you won't do what some of these young girls do, and come running every time a boy wants someone to go to bed with.'

Oriel tried to outstare her and found she couldn't. She started chipping notches out of the soap with her thumbnail instead.

'You see, they think it proves they're attractive if they sleep with lots of people,' Polly said. 'But it doesn't. It just proves they sleep around.'

'I thought you weren't going to lecture me,' Oriel said.

Polly sighed. 'I hoped I wasn't,' she said. 'What I was really going to tell you was that Eleanor phoned.'

Oriel looked up sharply. 'What for?'

'About some friends of hers who might give you a summer job as an au pair to their children.'

'What did she say? Has she asked them?' said Oriel eagerly.

'She said she'd mentioned it to them, and they are looking for someone, so she rang to ask how Dad and I would feel about the idea.'

'And Dad got raging mad and went to bed with his ulcer,' said Oriel gloomily.

'No, he was only angry about you not coming home and not letting us know where you were. I haven't mentioned this job to him yet. I wanted to know what you thought about it first.'

'I want to go!' Oriel said. 'It'd be great. I want to leave school right away.'

'There's no question of that,' Polly said, 'and this couple realize that. They want a girl for July and August, that's all, so you will stay at school till the end of the school year, and you will work harder than ever before. If you don't,' she added warningly, seeing Oriel about to protest, 'I can guarantee that your father won't agree to anything at all that you want to do.'

Oriel eyed her warily. 'But if I did . . . he still wouldn't agree, would he? Let me go to the States with people he didn't know?'

'I'll talk to him,' said Polly serenely. 'If this is what you'd really like to do, I'm sure he'll see the advantages in your spending the summer doing a proper job, taking on some responsibility and seeing a bit of the world at the same time. You do know that caring for children can be very hard work, don't you?'

'I don't mind that,' Oriel said.

'Well, if I were you,' Polly said, 'I'd put that across to him over the next few weeks – your willingness to work. Be a model schoolgirl and a paragon of virtue – inside and out.'

'And in return,' Oriel said, 'you'll work on Dad. Extra Saturday morning nooky and double bacon and eggs afterwards, yeah?'

'Oh, Oriel!' Polly said. 'Have a bit of respect for your parents, will you?'

Then they both started to laugh.

Harry sat in front of the television with a pre-dinner gin and bitter lemon in his hand, watching a documentary on Benidorm while Marie put the children to bed.

He should have been blissfully comfortable but he was not. Two things troubled his contentment: the wholemeal-based frozen pizza, flavoured with cardboard and onion, that Marie had given them for lunch, and the tableaux of Benidorm, where he had holidayed with Biddy several times. Watching the sun-whitened scenes unfold on screen, he was struck by the equally horrific realizations that the spectre of Biddy hovered in every Spanish street as irremovably as it did in every room of his and Marie's house, and that Benidorm was ridiculously unsophisticated.

Would other Logodata employees, watching this programme and cheerfully making fun of the pseudo-ethnic flamenco dancers, tavernas and bullrings, remember his glowing accounts of his holidays there, a decade ago, and laugh at him now? And would the figure of Biddy – somehow more solid in memory than she had ever been in real life – ever leave them alone? Ghosts were not meant to haunt you, surely, until the person was dead? There was nothing other-worldly about Biddy, living in respectable detachment from himself and Marie, in quiet, reassuring Buckinghamshire, yet her presence here with them in their daily lives seemed to grow stronger. Maybe, living a separate life, her character had grown more definite than when she was Harry's wife, overshadowed by his more dominant personality? Whatever the reason, it was she who now seemed the dominant influence in the house. Harry had not mentioned this to Marie. Biddy's name was never spoken between them, but Harry had an idea that Marie was also well aware that Biddy's departure was not as final and complete as it had appeared at the time.

Several times, Harry had had the impression, when he was fast asleep, of Biddy touching him lightly on the arm. Over the past few months, if he was honest with himself, he had to admit that Biddy had been scarcely out of his thoughts – even at work. Her presence was in no way threatening or vindictive; she seemed to be there rather because she felt she was needed, by them both. Harry hoped this was not an omen that something was about to happen to him, and dismissed the idea immediately.

'Both asleep,' Marie said, coming in. 'Must be a miracle. What are you watching?'

'Some rubbish,' he said. 'Turn it off, will you, pet?'

'I'll switch over,' she said, 'and we can watch that gameshow – the one with the couples, you know, and the stranger who has to guess who's married to who. Okay? You won't want supper just yet, will you?'

'No,' he said. 'No. In fact, I don't think I'll have anything tonight. Just a biscuit and a coffee later on.'

Marie looked at him. 'Have you got that pain again, Harry?'

'Just a bit,' he confessed.

She frowned. 'You can't have indigestion,' she said. 'It's ages since lunchtime. Is it up here again? Between your chest and your stomach, like before?'

'And across my back,' he said, 'and down my arms.'

Marie looked frightened. 'Shall I call a doctor or something?'

'No,' said Harry. 'No, it's nothing, love. I probably strained a muscle, that's all, putting up those shelves. Don't worry about it. Watch your programme.'

'We'll delay supper,' Eleanor said. 'We'd only get indigestion having heavy discussions while we're eating. Have a glass of wine.'

'I think,' Jake began, 'you shouldn't be too quick to turn down this job. You're already earning more than I could. I know the money isn't everything, but we are used to it. Even if you turn down the directorship, you could still keep your present job.'

'Jake, I don't know,' said Eleanor. 'This question of firing people whenever their faces or policies don't quite fit: even if I don't have to do the dirty work myself, this has just made me realize how much I've turned a blind eye to, over the years, and how much it has bugged me, at the back of my mind.'

'In business – let's face it, in any job – you have to do

what you're told. When I was working at the college, I had to take orders I didn't like,' Jake pointed out.

'I know, but there are limits, and I feel I've reached mine. Why this should trigger it off, I don't know, but I just feel as though the shutters have come down. Sarah said once she got to a point, with those hospital tests, where she heard her name called in the waiting room and her legs just refused to stand up and walk into the examination room. She said something inside her yelled, "No! I've had enough!" I feel like that.'

'What did Sarah do?' Jake inquired.

'Stood up and went in. Forced herself.'

'Sometimes that's what you have to do,' Jake said.

Eleanor looked at her wine glass, twisted it round very carefully once, and said, 'Sometimes you're lucky enough to have a choice. What is your choice going to be, about going back to work, now Gaby's at school? You never planned to stay at home indefinitely.'

'I didn't say I wanted that. But I want something better than I had before. Otherwise it's all been wasted. You know I always intended to write a book, before I looked for another job.'

Eleanor took a deep breath. 'Do you think you still have the enthusiasm for it? It's been seven years.'

Jake was silent. Dear Lord, Eleanor thought, let me say the right things. His pride has taken a lot of knocks, from people who don't think it's macho for men to bring up kids. I don't want to hurt him where he's already bruised.

'Don't forget you made a choice too,' she said gently, 'between Gaby and the book. You let her interests take precedence over yours. You may not have printed evidence of achievement to show a boss, but there's no way you could say that you've wasted seven years. Look at Gaby. She's your achievement.'

213

Jake's fists were clenched and his head was bowed almost to table level. He seemed to be undergoing some inner struggle. Finally he said tightly, 'You're not considering her interests much at the moment, Eleanor, are you?'

'If she's at school, I don't see it matters much which one of us works, does it?'

'I'm not talking about the job.' Jake's voice had a strangled note, as though he were exercising enormous control over his emotions. The tension was making him sweat.

'What is it?' Eleanor asked, suddenly alarmed. 'What was that other thing you wanted to talk to me about?'

'Your behaviour,' Jake said. His voice rose, but he calmed himself. 'Eleanor, what you do behind my back is your own business, and I don't ask, but don't involve my child in it – all right?'

Eleanor was stung by the deliberate 'my child'. 'What the hell are you talking about?' she demanded.

'I'm talking about the fact that I walked down to the park to meet you and Gaby today. I waited an hour. I scoured every inch of it. You didn't go there, did you?'

'No.'

'And before you think up some lie, Gaby told me. You took her to some man's flat. The one who rang you up yesterday morning. The one you skipped Marie's Gossip to spend the evening with. The one you keep sneaking out to see. God knows, Eleanor, I'm tolerant and I'm broadminded, but to drag a little girl into it – that's despicable!'

Eleanor stood up. 'I see,' she said. 'So you don't care what I do, as long as Gaby isn't involved?'

'I didn't say that,' he said.

'As good as,' she asserted. 'So you believed I was having an affair with somebody?'

214

'You have made it fairly obvious,' he said bitterly.

'Oh?' said Eleanor icily. 'And you thought it your duty to turn a blind eye, did you? Like you want me to turn a blind eye to what will happen to poor old Richard Shaw?'

'Don't try to put me in the wrong,' Jake said. 'You're the one . . .'

'You're damn right I'm putting you in the wrong,' Eleanor said. 'You prefer to turn yourself into a . . . male Sarah, a poor wronged little victim whose wicked wife abuses his good nature, rather than be honest with me and ask me straight out what's going on! Pretend you know nothing! Let me walk into trouble and never say a word that might get me out of it – is that it?'

'You're a mature, responsible adult,' Jake began.

'But I wouldn't be, would I,' Eleanor retorted, 'if I was getting myself into a messy situation like that? And you'd honestly just sit there, and let your wife screw up her life – and yours, and Gaby's – and never give me a hand, by a bit of plain speaking in the right place? Well, thanks a heap, Jake! Never mind me dragging Gaby into some sordid situation: you wouldn't mind letting me sink! No,' she interrupted as Jake started to speak, 'you can hear me out now. I took Gaby to a painter's studio, and I've been there a few times by myself, to get you a picture painted for your birthday. Believe me or don't, as you wish. I'll see you later. I'm going out, Jake.'

'Oh God,' he groaned. 'Is that it? Eleanor, I'm sorry. I really am. Look, don't go out.'

'I'd better,' she said. 'I'd better cool off. You know what I'm like when I lose my rag. Don't know when to stop.'

'No,' he said. 'It was justified. Come on, sit down. Come and kiss and make up, if you can.'

'I'll just go out for a walk. Honestly. I just need to calm down a bit. Ten minutes.'

'All right,' he said.

She went to the door, slowly.

'Eleanor,' he said.

She looked at him. 'Yes?'

'I'm sorry.'

'It's all right.'

'We'll work something out,' he said, 'about the job. I promise. We'll talk about it.'

'Yes.'

'It'll be all right,' he said. 'Won't it?'

'Yes, it'll be all right. It always is. It's a good marriage, Jake. See you in ten minutes.'

'See you, love,' he said.

12
Release

The weekend, designed as an island of peace and family harmony, finally encroached into the ocean of weekday work, and the advent of Monday morning caused many families to breathe a sigh of relief.

Gaby, who had been sick in the night, stayed off school. Eleanor, untypically, was also staying at home.

'What time is this advertising man coming?' Jake asked.

'Some time after nine.'

'I'm going out for a while,' he said. 'I'll take Gaby with me.'

'Okay. See you later, or else tonight. Bye, Gaby.'

'Can I stay with you?' Gaby asked.

'Mummy's going to be working,' Jake explained to her. 'A businessman is coming here for a meeting, because sometimes home is more peaceful than Mummy's office.' He caught Eleanor's eye and they both laughed. 'I said sometimes,' he excused himself.

'I know that,' Gaby said. 'I want to stay and see Mummy working. Can I?'

'I don't see why not,' Eleanor said. 'But it's only boring old talking, and looking at papers and things. And you'd have to stay very quiet. Sure you want to stay?'

'Yes,' Gaby said decisively.

'All right, then you can.'

So Gaby stayed, with her crayons and colouring book, in a corner of the sitting room, quietly. The meeting went very smoothly. Eleanor had forgotten how peaceful the house could be on a weekday, with the neighbours all out at work and their children at school, and the homely street sounds: the purring of the milk float, and house-wives calling greetings to one another as they passed with their shopping bags and trolleys. She had forgotten what it was like to be a housewife, to work out your own priorities for the day and go through it at your own pace. At one time, this only spelt boredom and monotony, but now she saw that their way of life could also hold freedom and peace.

Andy, the advertising executive, was also more at ease here than he had been in the Logodata offices, under Harry's critical scrutiny. He discussed designs and plans with cheerful confidence, and afterwards, while Eleanor made coffee, he enchanted Gaby by filling her sketchbook with patterns and designs and line drawings of little animals for her to colour in.

The phone rang. 'Excuse me a minute,' Eleanor said.

It was Jeannie, her secretary. 'Sorry to bother you,' she apologized. 'But Harry Kusek's secretary asked me to phone you. He's had a heart attack.'

At first Marie, when Harry's secretary phoned her, froze. She could neither answer her nor think what to do. The only thought that came into her mind was Biddy. She needed Biddy. Biddy would know what to do. But while her mind was preoccupied with this idea, her spirit resisted it fiercely.

Biddy's last words to Marie had been, 'Don't hesitate to call me if ever you need anything.' She had left her sister's phone number by the phone. Marie knew she would rather die than call on Biddy for anything. She now realized, with sick resignation, that she would even rather let Harry die, if what he needed at this time was Biddy's support.

'The ambulance should be arriving any minute, Mrs

Kusek,' Harry's secretary said. 'I'll give you the name of the hospital, and the directions. If you go straight there, to Casualty, that'll be the quickest way.'

'Yes,' she said. 'Okay.'

'Is there anybody you would like me to ring?' the secretary – Marie's successor – asked.

'Yes,' Marie said. 'Could you ask Eleanor Farringdon if she'd go with him in the ambulance, please?'

'I'm afraid she's out of the office; I've already tried. Mr Kusek asked me to phone her straight away. I believe her secretary's trying to contact her at home. Would you like me to call you back?'

'No,' Marie said. 'No, I'll leave straight away. Thank you for what you've done.'

Oh God, Marie thought, what am I going to do? She replaced the phone, and it rang immediately. 'Hello?'

'It's Eleanor. Are you all right, Marie? You've heard?'

'Yes.'

'I'll be round in two minutes. I'll take you to the hospital. Have you anyone who'll take care of the kids?'

'I could ring Harry's mother,' Marie said. 'But it'd take her a while to get over here.'

'The shock might be a bit much for her, Marie, at her age. She mightn't be able to manage the children as well. Shall I phone Sarah and see if she'll have them?'

'Oh yes. That would be better. Yes.'

'Okay, leave it to me. Make yourself a coffee or something. Lots of sugar. I'll be round as soon as I can, Marie.'

'Thanks.'

I'm a useless wife, Marie thought. I can't seem to think of anything. Everyone's having to organize things for me. But at least it's not Biddy doing it. Should I let her know, though? Twenty years of being married to him. No, I won't. She's nothing to him now. He's happier with me than he ever was with her. He's always saying so. Tears ran down her face. 'He's happy with me,' she sobbed, aloud. 'Honestly, Biddy, he is.'

Eleanor's first and very uncharitable thought was, 'Trust Harry to ruin my meeting, even at home.'

She went into the sitting room to tell Andy what had happened. He was full of sympathy, and offered to stay with Gaby till Jake returned. Eleanor accepted gratefully.

She phoned Sarah. Sarah agreed to go straight round to Marie's to look after Sorrel and Sacha.

She said goodbye to Gaby and picked up her car keys. The phone rang.

'Mrs Farringdon, it's Harry Kusek's secretary. I'm glad I caught you in time.'

Dear Lord, Eleanor prayed, don't let him be dead. Biddy would never forgive us for not looking after him.

'What is it?' she asked.

'He won't get into the ambulance.'

The relief was so great that Eleanor almost laughed. 'He what?'

'He won't go to hospital,' the woman said. She sounded near to tears. 'He says he's all right now and he wants to go home.'

'Are the ambulancemen there?'

'Yes, but he keeps on telling them to go away!'

'Is he able to come to the phone?'

'Yes, I think so. Shall I ask him to have a word with you?'

'Please.' Eleanor bit on her knuckles to fight down the hysterical urge to laugh. It's shock, she thought, or something. There's nothing funny about this. Control yourself.

'Eleanor,' said Harry. 'It's Harry.'

220

'Harry, are you all right?'

'Yes. Yes, all right now. Bit short of breath.'

'Then get in the ambulance and stop giving your secretary heart attacks as well, will you? Marie and I are on our way to the hospital. We'll see you there.'

'You will not.' Harry's voice took on a surge of strength. 'I'll see my own GP, in the privacy of my own home. I'm in no fit state to be tortured with electrodes, especially not on the NHS.'

'Hospital's the place for you, Harry, after a heart attack. You need to be examined straight away.'

'I need a bit of peace and a good rest first,' said Harry firmly. 'You have to be healthy to stand up to hospital treatment. I'm sending these mortuary attendants away and getting a taxi home. I'll see you there if you want to come and visit me. Save you a trip to the hospital.' He put the phone down.

His secretary cut in, on her extension. 'I was listening in,' she said, shamelessly.

'Good,' Eleanor said. 'Well, he can't be too bad if he's got the breath for a speech like that, can he?'

'What shall I do, Mrs Farringdon?'

'Oh, call the old bugger a taxi and take him home, will you?'

'Yes, I'll do that.' She sounded shocked by Eleanor's cheerfulness.

As well she might be, Eleanor thought, replacing the receiver. Why on earth do I feel so jolly about all this?

She phoned Sarah again. 'Sarah, cancel the babysitting. He's coming home instead.'

'Is he all right?' Sarah asked anxiously.

'He sounds in good spirits. Healthily bloody-minded. Sarah?'

'Yes?'

'I know this is meant to be tragic, but I can't help feeling that it's progress. Do you know what I mean?'

'Er . . . no,' Sarah said. 'Not really.'

'Oh. Well maybe I'm just being callous and unsympathetic.'

'No, no, I'm sure you're not.'

'Meaning I am. Sarah, I'll keep you informed. I'll phone you later from the Kuseks'. What time are you going to work?'

'Half an hour ago, actually. I've just phoned the matron; that's why I hadn't left.'

'Oh, I see. Well, look, you ring me whenever you want to, later on. Okay?'

'Okay, Eleanor. See you.'

Eleanor sighed, and dialled Marie's number again, to let her know that Harry was on his way home.

Jake came back while she was talking to Marie. She waved a hand at him, beckoning him to wait. Putting the phone down, she said, 'I'm glad you're back. Andy was going to mind Gaby; I've got to go out.'

'Eleanor,' he said, putting his arms around her. 'I've got some good news for us. I've been down to the college to see Clifford, and filed an application for my old job.'

'Jake, that's . . . Is it great? Is it what you want?'

'I think so. You know, after seven years away from work, I could find it hard enough to adjust even to the same job in familiar surroundings. I don't think it's really the time to aim higher. Perhaps in a year or two. There's no point in being ambitious for the sake of ambition, is there?'

'You're right there,' said Eleanor with feeling. 'We've just heard that Harry Kusek's had a heart attack at work.'

'No!'

'Yes. He's all right, or he sounds it. He won't go to

hospital: he's on his way home. I was just about to go round there.'

'Poor old Harry. Do you want me to go instead – or with you?'

'No need, unless you want to. I won't be staying long; it's just to make sure that Marie's okay really.'

'Will she be able to cope with him? What if he has another attack?'

'I think she'd be happier if he was in hospital,' Eleanor admitted. 'But she's ringing the GP now. I'll see you later, love. I'll call back here before I go in to work. Jake – this job. Have you got it, or are you just on a list of applicants?'

'They've been interviewing, and there are a few more to go yet, but Clifford says they haven't found anyone outstandingly suitable and he thinks there'll be no contest. He said if I want the job, it's mine, bar the formalities.'

Eleanor hugged him. 'Nice to be wanted, isn't it?'

Jake smiled. 'It doesn't feel bad, being one of the employed. But you – are sure you'll take to being a housewife again?'

'I don't know,' Eleanor said. 'Would you recommend it, after a seven-year trial?'

He considered. 'Yes and no.'

'What's the worst?' she asked teasingly. 'And the best?'

'I can answer that easily,' he said. 'It's five o'clock in the evening, the child is tired, there's tea to cook, the boiler goes out, the dog is sick, and Mummy won't be home from work for another hour and a half yet!'

'Tell me the good news, quick! What's the best thing about being a housewife?'

He raised his eyebrows exaggeratedly. 'I've just told you! You want to hear the worst now?'

They laughed.

'Aren't we awful,' exclaimed Eleanor, 'standing round cracking jokes when poor Harry's just had a heart attack?'

'Probably turn out to be the best thing that ever happened to him,' Jake said flippantly.

Eleanor looked at him. 'I have that feeling as well,' she said slowly. 'But why, would you say?'

He shrugged. 'Don't know why I said that really. You'd better go, hadn't you?'

'I had. I'll leave you to tell Andy he's relieved of babysitting duty. He and Gaby have been getting on like a house on fire.'

It was so like Eleanor, Sarah fumed, to call on her to perform some errand of mercy and then casually phone and say 'Forget the babysitting, Sarah: Harry's going home.' Nobody considers my job worth any notice, she told herself unfairly. She knew she was being unfair. Her hours were so irregular that no one could be expected to know when she was due to be at work unless she told them. She could quite well have said to Eleanor, 'Sorry, but I'm just off to work,' and Eleanor would have understood, and would have found someone else to mind Marie's children while Marie went to the hospital.

It was just that the matron had been so rude, when Sarah phoned to say she couldn't come in to work. 'It strikes me, Mrs Jepson,' she said, 'that we are just here to suit your convenience!' Sarah had felt like saying, 'Well, you could have fooled me! I'm not even given a rota for the week; I just take pot-luck, filling in the hours that no one else wants; I can never plan anything more than one day ahead . . .' She hadn't, of course. The poor woman had a hard job and enough aggression from other staff, not to mention the patients and their families. The least Sarah could contribute to the running of the place was to be unfailingly obliging and sweet-tempered.

Sweet-natured Sarah! If they only knew, she reflected despairingly, what went on inside me, behind the smiling face – none of them would want to know me.

Helen wondered why Eleanor had failed to turn up to collect her, as promised, to take her to meet Bob Fraser at Logodata. She considered whether to ring her, but realized she didn't know the number, or Eleanor's surname either, so she couldn't even look it up. In the end, she rang John at work.

'There's been a crisis here,' John told her. 'I'd not be surprised if she's mixed up with that. Harry Kusek had a heart attack, here in his office, this morning. The whole company's upside down with it.'

'Marie's husband? Poor thing! Is he all right? I mean, he's not dead, is he?'

'No, I think he's all right. But everybody panicked a bit at the time. I'd forget about Eleanor coming, if I were you. What time is your interview?'

'There was nothing arranged. She was just going to drop in and introduce me, on the off-chance. I could just call in, on my own, I suppose.'

'Oh no, you couldn't do that!' John said. 'If you don't go through the proper procedure, it could spoil your chances altogether.'

'All right; I'll leave it, then. See you tonight.'

'What are you going to do today instead?' he inquired.

'I've a few things to do,' she said, not wanting to be given a list of chores.

'I've a jacket that needs taking to the cleaners. It's the grey one, in the wardrobe. And if you're at a loose end . . .'

'There's someone at the door!' Helen interrupted. 'Okay I'll take your jacket in for you. Bye now!'

'Bye.'

225

When John rang off, she went to fetch the jacket, before she could forget. She slung it over one arm, put her sketchpad and a few tubes of paint and brushes into a carrier bag, and went off to Leon's to paint. I wish you no harm, Harry whatever-your-name-is, she told him silently, and I'm sorry you had to have a heart attack, but I think you've just given me a day off. I can put in a whole five or six hours on the portrait. It's an ill wind that blows nobody any good, eh? She went down the back stairs two at a time, whistling happily under her breath.

Sarah realized, when she stopped fuming, that she had just awarded herself a day off work. Having faced the matron's displeasure when she told her she wouldn't be coming in, Sarah was in no mood to phone back and say sorry, there had been a mistake. She would fill up the car with petrol and just get in and drive. She found it relaxing to do that, taking turnings at random, following signposts to places with interesting names. It felt like freedom. The best thing about it was that absolutely nobody knew where she was.

Ben spent the morning talking to his computer games supplier, to his secretary and to his sales reps. He informed the supplier he was taking on an exciting new job with fantastic prospects, which would leave him no time to operate the sideline. He told the reps the supplier had gone out of business; they could find their own supplier now if they wished, but without involving him, since he had lost interest in the venture. He told the secretary that Eleanor Farringdon had mentioned the matter to him, casually, as something of little importance to anybody, and that he had been able to reassure her that, although there had been no harm in the enterprise, he had been planning to end it for months now. The matter was finished and need not be mentioned again. If it was, the girl was to say she knew nothing about it. She agreed.

These conversations, which fooled no one, were all conducted over the phone – Ben having sat in the car a few streets from home for a while, and returned to the house when he judged that Sarah would have left for work.

His next phone call was to Eleanor. On hearing that she was out of the office, he left a message: 'Mission accomplished. Ben' to make quite sure she knew there would be no need to take further action. Then he phoned Mrs Gardener of the employment bureau, and was so polite and humble that she relented and gave him the good news without playing games with him.

'I have a prospective employer for you,' she informed him, 'who is suggesting an interview here at our premises at two P.M. this Wednesday.'

Ben felt his breath taken away. He hadn't expected events to move so quickly. 'Who is the client?' he asked. 'And what kind of job is he offering?'

'She,' said Mrs Gardener. 'It's a Ms Kareshi who will be interviewing you.'

A woman! Was this agency some kind of haven for feminists? And the name sounded Asian or something. Ben was blowed if he was going to waste his impressive sales talk – pitched to penetrate the defences of hard-headed business types – on some bird in a sari.

'What is she?' he asked. 'A personnel clerk?'

'Ms Kareshi,' said Mrs Gardener, 'is the personnel manager for senior sales staff for Beshel Ozone Incorporated, which, as I am sure you will have read in your *Financial Times*, has acquired the rapidly growing and highly competitive computer firm Tannix as one of its many subsidiaries.'

Ben was interested.

'Yes, I'd heard about that,' he said. Harry Kusek had mentioned it one day, in passing, at the end of a lengthy and nerve-racking progress meeting with all his regional sales managers. 'Tannix is rubbish,' he said, 'as far as marketing's concerned, but the products aren't bad at all. With a massive injection of cash – which Beshel can give – they could move from bottom gear into overdrive overnight.' Ben remembered the Beshel/Tannix takeover incident largely because of this phrase, which he wished he had thought of himself. He worked towards laying it on Mrs Gardener, to impress her. 'Tannix are at present bottom of the league,' he said, 'but with a massive . . .'

'The job they are offering,' Mrs Gardener continued, as though he had not spoken, 'is regional sales manager.'

'Oh, but I was intending to move up,' Ben said, disappointed. 'That's the same position as I hold here.'

'With respect,' said Mrs Gardener, without any trace of it in her voice, 'it is not. Not only are the regions more extensive but the market penetration is more intense because of the range of products now on offer, covering specialist applications as well as more general commercial uses. You would have twice as many sales reps as you have in the team at Logodata.'

I never told her how many reps Logodata had in its regional sales teams, Ben thought. She must have got to know the workings of the individual companies pretty well. I wonder how many other Logodata people have been ringing her up? Maybe even some of my own reps, looking to step into replicas of my shoes in other organizations? The idea made him feel insecure.

'Which region is it?' he asked.

'There are three posts being advertised: Home Counties/East Anglia, Midlands, and Scotland. I am not sure which one you'll be offered. One or two of those may already be filled by the time you are interviewed.'

Ben was alarmed. 'Don't I get a choice?'

'You can refuse the job, of course,' said Mrs Gardener smoothly, 'but if I were you I would consider the opportunity carefully. I am sure you are well aware that in your field of work you must be prepared to move, if you want to further your career. In my opinion, Tannix offers excellent prospects. But naturally I don't want you wasting my client's time. If you would not be prepared to consider this opportunity seriously, please say so now.'

'No,' Ben said, taking a deep breath. 'I'll take it seriously. Interview at two o'clock Wednesday, you said? I'll be there.'

So it was that Ben did not go to the office till two o'clock that afternoon. His secretary greeted him with the news of Harry Kusek's heart attack. 'Poor old sod,' said Ben automatically. He went into his office and shut the door. Perhaps he'll die, he thought. One less person to breathe down everybody's neck. Then he felt ashamed of himself. Harry was not a bad bloke.

'Poor old sod,' he said again, more softly.

Richard Shaw had mixed feelings about the news Stevie relayed to him so dramatically. His first reaction had been to rush up to Harry's office and offer to go in the ambulance with him. He had stopped himself. Harry, though a long-standing friend, was apt to pull rank over Richard if he considered that Richard was overstepping the bounds of familiarity.

Richard thought of how he would feel, himself, if Harry were to see him in the throes of one of his ulcer attacks. He realized that Harry might find it degrading to be seen by his old friend while he was out of control of his own body, in his own office where normally he wielded authority over everything and everyone.

So he would let someone else take charge of Harry while the poor old boy was blue round the mouth and clutching his chest. Later, he would get Polly to phone Marie, and when Harry had had time to recover his composure and dignity, then Richard would go and visit him. That is, if Harry would not be embarrassed to be seen in pyjamas, in a hospital bed, with his bodily functions recorded on charts at the end of it.

If Harry could not face Richard in those circumstances, then Richard would understand. He would rely on the women to care for Harry and exchange news bulletins on his state of health, and Richard would see him when Harry was back at work and once again fit to play boss. That was the way Harry liked it. Friendship, but with an element of patronage. Not a friendship on equal levels. That was the way it was, and Richard accepted it now, as he had accepted it for a long time.

When a man had a crisis like this, sometimes it made his friends take stock of what he meant to them. Probably today, a lot of people were thinking about their feelings towards Harry Kusek. Richard had never really considered how he felt about Harry. He was surprised to discover that he loved him.

It was not that Marie was not pleased to see Harry home; of course she was, but she was much more relieved to see Eleanor.

'What shall I do with him?' she asked, in a whisper. 'Are they meant to lie down or sit up?'

'They?' Eleanor asked, perplexed.

'Heart attack cases,' Marie said. She was very white. Fear made her look younger and more helpless than she was.

230

Eleanor put her arm through Marie's. 'Don't think of him as a heart attack,' she said. 'Just treat him as Harry. He'll tell you what he wants. He always does.'

Eleanor had a quick word with Harry's secretary, who had escorted him home in the cab. Then she followed Marie into the sitting room. Harry was in his usual armchair, slightly grey in the face, a little shaky, but sitting upright with rigid determination.

'I'm fine,' he said, in response to Eleanor's inquiry. 'Lot of fuss about nothing.'

'Would you be more comfortable in bed, do you think, Harry?' Eleanor asked him.

'I'm all right,' he said.

'The doctor said he'd be here in about an hour's time, unless . . .' Marie said, and then faltered. 'Unless we phone him again in the meantime.'

'I'm not going to drop dead,' said Harry brusquely. 'Leave me to have a word with Eleanor, will you? On our own.'

Marie looked at him and silently burst into tears. She ran out of the room. Eleanor went to follow her, but Harry said, 'Leave her. She'll be all right. I want to talk to you.'

Eleanor sat down, suddenly very grave.

'I don't want a meal made of this at work,' Harry began. 'I want you to put a clamp on the rumours, right away. Suspected heart attack but turned out to be a false alarm – that kind of thing. All right?'

'Why?' Eleanor asked.

'Because I'm telling you,' Harry said. 'I'll be back behind my desk and back at work by tomorrow. A few pills from the doctor in case of repeat performances, and nobody need be any the wiser. I'm not having anyone saying Harry Kusek isn't up to his job.'

'If you have a heart condition, Harry,' Eleanor said,

'you may not be up to the job, and it's wiser to be realistic about it.'

'I'll do what I damn well please!' he shouted.

'You have a wife too young to be left a widow, and two small kids,' said Eleanor bluntly. 'You'd better consider what they please. Pride may have its place, but it's not worth killing yourself for.'

Harry sat back and smiled bitterly. 'One of my oldest friends,' he said, 'comes round to cheer me up after a heart attack, and all you can talk to me about is death.'

'I didn't come to cheer you up,' Eleanor said. 'I came to talk some sense into you. What the hell do you mean by telling your secretary to phone Biddy?'

'What the hell business is it of yours?' he roared. 'And I'll fire her for telling you, as well!'

'Calm down,' said Eleanor coldly. 'You're behaving like a child. Marie is your wife now, Harry, and if you think she can't do your coping for you then you'll have to cope alone. The poor girl has been living in this . . . this shrine of a house, haunted by Biddy's shadow, for far too long.'

'Shut up,' he said. 'I won't listen to you. Go away.'

'You surround yourself with people to support you,' Eleanor continued, 'and you suck them dry. You've got to the top of the ladder by treading on people's heads, and I'm not going to watch you do it to Marie.'

'That's a lie!' he gasped.

'No, it's the truth. Oh, you're not the only one. I've seen enough high-powered businessmen, recklessly over-achieving in life at the expense of their wives and families. When they've used up their normal human quota of endurance and energy, they keep right on pushing themselves till they've used up everyone else's as well.'

He stared at her. 'What have you got against me?' he said pathetically. He looked suddenly old and tired.

Eleanor shook her head. 'I've known you a long time, Harry, and I'm very fond of you. Jake and I both are. You're a loving, fatherly, gentle and generous character, when you're being yourself. But you run your life like a machine – all function and no feelings. And sooner or later, machines break down.'

'I just happen to have a weak heart!' he said. 'It's not my fault. It can happen to anyone! If you want to blame anything, blame my heart, not me!'

'It's only a muscle, Harry,' Eleanor said, 'and muscles need exercise. I'd put your heart to a bit more use if I were you. Starting with the people whose failure, just by coincidence, has gone hand in hand with your success. Such as Richard Shaw.'

'Get out of my house,' said Harry.

Eleanor stood up and walked to the door.

'Eleanor,' he said.

'Yes, Harry?'

'Did Biddy confide in you?'

'From time to time.'

'Did she tell you what she said to me that last time, just as she was leaving?'

'No.'

'She said . . . something extraordinary,' he said, in bewilderment.

Eleanor sat down on a chair near the door. 'What did she say?'

'She said, "Harry, you've never understood what marriage is all about. You think you're separate from me, but you're not. Husband and wife are one flesh, you know, one spirit. It's as though they run off a common battery. You've drained all the power out of ours and you've never recharged it. You think you can just replace it with a new one, but you can't. Not without throwing half of yourself away." What do you think of that?'

233

Eleanor said nothing.

'Does it make sense to you?' he asked plaintively. 'Because I didn't understand what she was getting at, and I still don't, and now you seem to be blaming me in the same way. Are you?'

Eleanor came over and sat at his feet. She put her hands on his knees. 'I'm not blaming you,' she said more gently. 'You've been taught to believe that what real men do is go out and succeed, at any price. But Harry, be honest with me, how many men do you know who have a great important life, travelling all over the place, playing a prominent part in big events, top of their tree? How many of them have wives who are on tranquillizers, or are alcoholic, or are so drained and exhausted that while their husbands are living this public life, they have to hide away in private, too nervous to go out of the house?'

'What makes you think it's connected?' Harry demanded. 'Be fair, Eleanor. You're a sensible woman yourself, and you work, but some of these bored house-wives are just neurotic.'

'But where does it start? Biddy wasn't the neurotic type. She's sensitive, but down-to-earth; not prone to flights of fancy. Maybe her big mistake was waiting till you left, to tell you how marriage works. She should have told you twenty years ago, instead of sacrificing herself to the cause of keeping you going beyond your limits.'

'She held me back, if anything! Refusing to support me by going to functions, getting migraines and leaving me to go alone, half the time!'

'Well maybe – just maybe, Harry – if she hadn't failed in that way, you might have done, yourself. You say heart attacks are common, but it's even more common for middle-aged men and women to suddenly lose their nerve. If you hadn't had Biddy to be your weakness, that could have been you.'

234

'You're not associating me with mental sickness!' Harry protested. 'This is a purely physical . . .'

'It isn't sickness; it's health,' Eleanor said. 'It makes very little difference whether it's the mind or the body that goes on strike first. The fact is, something tells you you're only human, and human beings are weak. It defines your limits. If you have any sense, you'll take the hint that your body's giving you. Next time, the alarm bells could sound a lot louder.'

'So what am I meant to do about it?' he asked.

'Go easy,' Eleanor said. 'You're not Superman. Be yourself. And look on your wife and your friends as part of yourself. Don't expect Marie to have Biddy's maturity. Don't expect Richard to be a bright young executive.'

He looked at her. 'And you?'

She hesitated, then looked at the floor. 'Don't expect me to be a director. I'd like another chance at motherhood.'

He nodded. 'I see.'

'I love you, Harry,' she said. 'You'd be surprised to know how many people do. But we can't, any of us, hold you up. You've grown too strong. The ones you're used to leaning on are the weak ones now.'

'You make me feel an utter cad,' he said.

She laughed. 'That's a fine old-fashioned expression! No, Harry, you're not. You're a very nice man, but it's good to know your limits, and to allow other people's limits to slow you down as well, before you get the hand of God giving you the full-stop!'

'So the big successful director has to bow to human weakness?' he said wryly.

Eleanor stood up, and kissed him on the forehead. 'That's it,' she said. 'Join the club!'

* * *

235

Ben decided it was time to come clean with Sarah. Well, cleanish. There was no need to tell her about his off-the-record trading with Logodata's rivals and customers on Logodata's time. Sarah had never yet seen the need to ask why her husband always seemed to have a wallet full of cash but rarely had to visit the bank for it, so why should Ben need to tell her more than she wanted to know? Let the past bury itself, Ben decided. But the future – now that would have to be discussed, and before Wednesday.

Sarah, calm, smiling and refreshed from her day out, welcomed him home with a kiss. 'You're home nice and early,' she said.

'I wanted to talk to you about something. I want to leave Logodata. I'm applying for other jobs.' He told her the details, there on the doorstep, with no preliminaries, no excuses and no sales talk. She stood and listened to him.

'I want to go,' he said. 'I don't want to stay with Logodata. We're not discussing that. But what I'm saying is, I'll try my best to take a job that means we don't have to move, but I can't guarantee it.'

'The job you're applying for isn't London-based?' she asked. 'The one you've got the interview for?'

'It could be. I'll ask for the Home Counties region, if I'm offered the choice. If not – well, there are other jobs. I'll look around for a while, give it a fair chance, I promise. I know what this place means to you – the house, and your job and all your friends.'

'Oh no, you don't,' Sarah said. She started to cry, wrapping her arms around him. 'Please Ben,' she said, 'please can we move? Just pack up and go away some-where – anywhere – else? Oh, please!'

13
Finale

On the tarmac at Heathrow Airport, in the second week in July, a group of Logodata staff were about to board a plane for the annual sales conference in the south of France.

First in the queue for boarding, having extended a friendly and gracious welcome to lesser employees, were Logodata's UK managing director, Peter Halliday, and Gloria, his immaculately dressed and freshly permed wife.

Beside him, and part of the informal reception line, was the sales and marketing director, the impressively confident but approachable Harry Kusek. Kusek was acting against the advice of his doctors, who had warned him not to fly, but no one from Logodata knew this, apart from Kusek's very pretty but rather nervous young wife, Marie.

Marie, as most of the longer-standing employees were well aware, had been Kusek's secretary – or personal assistant – before he married her. After a three-year break to have their two children – excellently cared for by a nanny described by the Kuseks as 'a treasure' – she now occupied her former post again, following the resignation of the previous woman, whose name nobody could quite remember. The silly woman had taken it into her head, as a result of some small incident (probably just a bad bout of indigestion), that Kusek was prone to heart attacks, and had been frightened of what she termed the 'responsibility' of working with him.

Absent from the queue was Ben Jepson, the ex-Team Six regional sales manager, a brilliant and promising young executive, still much missed and lamented by his younger colleague, software sales representative, John Gee. Gee had seemed all set, at first, to rival Jepson's own record, being full of enthusiasm and flair and adapting easily from programme-designing to salesmanship. But somehow, since Jepson's recent departure to join a rival firm, based in the north of Scotland, the lad appeared to have lost heart. Of course, it was early days yet, and no doubt Gee would recover his youthful verve following this small setback. He was evidently looking forward to the sales conference trip, and was already chatting up one of the young female reps, with every expression of lively interest.

Right at the back of the queue, behind the gaggle of junior managers, sales reps and secretarial staff, stood Eleanor Farringdon – on her last sales conference now before leaving Logodata at the end of July – chatting with the senior sales administration executive, Richard Shaw, and his wife Polly.

Shaw, like Kusek, had at one time been rumoured to be suffering from ill-health – duodenal ulcer, or some such thing – but he showed no signs of it now, being pink-cheeked and lively of spirits. He was a close personal friend of Kusek's, who was often to be seen taking his coffee break in Shaw's office. This friendship was generally believed to have worked in Shaw's favour, in his recent promotion to senior administrative status with its accompanying pay rise, but no one appeared to begrudge him this small success since administrators were not in competition with anybody. He was a little over-zealous on expense fiddling and suchlike, but then that was only his job, and besides, he seemed mellower these days and easier to approach when genuine mistakes had been made in the young reps' paperwork.

The queue began to move. Eleanor Farringdon turned

and gave one last wave in the direction of the departure lounge, where her husband Jake and little daughter Gabriella stood watching her embark on her final business trip before taking a well-earned break in her career.

The giant aircraft, chartered by Logodata months in advance for this meticulously planned event, opened its mouth and swallowed up the people, all of them looking as tiny and as busy as little ants from where Jake and Gaby stood.

'Will Mummy ever get out again?' the child asked, alarmed.

'Oh yes,' Jake reassured her. 'She'll be back home with us soon.'

The plane finally managed to take off with such agonizing roars and reluctant lifting of its own bulky weight that it seemed that all the people inside must be straining every nerve to lift it by willpower off the ground.

Gaby and Jake made their way, hand in hand, to the other terminal and were just in time to wave goodbye to Helen and Oriel, sharing a flight to New York.

Oriel Shaw, newly kitted out in an attractive but demure grey cotton jumpsuit with a pink T-shirt underneath, was on her way to her first job as a family au pair. She would be staying a few days first in New York with Helen, who was a friend of hers. As well as fulfilling her lifetime ambition of seeing the big-city sights there, Oriel was looking forward to visiting the modest back-street gallery in which her friend Helen was exhibiting two small paintings. This would form a prelude to the grander occasion – an invitation-only private view evening at the more prestigious gallery where Rueben Farnheim had reopened an augmented exhibition of Grszinski abstracts, in addition to the highly acclaimed series of four small paintings collectively entitled *Tyrants as Victims*.

Gaby watched Oriel and Helen disappear from view. 'Everybody's going somewhere,' she said wistfully, 'except for us. Why aren't we?'

'I suppose,' her father said, 'because we have nothing to fly away from, and no incentive to leave.'

'What's incentive?' the child asked.

'It's a . . .' Jake stopped and scratched his head. Then he laughed. 'For the likes of you and me,' he said, 'it's cream cakes and orange squash in the airport café!'